A *Hidden Heiress* FOR THE **COWBOY**

SWEET RIVER RANCH ROMANCE - BOOK 6

VALERIE COMER

Greenwords Media

O Lord, you have searched me and known me!
Psalm 139:1 ESV

FREE BOOK?

Love cowboys? Me, too! That's why I'd like to offer you an ebook copy of *The Cowboy's Forever Crush* free as an introduction to the world of my Montana Ranches Christian Romance series. This story world encompasses the Saddle Springs series, the Cavanagh Cowboys series, the Sweet River Ranch series, and the Cavanagh Cowgirls series.

Come on in and be lassoed by love!

https://valeriecomer.com/subscribe-crush

CHAPTER ONE

J ude Kline focused on settling the helicopter on its brand-new helipad. Only a perfect landing would do. He tried to tell himself it was because his grandfather sat beside him, the man who had paid for both of Jude's pilot's licenses.

But it was mostly because of the audience gathered. He didn't take time to count, but there had to be at least 20 of his family members and coworkers present.

Never mind the group. A perfect landing was required only because Kaci Moore was among them. Impressing her was the only thing that mattered.

"Nicely done. Very smooth." Grandfather removed his headset and turned in his seat as he unbuckled. "Congratulations on your achievement, boy."

"Thank you for the opportunity, sir. I've dreamed of getting my pilot's license most of my life."

"My pleasure, and you did all the work." Grandfather tapped the dash in front of him. "Sightseeing tours will be a great asset to Sweet River Ranch. Thanks for the flyover."

"I can't tell you how much I appreciate—"

Grandfather's wave cut off Jude's gratitude. "It was the least I could do."

Which wasn't exactly true, but it seemed to be the old man's way of making up for not even knowing his daughter existed for over 50 years. And that had meant Grandfather had had no clue about Jude and his brother, either.

The past two years had been full of new... well, everything. Grandfather had bought Sweet River Ranch and summoned all six of his grandsons, Jude and Weston included, to bring it up to par and graft the family branches together. Mom ran the kitchen and loved it here. She'd met Keith Ralston, who'd taken over the head cattleman position last year, and the two had married on New Year's Eve.

Jude had worked in maintenance for the first while until he'd been brave enough to approach his grandfather with his dream of flying. A few blinks later, he'd been in Chicago for six months of personal, intensive lessons.

And here they were.

Jude shut down the engine, and the blades rotated to a stop.

Grandfather waved as a cheer rose from the gathered group.

Jude grunted in satisfaction. He'd done it. He slapped his grandfather's raised hand in a high five, opened the door, and hopped to the cement pad before turning to see if Grandfather needed a hand. Nope, the old man's confident descent proved he'd done this many times before.

Wally, the cousin Jude had never met, had preferred

flying choppers to planes. And a moment of inattention or weather or something had killed Wally and his three passengers before Jude ever met that side of his family. Everyone said Wally wasn't easily distracted and he was unlikely to be intoxicated. The fatal chain of events would likely never be known.

But the situation would be forefront of Jude's mind every time he flew. There was no room for distraction of any sort.

He was on the ground now, though.

His mother rushed over to hug him, tears flowing down her cheeks. "I'm so proud of you, Jude."

He patted her back awkwardly. "Thanks, Mom."

"Nice landing." Keith, Mom's new husband, gave him a sharp nod and a big grin.

"Thanks."

"Good job, little bro." Weston pounded his back, making Jude stumble under the impact.

"I can take you on anytime," Jude responded, his voice thick.

"Doubt it." Weston thumped again and stepped back. "All you've done is make it easier for you to run away. I'm not following you up there."

One by one, the other family members and coworkers offered their congratulations. Everyone but the woman he wanted most to impress. Finally, Kaci stood in front of him.

"Hey, Jude. Lookin' good." She gave him a quick side hug and stepped away.

"Thanks. Want a ride up sometime?"

Kaci's eyes brightened. "That would be fun."

It's a date.

But Jude managed to choke back the unuttered words. If those became audible, he'd be crossing the friendship boundary, and she'd almost certainly pull back. That awkwardness had rarely been there before he left for flight school in September, but things had changed while he was away. Or maybe it had been his imagination on his visits home. Guess he'd see now that he was back for good.

He forced a smile. "Sure. We'll figure out our schedules and go from there."

"Hey, we want in on flights, too!" Paisley slung her arm over Kaci's shoulder and turned to Grandfather. "All the staff who interacts regularly with our guests should, right, Mr. Sullivan? We need to be ready to brag about everything Sweet River has to offer." She batted her eyelashes at the old man.

Grandfather threw his head back and laughed.

The man looked younger than he had when Jude had met him not long after Wally's death. How much did that have to do with his love of relaxing at the ranch, and how much had to do with reconnecting with Nana and Mom? Probably some of each.

"I see what you're doing there, Paisley Kline. But maybe you can set up a roster for Wednesday. Six passengers at a time for 15-minute flights leaving every half hour. Two hours then Jude needs a 90-minute break for refueling and rest. You can schedule eight flights, and that's it." Grandfather nodded at Mom. "You and Keith will be on the first one, of course."

Mom beamed. Keith squeezed her to his side.

Jude looked away. So much for a special time with Kaci,

but maybe it was for the best. He could make sure she got the seat next to him so he could see her reactions. Maybe this would give her a taste of a bird's-eye-view of the area, and she'd agree to another flight, just the two of them.

Maybe he'd get brave enough to ask her on an actual date.

Except, she would shut him down. He knew she would.

Being just friends was getting old. Jude was ready for the next step. Why wasn't she? Was he not worth considering as a potential mate? Maybe she had a hangup with wealth like he did. Trusting someone with money could be tricky. He'd learned that by interacting with his newfound uncles in Chicago this past winter.

"Sounds great!" Paisley whipped out her phone.

It would be a miracle if the device wasn't on the verge of a dead battery, but maybe Weston had been a good influence on her in the month they'd been married.

"Okay, taking names." Paisley tap-tap-tapped then looked around. "First flight at 10:00. Nadine? Keith? Who else? Can Weston and I go on that one? Who else wants to?"

"Two o'clock sounds good for us." Cadence grinned at Graham. "I'll bring my camera and get lots of photos to post on our website and social media. We'll start promoting."

"And I'll try to figure out how to not lose money on the proposition," Graham muttered.

Everyone laughed at the number-crunching CFO.

Maxwell leaned toward Paisley. "Put Tate, Stephanie, the boys, Eryn, and me on 11:30. That makes a full flight, and it's after Simon's morning nap."

Jude hadn't realized Maxwell kept up on his nephews' schedules. Then again, he'd missed a lot being away from Montana for so many months.

Paisley kept tapping as others gave their preferred times.

Grandfather chuckled and shook his head. "That girl's quite something, isn't she?"

"She is." But Jude's sister-in-law wasn't the girl Jude cared about. Kaci had shifted off to the side and was poking at her own phone. Jude circled the group. "Hey. You should get your name on the list."

She glanced up, her smile not reaching her eyes. "I'm just one person. Paisley can tuck me in wherever there's space."

"I'll make certain she does."

Kaci looked down. "Thanks."

"Everything okay?"

She shoved her phone into her hip pocket. "Sure."

Jude studied her, his heart clenching. She was so pretty with her shoulder-length brown hair pulled back into a low ponytail, accentuating her high cheekbones. But there was no glimmer in her brown eyes today. Something was off, but she wouldn't likely let him in on the secret.

Once he hadn't minded not going deep.

That was then. This was now.

KACI MOORE TRIED to shove her niggling worries deep enough that no one would notice she wasn't quite herself, but she hadn't fooled Jude. Nothing much did. He was attentive; she could say that about him for sure. It was an excellent attribute for a pilot.

"I can't believe you finally got your license!" She poured all the enthusiasm she could muster into her words.

"Two licenses." Jude beamed. "Fixed-wing and rotary-wing both."

"Overachiever." She laughed.

"I can't believe it, either." He rocked back on his heels and poked his chin toward the group surrounding Paisley. "Can't believe my entire family trusts me enough to fly them."

"What's not to trust?" she teased.

"Wally crashed."

Now she felt like a heel for having forgotten. "Oh. But such accidents are rare." She studied his face. "Aren't they?"

"Of course, they are. But it's all up to the pilot to be vigilant every second. No distractions. Always looking for changes in atmospheric conditions. There's a lot going on."

Wow, she'd missed him far more than she ought to have. Friend zone. He had to stay there for his own good. For her peace of mind. She smiled at him. "I'm sure you're up for it."

And he would be. Jude was self-contained and conscientious. He'd be the best pilot Sweet River Ranch could have on staff, at least once he got experience. But he had enough hours to pass his — what had he called it? — PPL. Private Pilot's License.

Jude could achieve anything at all he put his mind to. He would simply put his head down and keep plodding forward until he had his prize in hand.

Which was why she needed to keep her distance,

because he'd been looking at her more speculatively since his return from Chicago. They'd been good friends for so long, but she would never ask him what he was thinking, because he might ask the same in return, and she was not in a position to divulge information.

"Kaci!" Paisley stopped beside her as she scrolled her phone. "Anyone in particular you'd like to fly with?" She smirked. "Besides the pilot."

"Hard to fly without a pilot." Kaci laughed. "Just stick my name with any group that needs a sixth. I'm flexible with the time." She avoided looking at Jude, but she could see the frown on his face.

"Okay. I'll make sure you have a spot, though." Paisley turned away, bumping heavily into Jude's shoulder. Accident? Not likely, even though she apologized. There was the smirk and wink, after all.

Everyone seemed to assume Kaci and Jude would demolish the friend-zone barrier at some point and admit they were madly in love. Nope, that rampart was high and strong. She'd keep shoring it up every time she noticed a weak spot.

It wasn't that she couldn't love Jude Kline. It would be easy. He was an amazing guy. But he was also an amazing guy who deserved life without looking over his shoulder the way life required of Kaci.

Maybe someday she'd be secure, but today was not that day.

"Make sure you get a seat." Jude studied her now.

"Oh, for sure!" Kaci managed a breezy tone. "I do have a lot going on this time of year, preparing all of the cottages before the season kicks off. My housekeeping crew doesn't start until next week, so I'm busy with inventory and all that."

"Do you like housekeeping?"

"It's great!" She was lying. On the other hand, the job suited her OCD personality well. She was driven to have everything in perfect order at all times.

Kaci couldn't control a whole lot of her life, but she could — and did — make sure every single cottage was spotless and welcoming as guests checked in.

Would Jude even understand that?

"If there's a job around the ranch you'd rather do, just talk to Tate about it."

Maxwell's fiancée, Eryn Ralston, was a good example of that policy. She'd started off as a kitchen helper, but she'd transitioned to running the gift shop, soon set to open for the season. The small space was bursting with local handcrafts that were sure to fly off the shelves.

Kaci shook her head. "I'm good where I am, honestly. It's not my dream job, but—"

"What is?"

Of course, Jude would jump on that. "I'll know it when I see it." Totally true. She *had* known. One day she'd be able to put her training to work, but it wouldn't be on a guest ranch in rural Montana, and it wouldn't happen until things settled down back home.

No. She wasn't going to think about that. There was no timeline. There were no guarantees.

Everyone at Sweet River Ranch would have to remain on the other side of her barricade, even Jude.

Especially Jude.

CHAPTER TWO

Paisley stood in front of Jude with her hands on her hips. "You need to get the headset repaired that I was wearing. It must be defective, because aren't they all brand new? It shouldn't have cut out like that."

Jude choked back a laugh and tried to look as though he was taking Paisley seriously. "I'll have a look." Not that he needed to. His sister-in-law had been babbling incessantly about nothing and everything while they were in the air, tying up the channel so others could hardly get their two-bits in. He'd eliminated the problem with the unobtrusive flip of a switch.

She flopped dramatically into the leather club chair at an angle to Jude's in front of the lodge's fireplace. "I was trying to say that there was a large flat rock overlooking the little lake where Weston and I took that group of tweens last summer. And I wanted to know if it was a big enough spot to land a helicopter."

"I did see that one, and I'm pretty sure the answer is yes. I'll need to get in there on horseback and do some scouting around. See if a trail is possible from there down to the campsite."

"It would be so awesome if we could fly in some gear. We could do way more of those trips if all the supplies didn't have to come in by packhorse."

Paisley was the family activities coordinator for Sweet River Ranch, and she'd dragged Jude's brother, whining and kicking, onto that excursion last year. Somehow, she'd gotten through Weston's walls on that multi-day trail ride, and they'd celebrated their one-month wedding anniversary just the other day.

If an out-trip would have the same softening effect on Kaci, Jude would sign up for 20 of them this summer, if her schedule would allow her to participate... but didn't she have enough cleaning staff under her to take some time off here and there? Not that she'd do it.

"What do you think?"

Paisley's question jolted Jude back to the lodge's cozy great room. "Uh, I can see that. Even if I can't land nearby, I can still haul in supplies and drop them off from a hover."

Paisley's eyes brightened. "Kayaks! Right, Kaci? Wouldn't everyone love to paddle way up in the high country?"

How had Jude not noticed Kaci coming up behind him? Now she stepped into his peripheral vision and perched on the arm of another club chair. "Do they need more activities at the end of a trail ride?"

"Yes!" Paisley nodded like a bobble-head. "Right now we can only offer fishing and more riding, but some of the participants groaned at the thought of riding more until their muscles eased... just barely in time for the return trip.

It was too cold to swim — though one boy fell in — but that might be an option later in summer. The ice was barely off the water in early June."

"It looked like a pretty spot from the air." Kaci sounded wistful.

"It's gorgeous," Paisley gushed.

"I've never ridden in, either." Jude glanced at Kaci. "Want to come when I measure that rock for a landing spot? It's hard to determine if it's big enough — level enough — from the air." He had a pretty good idea it would work, but caution was going to be his middle name every time he flew. He'd take nothing for granted.

Kaci bit her lip. "Maybe."

"Weston and I could come, too!" Then Paisley seemed to read Jude's expression. "Or not. Whichever."

"What are we doing or not doing?" Weston settled on the stone hearth facing them.

"Riding up to the lake together to see if that butte would work for Jude to land the helicopter. But he says he can drop off stuff even if he can't land!"

Weston nodded and kept his gaze on Jude as though trying to read him.

Good luck, bro. Everyone seemed to realize Jude's interest in Kaci had slipped out of the friend-zone. Everyone except Kaci. Or maybe she also suspected it, and that was why she was playing him cooler than she used to.

Jude's gut sank at that thought. There was a nod in his spirit confirming his suspicion, but that didn't help him know what to do about it. There had been several female pilots in his program. Cecelia had a crush on him and even asked him out a couple of times. He'd turned her down. A nice enough woman, but no spark. Jude was too intro-verted to date simply for something to do.

Was Kaci ready for an entire day of one-on-one? Jude doubted it, but he'd take what he could get. For now. He gave his brother a subtle nod. "Sure. Four riders sounds like a decent-sized group. The return trip is doable in one day, right?"

Weston smirked. "You might have a pansy butt after not riding since last summer. The rest of us will be fine." He turned to Kaci. "What day works for you?"

"I... um..." Kaci shot a panicked look at Jude. "Next Wednesday?"

"Good choice." Paisley nodded. "It's a lighter work load for all of us that day. When are the public flights starting, Jude? Cadence needs to know for the online registration."

"Uh... Memorial Day weekend?"

"That's in under two weeks!" Paisley leaped to her feet. "Why didn't you say anything?"

"I just did." Jude shrugged, forcing his expression to remain impassive.

Kaci snickered.

It wasn't often he got one up on his sister-in-law. She was an interesting combination of on top of everything and totally scatterbrained. She blamed ADHD. Whatever the cause, she was fun to tease.

Jude nodded at his brother. "Meanwhile, I'll take Pepper out a few times and try to get back in shape." He'd gone to the gym in Chicago, but that was unlikely to be helpful for horseback riding. "Anyone been keeping her exercised?"

Weston's mouth twitched. "Kaci has."

"You?" Jude turned to Kaci, who was studying her

hands. "Thanks. She's such a great mare. I'm glad you got a chance to work with her."

Kaci glanced up, her face flushed. "She's great. She missed you, I think."

Had Kaci missed him? He didn't dare ask, especially with Paisley and Weston so attentive. "I missed her, too. I don't think there'd ever been a time since I was about three when I didn't ride at least once or twice a week."

"I'll find a different horse to ride now." Kaci turned to Weston. "Suggestions?"

"Any you want, really. You're a solid rider." Weston smirked. "You could even try Ranger."

Jude snorted a laugh. "You don't let anyone ride Ranger!"

"Except Graham that one time." Weston shook his head. "That was a disaster. But I trust Kaci."

Kaci blinked at him. "I was thinking more of Mirage or Enchantment or one of the newer ones."

"How about Sparkles?" Jude tried to keep a straight face. Failed.

Kaci giggled. "Jamie's pony? I'll pass. Thanks, anyway."

"Hey, I tried." And got a laugh. Score.

"OUR GUESTS SAY there were dust bunnies under their bed and cobwebs in the closet when they checked in." Kaci leveled a glare at her newest chambermaid.

"It was clean." Giana's chin jutted dangerously.

"Sweet River Ranch requires a deeper level of attention from its staff." If the girl snapped her gum one more time,

Kaci would fire her. It was plenty tempting as it was, only there hadn't been an overabundance of applicants to pick from.

"Okay, fine. I'll tell the dust bunnies to multiply elsewhere."

"You do that. All of the cottages are booked for Memorial Day weekend, so please go through each unit on Dragonfly Lane and Firefly Lane in the next two days and put every single surface to the white-glove test."

"Yes'm." The gum smacked.

"And make sure you don't dump that gum in any of the cottages' trash cans." Or yards... but surely the girl was smart enough for that? One could hope.

Giana turned away, rolling her eyes and shaking her head.

Man, they didn't make hired help like they used to. Dad would make short work of Giana's work ethics... or lack thereof. Kaci huffed a breath. Not that her parents had anything to do with Sweet River Ranch. Thankfully.

But there was still an emotional tornado just under the surface whenever she thought of home. Would she ever be free to return to being Kirsten Catriona Moorehouse-Atkinson again? Most days she didn't even want to, but family was a big thing to the Sullivan crew around her. Even Paisley, with her messed-up drug-addicted mother, had a couple of sisters who stayed in touch.

Grr. Paisley's touchy-feely sister Kait had draped all over Jude at Weston and Paisley's wedding a few weeks ago. Ugh. Nothing had ever made Kaci want to scratch someone's eyes out like watching Kait. Nothing had tested her resolve to keep Jude at arm's length more than watching him try to disentangle from the woman's clutches dozens of times over the days of her visit.

Kaci descended the steps of cottage four, hopped on her golf cart, and cruised over to Ladybug Lane. Maxwell's construction crew had worked miracles over here last summer, including making half of the single-level units wheelchair-accessible. It turned out that folks with mobility issues were super grateful to have a place to enjoy nature. She knew she would if she were in their boots.

Kylie was the cleaner over here, and Kaci found her arranging a bouquet on the dining table of cottage five. That was more like it.

"Hey, looks great! Are you finding everything you need?"

"Yes, I think so. Did I... can I help you with anything?"

Meaning was she in trouble. Nope, that was all the other chambermaid. Kaci shook her head. "Nothing specific. I just want to be available as you and Giana learn the ropes around here. I'd much rather you asked than guessed. We're not a typical hotel setting, for all we're part of the Sullivan Hotel chain."

"I did work for them last summer in Boston."

"I saw that on your resume! Which do you prefer, city life or country life?"

"I'm not sure yet." Kylie's smile warmed her face. "That's why I wanted to experience how the other half lives. You must love rural life. This is your third summer?"

Did she love rural life? Well, it had grown on her. "It's great here. And, yes, this is my third. Trish over in the lodge is starting her second year."

"Where did you come from? I catch a hint of Texan but then I'm not sure."

Kaci rapped the table twice. "I once lived in Texas, but Montana's home now. If you don't have any questions about our cleaning processes, I'll head out. I'll be away all day tomorrow, so ask now."

"Oh? Your day off?"

"Yep!"

"What's to do around here on days off? Are you going down to Jewel Lake?"

"No, I'm going on a trail ride. But the town is nice, too. And Missoula isn't that far away if you have a hankering for more extensive shopping."

"Trail ride? I want to learn to ride."

Of course, Kylie had picked up on that. "I think they're still offering orientation classes for our new staffers. Did you check on the whiteboard in the dining hall? Mr. Sullivan wants each of us who meet the public to have a working knowledge of all the activities our guests might wish to do. You can also sign out kayaks or some of the lawn games."

"Helicopter rides?" Kylie clasped her hands under her chin and her eyes grew soft and distant. "Although I'm not sure I'd look out the window. That pilot is gorgeous."

"Jude Kline?" Kaci laughed. "You do know he's one of the owner's grandsons, right?"

"I know, but a girl can dream."

Right. Kaci couldn't shoot her down, because stranger things had happened. "Well, he is kind of cute. But don't get your hopes up."

"So, are you saying helicopter rides are out of the question... or that the pilot is?"

Kaci managed a light laugh. "Take it however you like, but I do know they're not tossing out sightseeing tours like candy at a parade. You'd get a staff discount, but no freebies."

"I'll check into it, and look up the riding lesson, too. Where are you going on your trail ride?"

"Way back in the mountains. Apparently, there's a little lake up there."

"Aw, nice. Who all is going?"

"A group of friends. Now, if you don't have anything else?"

"Um, no. I'm good. But I think I want your friends."

"They're pretty great. Be nice to everyone, and who knows what friendships will come of it?" Kaci smiled to remove any sting.

This was one staff member she wasn't about to introduce to Jude. Kaci might not be in a position to claim more than friends with him herself, but she wouldn't be able to stomach watching him fall in love with someone else. She'd have to leave for her own sanity.

Her attorney had told her she was all legal and protected, but Kaci had no desire to test it out in a new situation.

Hopefully, she wouldn't need to disappear again.

CHAPTER THREE

Six in the morning, and the sun would be rising soon. There was already a little contrast visible as Jude entered the stable. He'd been out on Pepper several times over the past week, but today would be a solid test for both of them.

Voices beckoned him further into the stable, low lights illuminating the alley between the box stalls.

"Hey, girl," Jude murmured as he unlatched Pepper's gate. "Ready for a long day?"

The mare nickered and bobbed her head.

Jude grinned as she eagerly accepted a carrot. "Me, too. It's gonna be a good day. I promise even though I have a new love, we're going to spend a lot of time together from now on. I'll have more free time than when I was in maintenance." At least, he hoped so. Upkeep on the chopper was going to take some of his time, for sure, but he wouldn't be working an eight-to-five anymore.

"Jude?" Weston's voice came from the corridor.

"Yeah?" Jude turned.

"Mom sent along a sack lunch so big it might take two sets of saddlebags."

"Gotta love it. I missed her cooking."

"I bet. Never thought I'd be one of those grown men whose mothers still cooked for him."

"And for dozens of other people who work here."

"Plus all those tourists." Weston shook his head. "She loves it, though."

Jude figured it was Keith she loved most. He'd missed his mother's entire romance and early marriage by being away for six months, but he'd never seen Mom so happy. So contented. Keith seemed like a great guy. Mom thought so, for sure, and that was all that mattered.

Jude swung a saddle pad onto Pepper's back. "Is Kaci here yet?"

Weston smirked. "All saddled up and waiting out in the corral."

"So, I'm the late one, huh?"

"You said it, not me."

The saddle came next. "I'll only be a minute."

Weston came closer and lowered his voice. "I'm not sure what your status is with Kaci these days..."

A leading comment if ever there was one. "Just friends, remember?" Jude replied lightly.

"Right." Weston rolled his eyes as he slid another carrot into Pepper's eager mouth. "Heads up, though. There's something going on that she's not talking about."

"There's always stuff she's not talking about." Like anything about her family or her childhood. One big, vacant history.

"Paisley thinks there's more."

"And you're warning me about this why?" Jude cinched the strap beneath the mare's belly.

"Because I thought you needed to know. Don't get in too deep, bro. She's a flight risk."

Jude scoffed. "She's been here for two solid years." And not left the property other than for church on Sunday and very occasional brief excursions into Jewel Lake or Missoula with the other women.

"Just a feeling. Be careful."

"Always. You're talking to the king of caution."

Weston snorted as loud as any horse. "Absolutely not true or you wouldn't get your jollies bobbing around in the sky in nothing more than a tin can."

"A tin can with an engine and rotors." Jude couldn't help grinning. "Although I could see jumping out with a chute. Want to join me sometime?"

"Not one ever-lovin' chance. The farthest from the ground I want to be is on Ranger's back."

Jude slid the bridle over Pepper's head and settled the bit in her mouth. "You didn't seem to mind the flyover last week."

"Ask Paisley if I crushed every bone in her hand or not."

"I'm guessing not, or she wouldn't be up for a ride today."

"Pfft." Weston stepped aside so that Jude could walk Pepper out to the corral.

How could two brothers be so different? Jude had dreamed of the skies his entire life, but there sure hadn't been any money for lessons in his teen years, let alone airplanes and helicopters. Now he had both at his disposal, thanks to Grandfather.

It chafed his spirit that he'd been so easy to buy. Dangle a pilot's license in front of him, and he'd been all in.

"Good morning, Paisley. Kaci." Jude tucked his boot into Pepper's stirrup and swung into the saddle. Man, he'd missed this. "Lovely day for a ride."

"I'll get the gate." Weston opened it and led Ranger through behind the others before closing it again and mounting up.

"Thanks, bro."

Paisley and Kaci had already struck out ahead of the brothers. Jude watched Kaci's lithe body shift comfortably on Nutmeg's back. She must have ridden in her former life in Texas. She'd also admitted to having flown in a helicopter before. She'd confidently adjusted her headset without instruction, so likely she'd flown more than once.

Who was Kaci Moore, really? If she ever opened up to Jude about her past, he'd know they were getting somewhere. Today didn't look to be that day, but at least it was time together. Maybe it was less weird with Weston and Paisley along.

Weird? It had never been awkward before. They'd hung out so many times before he'd left for Chicago. Had she felt deserted while he was away? If so, she was a good liar, since she'd encouraged him to follow his dreams.

Now? Weston was right. Something had changed. Her defenses were higher and more solid.

"I love mornings like this." Weston gestured downslope, where shafts of early morning sunshine angled between the hills.

"Who are you and what have you done with my grumpy brother?"

"I wasn't grouchy."

"Duh. Tell that to someone who hasn't known you your entire life."

"You're two years younger, so you haven't—"

"You're dodging the subject."

Weston shrugged. "Blame Paisley. Blame God."

"You're telling me true love can change an entire personality?" Jude couldn't keep the mocking tone out of his voice.

"You bet. Not sure I'd have listened to God if it hadn't been for Paisley, though."

Jude's relationship with his Heavenly Father was just fine. It could always be improved upon, of course, but he was doing his best to keep tuned for nudges from the Holy Spirit.

Was it God showing him Kaci's extra layer of reticence, or was it all Jude's imagination? Not if Weston and Paisley had seen the same thing.

Jude turned to his brother. "We've got a lot to be thankful for, I guess."

"Yeah, we do. Not gonna lie, I was worried when Mom headed to Chicago to beard the old man in his den. Figured she'd get tossed out on her butt. That Grandfather would prove to be nothing but an entitled jerk."

"It was a nerve-racking time."

Weston shook his head. "She was determined; I'll grant you that. And it turned out okay."

"More than okay." Jude studied his brother.

"Easy for you to say, flyboy."

"Easy for *you* to say, married man."

Weston huffed a laugh. "There's that. I'd never have met

Paisley if not for Mom's nerve that resulted in Grandfather buying Sweet River Ranch."

And Jude wouldn't have met Kaci. But was there any chance of a happy ending for the two of them? Being pals was a great foundation for more, but what if she kept him in the friend zone all summer?

For years?

Forever?

"WE NEED a games night now that Jude's back." Paisley beamed in Kaci's direction as their horses trotted along up the trail.

"Sure. Sounds fun." What else could Kaci say? It sounded like Paisley was building a double date instead of friends hanging out, but maybe Kaci was reading too much into it. Over the past couple of years, most of the original gang had paired off. At least, all of Mr. Sullivan's grandsons were married or engaged with the sole exception of Jude.

Did he feel the target on his back the way she did? She'd never felt like she needed to avoid him before, but now? Now they couldn't blend into the field of singles, unless she purposefully made new friends.

New friends asked questions, and Kaci wasn't answering them. That always took a bit to get past. Emma Cavanagh was her roommate this summer, and she tended to mind her own business. Thankfully.

"It will be like old times." Paisley sighed contentedly.

Kaci forced a laugh. "Not so much, since you and Weston are newlyweds."

"At least no one has to watch the awkward interplay between us trying to avoid our feelings. Admitting them — and embracing them — has been amazing."

Kaci stuck her finger in her ear. "Lalala."

Her friend giggled. "I didn't mean *that*."

"Sure, you didn't." Paisley couldn't have noticed the onlookers as much as Kaci had. No one seemed to believe that a woman and a man could remain just friends indefinitely without conceding more.

If Kaci's life wasn't so complicated, she could totally see diving in and seeing where "more" with Jude might lead.

Hello? Her life *was* complicated. A boyfriend — let alone a fiancé or husband — deserved to know his woman's history.

Honey, it appears my dad is an attorney for the mob.

Yeah, that wasn't exactly the stuff of casual conversation. Any man in his right mind would drop her like a hot potato. Even a casual friendship would go poof. She'd save Jude the bother. He was a stickler for honesty, and she liked having him around. They'd shared so many movie nights, card games, and horseback rides. She needed him to stay in exactly the role he'd chosen.

At the time, he'd been all in on the *just friends* option. But was he rethinking that position now that he'd managed to achieve a major goal he'd been striving for? Didn't everyone begin to contemplate settling down as they approached 30?

She was 24, still a few years off from that magic number, but Jude was 28.

"—so great if we can drop half a dozen kayaks off at the lake."

Right. Paisley was talking, as always. It was so easy to tune her out, but this wasn't the time. Not when they were one-on-one for an entire day with the guys not many horse-lengths behind them. If anything, Kaci needed to be triply alert.

"I can't wait to see your lake from the ground. It looks like quite a gem from the air!" Jude had circled it twice on their flight the other day.

"The lake needs a name. Can you believe there isn't one on the topo maps?"

"Huh."

"Any ideas?"

"Um, no. Maybe after I've experienced it."

"You should come on one of our overnight trail rides. We always need another female chaperone."

Kaci shrugged. "I have a full-time job already."

"You've got staff for that."

"I still need to do my share."

"Well, if we ever come up short-handed, I'll ask Tate to rearrange your schedule."

"Don't I get a say?"

"Aw, you know you'd love to come."

Kaci knew no such thing. On the other hand, Jude would be busy flying, so Paisley couldn't rope him into being one of the chaperones. Maybe it would be good to get out of his orbit from time to time. She wasn't about to admit that to Paisley, though.

They rounded a bend in the trail. Whoa. Kaci reined Nutmeg to a halt and stared across the valley where a grove of aspens was leafing out, caught in the glow of spring sunshine. The beauty was all but blinding.

"I missed this." Jude's quiet voice came from beside her.

"Yeah, it's… spectacular." She shook her head. Why had she never ridden beyond the usual tourist trails near the stable?

"I know. I don't ever want to leave Montana again. At least not for longer than a vacation." Jude's exhale lingered. "I've come home."

Kaci didn't have that sort of safe place. Never had. "I can see why you feel that way."

"A little different than Texas, huh?"

She stiffened. Was that a leading question? "Sure is." She pressed her knees to Nutmeg's sides and urged her forward to catch up with Paisley.

"Hey, Kaci?"

"Hmm?" She glanced back at Jude.

"I wasn't pushing."

And I wasn't running from you. Except, she had been. What would it be like to be a normal person with nothing to hide? It had been so long that she honestly couldn't remember. "Okay."

Dad's irregular business dealings had come to her awareness when she'd been in college. Nothing specific, not at first, just a few things that had made her wonder what sort of clients he really worked for. Whom he protected. Who protected him. Was that normal for attorneys?

She didn't know, but she sure couldn't ask Dad or Mom. She'd commented to her big brother about a specific questionable client after he'd started working with Dad. Duncan had tweaked her nose and said not to worry, everything was above board.

Kaci had zipped her mouth, but once she'd noticed, she couldn't quite rest. There were too many things that didn't add up. They'd never been shy of money, but her parents had bought a much bigger, nicer, country home than the one of her childhood. Dad's cars were newer and fancier. So were Mom's. Duncan's.

What was she supposed to think? The only person she could confide in was Grandad Moorehouse. He'd definitely taken her concerns seriously, but when he'd mentioned something to his son-in-law, Dad had punted the question to the side with some reply that didn't even make sense.

Then there'd been the untraceable threat she'd received by text.

"From the rising of the sun to the place where it sets, the name of the Lord is to be praised." Jude's reverent tone brought Kaci back to the vista of sunshine spreading across the valley below.

"Sounds like a psalm."

"It is." He grinned at her. "Psalm 113:3."

She tore her gaze from his.

God, why can't I see where things could go with this amazing man?

Kaci gritted her teeth. Life wasn't fair.

CHAPTER FOUR

Well? What do you think?" Paisley twirled around on top of the flat rock, hands in the air.

How had this woman gotten past Jude's brother's defenses? Weston was clearly not in the least intimidated by her. Not like he'd been the first year. How had things changed?

Jude truly wanted to know, because he needed optimism like Paisley's. How could he be the friend Kaci wanted and needed and still become more? But it wasn't like he was ready to have a heart-to-heart with his sister-in-law. It wasn't like he was ready to admit that he was obsessed by Kaci Moore. Not that it would be a shock for anyone.

Now he clambered up on the rock, tugging his tape measure free of his belt. "This isn't something I'm willing to trust to my eyeballs alone." He knelt at the edge. "Hold the tape here, and I'll get a read on it over there."

"Sure!" Paisley dropped beside him and pinned it down.

Jude noted the distance. So far, so good. "Now the other direction." The rock wasn't perfectly circular, of course, but it looked like it might check out okay. With dimensions confirmed, he stood with his hands on his hips studying the surface.

"Need those bushes out of there?" Weston asked.

Jude nodded. "And any of those loose smaller rocks."

Kaci pulled a pair of work gloves from her backpack before setting it down. "Where do you want the rocks?"

"Dump them over the far side. On this side — toward the lake — we're going to need to see what we can do to create better access. It's a bit steep and rough for hauling supplies."

"We made it up okay," Paisley protested.

"Not sure my grandfather can make the climb." Although he probably could. The old man surprised Jude nearly every day. "And would you want to haul heavy, awkward items?"

"Point taken. Hey, Weston, did you bring those foldable shovels?"

He smirked at her. "Sure did. And a few pairs of pruners, so there's no excuse for everyone not to put their backs into it."

A rock clattered down the slope, and Kaci turned for another one. She was already outworking them all. Jude grabbed an irregularly shaped boulder the size of a basketball and heaved it over the edge.

"Here, hold that bush aside while I cut the stems," Weston said behind him. "The roots are probably shallow because of the rocks, but I can't quite pull them."

The spring sun beat down on the quartet as they

worked to clear the area. Jude kept an eye on Kaci. She wasn't overdoing it, was she? Didn't seem to be.

"You must've been working out over the winter," he joked.

She grinned. "Of course. There's not much else to do around here when we're neck deep in snow."

"Was there a lot of it this year?"

She pried another rock loose. "We had a couple of good storms like the one that knocked out our power for a few days early in the new year. It was good having your grandmother here during that time. She kept spirits up and helped Eryn and Madison figure out how to cook with limited resources."

"Yeah, I heard about that storm." Jude had missed a lot by being away for so long. "I got away just before it blew in. We didn't even get the tail end in Chicago."

"Maybe the wind just blasted it on by." Kaci surveyed the area she'd cleared.

"Could be." Jude chuckled. "I now know how the city got its nickname."

"I bet."

"Ever spent much time in Chicago?"

Kaci flicked a narrowed gaze his direction. "I've been a lot of places."

Right. He kept forgetting all the subjects to avoid. Anything to do with her family and her past. In the early days of their friendship, it hadn't bothered him. Chatting about day-to-day life at Sweet River Ranch had been enough. He hadn't clued in for a long time how deftly she avoided most topics. Now that he'd noticed, he wondered how he could ever have been blind to it.

"I haven't been many places." He sat and pushed a larger loose rock with his feet. "A mission trip to Mexico when I was a teen. We joined with another group and changed planes in Dallas, so I count Texas as a place I've been."

He kept an eye on Kaci in his periphery. If he hadn't been, he wouldn't have noticed the quick set to her jaw before she turned her back.

"Now I've been to Kansas and landed in multiple other states."

"Great!"

Her enthusiasm was totally false. It didn't even take having hung around Paisley's genuine exuberance to recognize the sham.

Jude glanced to where Weston and Paisley worked together removing another clump of bushes. He turned back to Kaci and lowered his voice. "You can trust me, you know."

"Of course, I do!"

He studied her profile. "Which means you can talk to me and know it won't go any further."

"We talk."

"On a very limited number of topics."

She dropped a rock from a few inches then bent over her foot. "Ouch. I need to be more careful."

Had the rock even touched her? Jude didn't think so. "Kaci."

"Looks like Paisley needs help."

"*Kaci.*"

"Jude, don't."

"Don't what?" He couldn't get an ounce of curiosity in

his tone. He knew exactly what she meant. He was simply tired of playing her game.

"We're just friends, remember?" Her gaze ricocheted off his.

"I have vague acquaintances I know more about than I know you after hanging out for two full years." Minus the months he'd been away.

"I don't like to talk much."

"You're hiding things."

"And you're too pushy."

"Because you don't trust me."

Kaci huffed and rolled her eyes. "You're like a broken record."

"And you're not?"

"Can we drop the subject, please?"

He studied her flushed face. It wasn't all from exertion. Her averted gaze wasn't her normal, either, unless he asked questions she didn't want to answer. Should he push? Would he ever get past her barricade by doing so? Or just make her avoid him? Yet, how could anything be worse than staying in the superficial relationship where she'd placed him?

"Are you in trouble with the law? My grandfather could help."

Kaci's jaw set. "Are you quite done speculating?"

"Not really. The more you put me off, the more random scenarios my imagination comes up with."

"Find other things to be curious about. Tell me how you expect to use this helipad to access this mountain lake."

Jude gritted his teeth. Where was the discussion in that?

KACI SIDLED toward where Paisley worked with Weston. Maybe it wasn't too obvious that she was trying to get away from Jude. Why couldn't he leave well enough alone? Why keep pushing her?

She'd thrived on their early relationship. It had been fun to have a guy friend, a buddy who was up for a games or movie night, a water fight out in the kayaks, or a head-clearing horseback ride.

Once, she'd daydreamed of more, back when she thought she'd be out of hiding in a few months. Now, months had dragged into years with no end in sight.

How long, oh, Lord?

Yeah, her heart cry echoed the ancient Jewish people's plea for a Messiah, but didn't she need a redeemer of her own? The monthly missives her lawyer — ironically, Jude's Aunt Bridget — forwarded from Grandad did not hint that an end was in sight.

But her maternal grandfather did want to meet with her in Chicago. He'd set a date for early June. Clearly, he did not understand how hard it was to get away from Sweet River during the tourist season. He definitely didn't understand why she'd taken a job as head housekeeper, of all things... even though it was his decades-long friendship with Walter Sullivan that had procured this position for her.

And, of course, Mr. Sullivan would cheerfully give her the time off, but he'd handed over the reins of running the business to Jude's cousin Tate and was no longer in charge of day-to-day operations. That complicated everything.

"You're a long way off," Paisley observed.

Kaci glanced over with a start. She'd been tugging at a bush without paying attention, and the bush hadn't budged so much as an inch. "Just thinking."

"Thinking is over-rated." Paisley handed her a pair of pruners. "Although it can be productive at times, if it means finding the right tools for the job."

Kaci managed a chuckle. "Thanks. It seems with all the rock, these roots should be shallow enough to pull out."

"That's what Weston thought, too. You were both wrong."

Weston huffed a laugh. "You wound me, woman."

Paisley rolled her eyes and leaned toward Kaci. "Men and their over-inflated egos."

"Still getting me right in the heart." Weston grabbed his chest and sank to his knees.

"So dramatic," Paisley whispered.

Kaci shook her head but couldn't stop a grin. She could still hardly believe the change in the surly cowboy. She wouldn't have bet a nickel on him having a sense of humor when they'd first met. He'd seemed gruff and angry all the time.

The power of love.

Yeah, well, love was fine for other people, but Kaci needed to keep strong against it for herself. God's love was all she needed, right?

Tell yourself what you need to hear, girl.

She didn't dare glance behind her to see what Jude was doing over there. Besides, the clattering of rocks proved he was still intent on clearing the loose rubble.

She clipped the bushes at ground level and moved on to

another clump before pausing to look down on the lake. Beside where they'd staked the horses was an open area with a campfire spot at the edge of a rocky beach leading to the water. It looked inviting.

Kaci had worked up enough sweat she was almost tempted to take a cooling dip, but the mixed company and the fact that it was only mid-May put that thought on pause. The lake had probably been covered in ice last week. Some northerners thrived on Polar Bear Swims, but to a Texan born and bred? That meant coolish water, not with ice cubes all but floating in it.

"Break time!" Paisley sang out.

"We just got started!" Weston protested.

"It's been at least an hour. Right, Kaci?"

No way was Kaci getting in the middle of this.

"Okay, fine. I just need to use the facilities. And, while I'm thankful for the privacy screens around the latrines, it occurs to me that we need actual outhouses with roofs if people are going to be up on this rock."

"I'm working way over here, Paisley," Jude called. "Promise I won't peek."

Weston snorted a laugh.

"A pee break sounds good. I'll go with you."

"What's with women and their need to go to the bathroom in groups?"

Paisley glared at her husband, who put up his hands in mock surrender. The guy was learning quickly.

"It's the power of suggestion," Jude hollered from across the rock.

"Quit while you're ahead," Paisley yelled back. "Come on, Kaci. Let's leave these lugs to the hard labor for a bit."

"Too hard on your delicate little muscles?" Weston taunted.

"Them's fightin' words, darling."

"Oooh, a fight! Then we can make up. I like making up."

Kaci stuck her fingers in her ears. "Lalala."

Paisley laughed and grabbed Kaci's arm. "Come on, girlfriend. Maybe we can figure out a better route off this butte while we're at it."

Kaci eyed the descent. "We need one, I think. Coming up wasn't bad, but it looks harder going down. I can't see my handholds from here."

"Maybe we'll need a pulley system for loads."

"You mean for people."

Paisley chuckled. "Don't be a wimp. We were right over here." She took a step down then grabbed at a bush to keep her balance as loose pebbles cascaded from beneath her feet.

"I'm not sure how many times I want to climb this thing." But Kaci followed her friend's lead.

"Yeah, it's a bit steep. Mr. Sullivan isn't the only one who'll have trouble with it."

They stood at the bottom and eyed the route they'd just descended.

Kaci shook her head. "A ladder bolted into the rocks might not be a bad idea in some places. That's a bit of a scramble."

"Maybe there's a better route a little further to the south."

"Maybe."

Paisley tugged on Kaci's arm again. "After we use the

facilities, we can circumnavigate the base and see if there's a better way up."

"Sounds good." Kaci lowered her voice. "Also, I didn't want to mention it up there, but I need to pee, too. Guys have it so easy."

"Don't they, though? But don't tell Weston that my hours behind a desk are totally showing in my stamina. Once the season gets into full swing and I'm active with visiting kids and their families, I'll get back in shape."

"There's a staff gym, you know."

Paisley wrinkled her nose. "Over my dead body."

Kaci laughed. "I needed something to do over the winter."

"With Jude far away in Chicago."

Shoot. She'd totally opened herself up for that one.

CHAPTER FIVE

J ude started a small blaze in the fire-blackened ring of stones near the waterfront while Weston and Paisley hauled more branches and Kaci spread out the picnic lunch from the saddlebags. He eyed the containers she laid out on the log. "Whatcha got there?"

"Your mom sent roast beef sandwiches and the leftovers of that broiled oatmeal cake she made yesterday." Kaci peered into a large container. "And a whole lot of fresh veggies."

Jude chuckled. "That's my mom. Always with the veggies. I can't tell you how many times I buried them in the garden when I was a kid. I hated anything green."

Kaci leaned back on her heels and eyed him. "You outgrew that, I hope."

"More or less. They're still not my favorite thing, but I'm a big boy now and know they're good for me." He narrowed his gaze. "She didn't send broccoli, did she?"

Kaci held up a piece.

"Drat. She knows I hate those."

"Jamie calls them little trees and gobbles them up." Humor danced in Kaci's eyes.

He'd do nearly anything to see more of that. "Well, I'm not a three-year-old, and I wasn't raised by Stephanie and Tate. But kudos to the kid."

"What's not to like?" Eyebrows raised, Kaci chomped into a piece. "Mmm. Good."

"Are you making fun of me?"

"Maybe?"

"They get stuck in my teeth. I was never so glad to wear braces as when broccoli was on the menu. At least Mom didn't nag me then."

"Broccoli is a superfood."

Jude rolled his eyes. "You're making that up."

"Not at all. It's packed with nutrients, vitamins, and fiber. It's even been shown to have anti-cancer properties."

"You sound like an encyclopedia. Why do you care so much?"

She flushed and looked away.

Jude blinked. Hadn't that been an innocent question? But with Kaci's many secrets, nothing was innocuous. He had no clue what random point would set her off.

"Enough wood, Jude?" Paisley dropped another load beside the big log.

"Probably." He gave another speculative look at Kaci, but she was fussing with one of the containers.

"Weston's gone for water." Paisley unscrewed the top of her thermos. "Why he insists on brewing coffee over the fire instead of filling a thermal mug or two from the dispenser at the ranch, I'll never know."

"I brought myself tea," Kaci said.

Paisley shook her head. "You drink herbal stuff with honey. I'll take my Earl black and straight, thank you very much."

Women. Jude cracked a stick against his knee and fed it into the flames. "Don't knock cowboy coffee. It's great stuff. West and I have lots of memories of camping and fishing with our Grandpa Kline. He loved his coffee the way you like your tea, Paisley." He broke another stick and eyed his sister-in-law. "Thick enough to keep a spoon upright."

Kaci shuddered.

Neither of them needed to know Jude preferred his less like tar. He'd even found he liked an occasional frou-frou beverage during his months in Chicago, not that he'd ever admit it to his brother.

Weston tucked his billy can into the coals on the edge of the fire and eyed his wife. "Disparaging my preferences again?"

"Never." Paisley fluttered her eyelashes. "After all, you chose me, so I can't make too much fun of your life choices."

"Nice comeback." Kaci snickered.

"I also can't complain about a lengthier lunch break while we wait, not only for you to brew your mud, but also for you to drink it."

"No one's stopping you from climbing that butte and clearing more bushes, woman." Weston grabbed Paisley and pulled her into a hug.

Jude turned aside to keep his smirk from showing. Those two were at it constantly, punctuating every snarky conversation with a dozen kisses. There they were, smooching again.

Why did he have to choose a woman who didn't want him? It had been the opposite with his brother. Paisley had done the pursuing until she wore Weston down, but that had been Weston's insecurities speaking. He'd come around after a while and realized what a treasure he had in front of him. Paisley might be a scatterbrained chatterbox, but she was loyal, loved Jesus, and was completely devoted to Weston.

Kaci's barriers seemed deeply rooted compared to Weston's, but what did Jude know? She didn't share enough to give him a clue what was going on.

"Let's pray over this lunch." Weston took Paisley's hand in his and bowed his head. "Thank You, Lord, for this food. Thank You for Your amazing creation we get to enjoy. Please grant us wisdom and safety as we navigate through this day. In Jesus's name, amen."

"Amen," Jude murmured.

Kaci handed out the sandwiches, and they all dug in. Jude fed a few more sticks into the fire, and Weston dumped coffee grounds into the water boiling in his billy can. Jude was with the women on this one. He'd rather have brought his own thermos and had sips of hot coffee to enjoy all morning rather than this sludge over lunch, but offending his brother wasn't a good option. Weston was right in that campfires just like this one were the stuff his memories were made of.

"Remember that time we caught all those bass with Grandpa?"

"Yeah." Weston's grin looked far away. "Good times. We cooked them over the fire. Best meal of my life."

Kaci elbowed Paisley. "Is that some kind of slur on your marriage?"

Paisley chuckled. "Good thing we eat in the dining hall is all I can say."

"You guys are building a house, though? You might have to cook eventually."

"Over near the stables. Close to the lodge, so I think I'm safe. Besides, Weston can cook."

Weston snorted a laugh. "Good thing, since Paisley can burn water."

"Only that one time."

Jude looked between them. "There's a story I need to hear."

Paisley glared at him. "I got distracted, okay? It was Weston's fault."

"That's probably all the story we need, then." Kaci held out the veggies. "Here, who wants some?"

"Anything but broccoli." Jude grabbed at the container, his fingers brushing Kaci's as he did so. Awareness surged through him as his gaze met hers.

The container tumbled to the ground between them, scattering carrots, broccoli, and sugar-snap peas into the rocky crevices. "Oops. Sorry about that." He dragged his gaze from hers.

"Did you dump the broccoli on purpose?" Weston taunted.

"No, I… never mind." Maybe Jude should have owned it, but it was too late now.

His brother picked up a few of the vegetables, brushed them off, and dropped them back into the container. "Good thing that wasn't glass."

"Uh, yeah. Good thing."

"I'm not eating dirty veggies." Paisley's nose curled as she shook her head.

"Nothing a swish in the lake won't cure." Weston brushed sand out of a piece of broccoli.

"Um. No."

But Jude's brother and sister-in-law's banter was background babble. Jude was still wondering what that spark of energy had been all about.

KACI GULPED down the last of her sandwich and washed it down with a swig from her water bottle. "Time to get back to work." She carefully kept her gaze averted from Jude.

"I'm just making coffee now," Weston drawled. "You go ahead, though."

"I'm taking a longer break." Paisley nibbled at her sandwich.

That left Jude, the one Kaci was determined to avoid. What had that jolt been all about, anyway? It had been like static electricity. Her little brother used to scuff across the carpet then touch her, hoping for a reaction.

But Jude hadn't tried, and neither had she. He'd dropped that container like a hot potato, so she had to assume he'd felt what she had.

It was bizarre. Made no sense. She touched people all the time... okay, so maybe she didn't. When was the last time she'd done it on purpose? Days? Weeks? She'd never been touchy-feely. That was for needy girls like Paisley's sister Kait who'd draped all over Jude at the wedding last month. Maybe it was for girls who'd had affectionate parents.

Kaci really, really didn't want to go down this rabbit trail. She packed up the remains of lunch then offered the pieces of cake to the others, keeping her fingers well back from the edge... and her gaze averted from Jude's.

"Good dessert." She dug into her own piece. "I've never had cake with a broiled topping before. It's amazing."

"I hadn't, either." Paisley shook her head. "Nobody baked in my house unless it came from a box. Even that was rare."

In Kaci's experience, cake hadn't come from a mix but from a caterer, but that wasn't information she was going to drop in present company. She licked the last remnants of toasted coconut and walnuts from her fingers.

Weston poured himself and Jude each a coffee before leaning back against the log with a contented sigh.

This was going to take forever. She bounced to her feet. "I'll be back in a few." After using the latrine and washing her hands in the lake, she grabbed the salvaged vegetables and fed them to the horses.

Nutmeg nipped the broccoli from Kaci's outstretched palm and snuffled for more.

"Glad someone likes it," Jude said with a low chuckle.

Kaci jumped. She hadn't even heard him coming.

"Hey, I didn't mean to startle you. I thought I was making enough noise to wake a winter bear."

"Nope. Not nearly enough." She meant it to sound light, casual, maybe even funny. Instead, her panic was likely obvious. When had things become so awkward between them? She'd been content with friendship for two full years. So had he or, if not, it hadn't shown.

Or maybe she'd been oblivious. Hopefully not that, because her very safety — maybe even her life — depended on awareness of her surroundings.

If she'd missed this, what else had she missed? Any newcomer to Sweet River, whether staff or guest, had the potential of being someone who'd known Kirsten. Longer hair was not the stuff of disguise, nor was a lighter style of makeup.

Panic welled up her throat. She wasn't safe. Someone could find her at any minute.

Okay, maybe not up here by this mountain lake. If Paisley or Jude or Weston had already figured out her identity, her gig would have been up a long time ago.

"Sorry, Kaci. I didn't mean to throw you for a loop." Jude sounded contrite. "It seems like I can't say anything right anymore."

If he limited his topics to Sweet River Ranch and what was for dinner, they should be fine. *That* was what had changed. He'd started to look at her in a different way and to probe more about her past, but she couldn't exactly say that outright. She'd come pretty close, and he hadn't backed off.

She went around to the other side of Nutmeg, where she could stroke the horse's face and keep an eye on Jude. "Are sightseeing flights filling up?"

His eyes lit up.

Bingo.

"Pretty well. We had to cancel a few reservations because Grandfather wants me in Chicago week after next.

He has some people he wants me to meet, and then he wants to come out to the ranch for a while."

"To see Eleanor?" Kaci guessed.

"My nana? Probably."

"Do you think they're going to get back together?"

Better someone else's love life than hers, not that she didn't want one. It just had to wait until things had cleared up back home... which would likely mean her father and her brother in prison. Why, oh, why did she hear so little from Grandad?

Jude lifted a shoulder. "Maybe? I guess you're never too old to get married, or so I hear."

Alarm bells rang in Kaci's head. Somehow, it didn't seem like a safe subject anymore. "He's over 80, isn't he?"

Jude nodded. "And Nana's 77 in a couple of weeks."

"Maybe he wants to be here for her birthday."

"I guess. At any rate, we had to cancel some bookings for flights. My grandfather is the boss, so what he says goes."

"Will you be gone long?" Kaci kind of hoped so. She could use a reprieve.

"Four or five days, it sounds like. He's still trying to line things up with his friend he wants me to meet."

"Maybe it's a young lady."

Jude practically got whiplash from pivoting to stare straight at her. And had his eyes somehow turned to laser beams? "He knows better than to pull a stunt like that."

"You're his last single grandson." And she should definitely zip her face.

"Bryce and Maxwell aren't married."

"But they are very taken, and didn't your grandfather

play a large role in getting Madison here to the ranch to make up with Bryce? I wouldn't put it past him to meddle."

"Well, he can butt out."

Kaci tried to tear her gaze away from Jude, but it was impossible.

"I have my own ideas."

And she had a sneaking suspicion just what those were. Why couldn't she keep her mouth shut? "It takes two to tango," she threw over her shoulder as she strode back toward the fire.

CHAPTER SIX

I have news for you." Mr. Sullivan's voice came through the airwaves.

Kaci clutched her cell phone. "What kind of news?"

"Your grandfather will be in Chicago next week and wants to meet with you."

Hope and joy shot through her, followed immediately by a wave of panic. "Is it safe?"

"I believe so. Frederick has booked a suite at the Waldorf Astoria, and I've booked one for you a dozen rooms away. He has some meetings planned, so there should be no suspicion."

"Wouldn't he usually stay at a Sullivan hotel?"

Mr. Sullivan hesitated. "He would, but we don't think this will cause a red flag. Bridget feels it seems safer for you."

Kaci's gut twisted. Oh, how she wanted to see Grandad! How she wanted to feel his arms around her and his whispered assurance that everything would work out all right. She'd missed him so much.

But it seemed risky to meet with him, even so far from Texas or Montana. "Are you sure?"

"As sure as we can be. We'll have additional eyes over there as well. But Frederick feels it is important to speak with you in person."

"That sounds ominous."

"On the contrary, he sounded fairly upbeat when we spoke."

That should be more comforting than it seemed.

"You'll be flying in with Jude, so there will be no airline ticket attributed to Kaci Moore, in case anyone's watching."

Not Jude. "I should drive. That way, I won't have to depend on a taxi or Uber to get around the city."

"I've made all of the arrangements."

Of course, he had. Jude had mentioned the other day on their horseback ride to the lake that he was going to Chicago. She'd had no reason to suspect she might be going, too. "I don't think—"

"Kaci." The old man's voice was tender, like a grandfather.

"Yes, sir?"

"You can't hide forever, and it sounds like Frederick has something important to discuss. It's worth the trip."

"Did he tell you what he knows?"

Did Kaci imagine the brief pause?

"Only a hint. Jude is taking the helicopter to the Missoula airport early Tuesday morning, where he'll switch to the company jet. You'll be in Chicago by lunchtime."

Half a day with Jude. Probably more in Chicago, unless the Sullivans were all keeping a low profile to not draw attention to the link. Then the return flight. "How much does Jude know?"

"Nothing."

"Won't he wonder why he's chauffeuring me to Chicago?"

"We'll just tell him you're looking for a few days off for shopping or a break."

"He won't buy that." For starters, Kaci hadn't left the ranch for more than a few hours in the two years she'd been employed there. Now, as the tourist season ramped up, was *not* when she'd choose to take personal time.

"Sure he will."

"I don't think so. He already asks too many questions about my past. He won't accept this at face value."

"You're reading too much into him."

"With all due respect, sir, I'm not." How could a man who headed up a powerful hotel empire not be more observant? Granted, he hadn't been around the ranch a whole lot since Jude's return six weeks ago, and maybe he'd believed the 'just friends' line both Kaci and Jude had presented for two years. Not many had truly believed it, though. Their friends sure hadn't.

"You'll think of something. I'll be returning with the two of you on Saturday, so I can provide a buffer then."

Kaci sighed. "Do I have a choice?"

"Yes, you do. I can cancel your reservation. Frederick will still come. As I said, he has meetings lined up."

And she might never know what Grandad wanted to tell her. The old man wasn't one for phone calls, preferring to observe body language. He detested texting with a passion shared by many octogenarians. So, while she might get him to talk on the phone, it would likely be cryptic. He might worry who could overhear on his end. He was going a long way out of his way to meet her in person, and she was so afraid of Jude's curiosity that she'd forego this opportunity to put the past in perspective?

Kaci straightened her back, though Mr. Sullivan couldn't see her. "Okay, fine. I'll make up some excuse and come. Hopefully my staff will do an adequate job while I'm gone."

"I'm sure they will. And Kaci? You won't regret this. We'll keep you as safe here as you are at Sweet River."

Hadn't she worried recently that any new guest could be a former acquaintance from Texas? She didn't always feel very safe, keeping a surreptitious eye on folks in the dining hall, staying aware of her surroundings, and watching for anyone who might be paying her extra attention.

Ultimately, her safety wasn't Mr. Sullivan's problem. It was hers, and she could be just as aware in an urban environment as here at the ranch. She'd lived in the city most of her life. She could blend in.

"Thank you, Mr. Sullivan." What else could she say?

"See you on Tuesday."

He didn't mean that literally, did he? What of keeping a distance from her and Grandad? No, he had done everything by protocol for two-and-a-half years. His daughter-in-law, Bridget, was the attorney managing Kaci's identity. If she couldn't trust him now, she couldn't trust him at all.

"See you Tuesday."

Kaci set her phone on the table and looked out the window of the tiny duplex she shared with Emma Cavanagh, one of the kitchen staff. The fresh green of spring leaves warmed the trees from the stark skeletons they'd been for so many months. Sunlight dappled on the lake, a sliver of which she could make out between another pair of duplexes across the way.

She'd been safe at Sweet River Ranch, at least as much as anywhere. What would Grandad divulge? Would she return to the ranch, or be off to a new, safer hideout? Was it even possible that she'd be able to return to Dallas and assume her own identity sometime soon? Take a job as a nurse the way she'd planned and trained for?

Not if the investigation against Dad's law firm wasn't concluded and any wrongdoers in custody. Her heart cried at the thought of Dad and Duncan in prison, but the evidence — the things she'd heard and seen — pointed strongly to guilt.

Oh, Lord!

Tears dribbled down her cheeks.

I long to have this chapter over with, but my daddy! My big brother! I don't know what to pray, how to feel, how to act.

That's why the Holy Spirit interceded when believers didn't know how to pray, but faith had never been so difficult.

"TODAY'S TEXT is from the first few verses of Luke chapter 12," intoned Pastor Marshall on Sunday morning. "'Meanwhile, when a crowd of many thousands had gathered, so that they were trampling on one another, Jesus began to speak first to his disciples, saying: 'Be on your guard against the yeast of the Pharisees, which is hypocrisy. There is nothing concealed that will not be disclosed, or hidden that will not be made known. What you have said in the dark will be heard in the daylight, and what you have whispered in the ear in the inner rooms will be proclaimed from the roofs.'"

Jude shifted restlessly in the pew of Creekside Fellowship between his mom and his brother. He didn't dare glance across the sanctuary to where Kaci sat with several of the housekeeping staff.

Take that, Kaci Moore. Your secrets can't stay hidden forever.

Not that her secrets had anything to do with the Pharisees of Jesus's day.

"Or, as the Apostle Paul put it, 'for you were once darkness, but now you are light in the Lord. Live as children of light.' What did Jesus mean? What did Paul mean?"

Jude hunkered a little deeper in his seat. He lived as a child of light, didn't he? Jesus had saved him from living for himself when he was a teen. The mission trip to Mexico had solidified it. He'd tried hard not to let the Sullivan money taint him in the past couple of years. Had he been pulled to the dark side on account of it without even noticing?

"The Pharisees were big on following rules. They never had enough laws but kept making more of them. It was like a competition. After all, you couldn't be the best rule keeper of all if there were only two, and they were so easy that anyone could follow them, right?"

Where was the pastor going with this? Jude much preferred uplifting sermons.

"So the more laws they had and the more nuanced they were, the harder it was to follow them all. Then it became possible to be better at being a Pharisee than the guy next to you."

Pastor Marshall rearranged his notes on the lectern as his gaze scanned the congregation. "Jesus accused the Pharisees of being like whitewashed tombs, sparkling clean and white on the outside, but full of rot and decay on the inside. Their very lifestyle demanded that they hide their failures from others. Perception was everything."

Ugh. Jude had spent so much time wondering what Kaci was hiding he'd pushed aside the fact that he, too, chose what to divulge and when to share it. He was far from an open book himself, but that didn't mean he had big things to hide. Just… it wasn't anyone else's business what went on inside his head. He had a feeling Kaci's reticence was based on something more, but how could he know for sure without pinning her down?

Grandfather had told him Kaci was coming to Chicago with him on Tuesday, and that she'd be met by a taxi while he'd be met by the Sullivan limo. They'd be going their separate ways, Grandfather stressed.

The questions he'd asked resulted in deflection. It was like Kaci and the old man were in cahoots together, but that couldn't be. Could it?

"In Luke 18, Jesus tells us a related parable. It goes like this." Pastor Marshall lifted his big leather-bound Bible and began to read. "'To some who were confident of their own righteousness and looked down on everyone else, Jesus told this parable: "Two men went up to the temple to pray, one a Pharisee and the other a tax collector. The Pharisee stood by himself and prayed: 'God, I thank you that I am not like other people — robbers, evildoers, adulterers — or even like this tax collector. I fast twice a week and give a tenth of all I get.' But the tax collector stood at a distance. He would not even look up to heaven, but beat his breast and said, 'God, have mercy on me, a sinner.'

"'I tell you that this man, rather than the other, went home justified before God. For all those who exalt themselves will be humbled, and those who humble themselves will be exalted.'"

Pastor Marshall set his Bible aside. "You may wonder how all those dots connect. The Pharisee hid his true self and only revealed what he wanted the public to see. In fact, he likely even believed it to be true. But the tax collector? He knew who he was. Everyone knew who he was. He didn't try to hide it, but he also didn't embrace it and say, 'well this is just who I am.' He acknowledged his identity… and begged for mercy."

Silence hung over Creekside Fellowship. It seemed everyone was clinging to the pastor's words.

"There's a balance, of course, between hiding our innermost being from those around us and letting all our dirty laundry hang out. This is where Paul's words in Ephesians five clarify what's going on. He says, 'For you were once darkness, but now you are light in the Lord. Live as children of light (for the fruit of the light consists in all goodness, righteousness and truth) and find out what pleases the Lord. Have nothing to do with the fruitless deeds of darkness, but rather expose them. It is shameful even to mention what the disobedient do in secret. But everything exposed by the light becomes visible — and everything that is illuminated becomes a light.'"

Pastor Marshall leaned over the lectern. "Darkness or light. Hidden or revealed. Lies or truth. How do you want to live? Which side aligns with the abundant life Jesus came to provide? Let us pray."

Jude ducked his head. The pastor probably prayed, not that Jude was listening. He wanted to grab Kaci by the shoulders and ask her the same question. Why was she choosing secrets rather than trust?

He was dependable. He was. He cared a lot about her, but if she wouldn't be honest toward him, what was left? Maybe he didn't even know enough about her to know for sure she was a good person.

That was silly. Of course, she was. She wasn't hiding her innate personality, just her entire past. Wasn't that enough?

Relationships couldn't be built on lack of trust. On secrets.

Maybe she'd hear this message and come to him afterward, ready to tell all.

But when the closing hymn had been sung, she'd disappeared from the building.

CHAPTER SEVEN

Could this be any more awkward? The senior Mr. Sullivan must be playing some sort of game here, which didn't bode well for the next five days.

The hop via helicopter from the ranch to the airport hadn't been conducive to conversation since the rotors and engine were so loud. But now, as Jude guided her to the small jet sitting on the runway, all Kaci felt was fear that this next, longer leg would be more difficult. Only the thought of seeing Grandad kept her moving forward.

That, and Jude's hand at the small of her back. She tried to step aside, to out-walk his touch, but it remained steady. Realization sifted over her like a cozy down blanket. She craved human touch. There'd been so little in her life, and she'd allowed even less in Montana. She could count on one hand the number of times she'd willingly hugged one of her girlfriends here.

As for the guys? Nothing beyond an occasional dance or an accidental brush of arms while working together. Even Jude.

Especially Jude.

Now he ushered her up the airstairs into the jet. It wasn't a large plane — not nearly the size of Dad's personal jet — but the seats faced each other in conversational groupings. Good. She could get comfortable in the cabin while Jude settled in the cockpit.

Kaci slid her roller bag into the cabin.

"You're up front with me, of course." Jude laughed. "Ever ridden in the cockpit before?"

She froze, avoiding eye contact, her memories of flying with her father unfolding in front of her like the 3D book she'd read to Jamie the other day. *Close the book, Kaci. Let the pop-up fold away again.*

"I thought I'd catch up on some reading. This looks comfy right here." She dared shoot a glance at Jude.

A look of concern, maybe even worry, crossed his features. "I'd love your company."

How could she refuse? Friends. They were friends, and it was natural for them to hang out in the same space.

"Okay. Sure." But trepidation sank in her gut. Man, this was awkward. She longed for the easy relationship they'd once enjoyed, but Jude had changed since his return. He looked at her differently.

It might not only be Jude who'd changed. Maybe she had, too. Her friend group all had significant others now. People were pairing up all around her.

And Kaci couldn't help but wish she were free to do the same. She stiffened her back. Maybe this meeting with Grandad would clear the way to a future where she'd be free to be herself.

Truth? Kirsten Atkinson was a distant memory. Kaci

had an entire life — albeit without a backstory — that did not intersect with Kirsten's.

Maybe it would now. That would be good, right? Reuniting with her parents — except that was unlikely to happen. Dad was going to end up behind bars sooner or later. The relationship Kirsten had enjoyed with him as a child had been a sham and would never return.

With a start, she heard Jude requesting permission to prepare for takeoff from air traffic control. She'd buckled and adjusted her headset without paying attention.

Kaci's hands trembled as she clenched them tightly in her lap. She had to get a grip, or Jude would think it was his skill level that had her nervous. No, she trusted him completely. It was her own issues that had her shaken.

The brief conversation with the tower paused as Jude positioned the aircraft for takeoff. Then he received the all-clear and flipped a sequence of switches. He grinned at Kaci. "Ready?"

She managed a smile in return. "Ready."

Jude turned his attention back to the instrument panel and sent them hurtling down the runway and into the air.

The heavy feeling of gravity pushed her hard into the seat until they were airborne. Then the plane banked to the east and leveled off.

Jude flexed his shoulder muscles and grinned over at her again.

"Good job!"

"Thanks." He beamed.

Why was her approval so important to him? She'd been trying to deny it, but it wasn't really possible. Jude was hoping for more from her than she could give.

A flicker of hope stirred. Maybe this conversation with her grandfather would put to rest all the reasons why a relationship with Jude was a bad idea.

Did she want that?

She didn't dare consider it. Sure, Jude was an attractive man. He was genuinely kind. He truly desired to follow the Lord's direction in his life. Kirsten would have been all in.

But Kaci wasn't sure. Who was she, anyway? No longer Kirsten. Not exactly Kaci. Who would she be when those two identities merged?

If they ever did. She shouldn't put the cart before the horse. Kirsten Catriona Moorehouse-Atkinson was not in this cockpit with Jude Kline. Kaci Moore was, and Kaci Moore had many issues she couldn't drag Jude into.

She turned to Jude. "Tell me about your first flight." Maybe she could keep the conversation rolling in directions that didn't hinge on her own past, present, or future identity.

THIS WAS MORE LIKE IT. The three-hour flight had flown by — no pun intended. Jude reveled in the familiar comfort of time with Kaci the way it used to be before he'd noticed what all she left out of conversations. Before he'd noticed *her*.

Wheels down.

The small jet bounced a little then rapidly slowed.

Jude followed instructions as he taxied to the private area of the airport, finally coming to rest in the designated area. He depowered the plane, checking all the gauges as he did so. Finally, with the engine off, he removed his headset and grinned at Kaci. "Here we are."

"So I see."

The smile didn't reach her eyes. He'd been dying to ask for three days why she was coming to Chicago, but he'd chopped off the question each time. Surely, she'd tell him. But apparently not. Her secrets were tightly in place, sewn up, locked down, completely hidden.

Jude reached over and touched her arm. "You okay? Someone's meeting you?"

"Sure! And yes, I have a ride, thanks."

"Can I see you while we're here?"

Her lips tightened.

And... he shouldn't have let the question blurt out. He *knew* that.

"Just text me when to meet you back here. Saturday morning, right?"

"Yeah. Saturday morning at eight, local time. Just inside the private terminal."

"Your grandfather is returning with us?"

Did she have to remind him they'd have company on the return trip? "I believe so."

"All right then." She set her headset on its hook and reached for her carry-on.

"I'll get that for you." He grabbed her handle then his own. "After you."

"Don't you need to lock up?"

"Electronic. It's all good."

He followed her down the airstairs into the warmth of noonday sunshine. They crossed the tarmac and through the terminal.

On the other side, Kaci pulled out her phone and tapped into it. Then she gestured toward a waiting Highlander. "That's my ride."

Jude frowned. "You're sure? Kenneth is right there in the Sullivan limo. We can drop you off wherever you're going." It occurred to him he didn't even know where that was.

"No, it's all good. I promise." Kaci flashed him an eye-contact-less grin and took the handle of her roller bag. "See you Saturday."

Jude couldn't help snapping a photo of the Highlander's license plate as the young driver in dark sunglasses stowed Kaci's bag and held the door for her. Letting her go like this went against every impulse in his body. He might not have always respected his dad as much as he should have, but Michael Kline's dedication to chivalry had never varied. He'd taught Weston and Jude to look out for all women, not just the ones in their lives.

Kenneth stood beside the black Sullivan limo. "Jude?"

"Yes, sir." Jude strode over as the Highlander shifted into traffic and disappeared. "Thanks for the pickup."

"No problem, sir. It's my pleasure." He loaded Jude's bag. "To Sullivan Tower?"

Jude chuckled as he took his seat. "Wherever my grandfather told you to take me." Just imagine Kaci with a chauffeur. Even after six months in Chicago, he'd barely become accustomed to being driven around. To be fair, mostly he'd driven himself, but the limo was always at the ready, and his grandfather and uncles had sent it for him on numerous occasions.

They merged into traffic, and Jude's eagle eye spotted

the Highlander up ahead. He choked back orders to follow the other vehicle. This trip had been arranged by his grandfather — for both him and for Kaci, as far as he could figure out — and he had to believe the old man knew what he was doing.

Ultimately, he had to trust that God knew what He was doing, even though life seemed to keep spiraling. Okay, maybe not his entire life, but the part that was Kaci? Definitely in a tailspin. A safe, soft landing seemed impossible.

So busy! The Highlander wended between other vehicles on I-55 then merged with Lake Shore Drive.

Kaci gazed at the blue waters of Lake Michigan beyond McCormick Place as they zipped northward. She hadn't set foot in a city since the day she left Dallas two and a half years ago. At first, she'd missed the hustle and bustle and the energy from the crowds, but she'd gradually come to appreciate the call of the loon on a still, quiet evening. Slowly, the tenseness in her shoulders had dissipated as she settled into remote rural life.

Sure, she'd remained aware of the fact that any visitor might be from Dallas and a friend of her family, but fear hadn't overwhelmed her.

The tension tightened in her shoulders now and created an aching band around her skull. Eagerness to see Grandad warred with dread of what he might say and the distinct possibility he was being watched and that her cover would be blown. Buildings loomed over East Walton as they turned in at the Waldorf Astoria with its distinctive blue awnings and tall towers.

Her driver deposited her at the doors, and Kaci took a deep breath before striding into the lobby, her roller bag gliding beside her. Check-in went smoothly, and she stepped into the elevator for her floor. Soon she stood in her luxurious room wishing she'd stopped for lunch. Maybe she should order room service — the fewer times she emerged in public during the next few days, the better.

But before she could consider it further, her phone buzzed with a text from an unknown number. She narrowed her gaze and opened the text.

Please join me for lunch. Fred

The room number was given.

Fred could only be Frederick, her grandfather, right? Who else knew she was here, besides Walter and Bridget?

Kaci hated walking by faith, but that's where her life was right now. There'd been so many shadows that stepping into the light was a jarring experience.

Into the light? She scoffed a laugh under her breath. More subterfuge. But maybe it would soon be at an end.

I'll be there shortly.

No need to leave a name or initials. If 'Fred' didn't know to whom he was texting, her problems were much, much greater than she suspected.

Kaci took a few minutes to freshen up before tucking her room card in a slot in her phone case and making her way up several floors. The door to the suite sprang open at her approach, and she entered, heart pounding.

The door closed behind her, and her grandfather

emerged from the space behind it, holding out his arms. "Kirsten."

"Grandad." She stepped into his once-familiar embrace, and the tears began to flow. "Oh, Grandad, I've missed you so much."

"And I, you. Pure follower of Christ."

This meaning was what she'd given up by relegating Kirsten Catriona to the sidelines. She might have adopted Kaci as a result of her initials, but the actual meaning spoke of being watchful in times of war... all too apt.

Grandad held her at arm's length as his gaze roved her face. "Why tears today?"

"Tears of relief. Tears of joy. Perhaps also tears of trepidation."

He nodded and pulled her in for another squeeze. "I understand. Shall we have a bite to eat? And then we must talk."

Kaci nodded, but food? A few minutes ago, she'd been hungry. Now, she couldn't imagine having an appetite. Not when information — and perhaps an end to her exile — lay just beyond.

CHAPTER EIGHT

T hanks for the lift." Jude knew better than to open the limo's back door. That was Kenneth's duty, and he took it seriously, though it drove Jude crazy.

"You're very welcome, sir. Give me a ring if you're leaving before Mr. Sullivan."

"Will do. I appreciate it."

The man smiled and tipped his head. Grandfather had told Jude last winter that Kenneth was astonished about how much more polite all the young men were after spending a couple of years in Montana. They no longer looked on him as part of the furniture but as a human.

What must it be like to have a completely invisible job? Even as head of maintenance for the first two summers, Jude had received more respect than that... maybe because everyone knew he was the big boss's grandson.

Jude tried to shake off the feeling of unease. He'd been to the Sullivan Tower numerous times over the winter, but the sense of not-belonging had never quite dissipated. He was just a simple cowboy from backwoods Montana.

He straightened his shoulders as the door slid open in front of him.

No, he was more. He was a child of the King, which was so much more important that being Mr. Sullivan's grandson. He wasn't a nobody.

He flashed his ID to security. How had Mom ever gotten as far as Grandfather's office without being thrown out of the building? There was no answer but God.

Jude rode the elevator up and emerged on the top floor. Grandfather's secretary looked up from her desk and greeted him with a smile. "He's expecting you. Go on in."

"Thanks, Tammy."

Grandfather met him at the door of his expansive office with its view of the city below and the lake beyond. "Jude! Good to see you, boy."

Jude grinned and grasped the proffered hand. "At your service, sir."

"Come on in and have a seat. I've had Tammy order us some lunch. It will be here in a few minutes."

"Thanks. I'm hungry enough to eat a horse."

"A steak will have to do." The old man grimaced. "A small one on a salad. My physician insists I need less red meat and more greens."

Jude chuckled. "Sounds good, though." At least, it wasn't broccoli.

"Of course. Your mother raised you right."

"She did." Jude settled into an easy chair by the fireplace in the office suite's sitting area. A low flame flickered, not that the late-May day needed additional heat.

"How are things at the ranch?" Grandfather lowered himself into a seat nearby. "How is your grandmother?"

"Good. And good." Jude eyed the older man, who never failed to ask after Nana. "I'm curious why you summoned me to Chicago this week. What's on the agenda?"

Grandfather waved his hand. "We'll talk about it after lunch. We have several days to go over things."

What kinds of things? Maybe Uncle James had refused to fly to Kansas to pick up his ex-wife for corporate meetings. Maybe Uncle James was busy, and Jude was needed to escort the old man to Sullivan hotels in other states for a few days.

Tammy brought in a tray and set it on the round table by the window, and the two men shifted location.

Before Jude could so much as sniff the delectable steak, Grandfather began to pray. "Father God, thank You for bringing Jude and Kaci safely to Chicago. I pray that you will bless both of their endeavors over the next few days. Thank You for this food. I ask You to bless it to the use of our bodies, and bless the hands that prepared it. In Jesus' name, amen."

Jude removed the dome from his plate before glancing at his companion. "Isn't Kaci here just to do some shopping?" Seemed strange to ask for blessing on that kind of endeavor, but maybe she was looking for all-new linens for the resort or something like that. But wouldn't she have just said so? Besides, everything had been replaced two years ago. They couldn't possibly be ready to be tossed out yet.

"She will likely do some of that." Grandfather lifted a

bite of steak, dripping with blue cheese dressing, from his salad.

Well, Jude had tried. "And what will I be doing?"

"Enjoying your lunch, even though your mother could doubtless have made it better."

He knew when he was beat. "She probably could, though blue cheese isn't the dressing she prefers on something like this." Probably wasn't Grandfather's doctor's first choice, either.

"Oh? What is?"

Jude smirked. "Ranch. Need you ask?"

Grandfather chuckled. "Of course. And hers is much better than anything that comes from the supermarket. Tell me about the flights you've taken so far this season."

"Well, it's only been a few weeks, but it's been fascinating to see the same areas over and over as the snow recedes. The trees are leafing out, and wildflowers are beginning to bloom."

"You kids established a helipad up by the mountain lake?"

"We did." A memorable day spent with Kaci, Weston, and Paisley. A day when his relationship with Kaci took a step forward and a step back, a dance they seemed to be doing ever since he returned two months ago. "Want to go up and see it next time you're in Montana?"

Grandfather scrunched his face. "It looked like a steep butte to access by foot."

"Weston and Paisley have been out there a couple of times working on a proper trail with some steps formed and a railing along the steep parts."

"Keep me apprised. It's a possibility. Have you taken your grandmother up in the helicopter?"

"She refuses."

Grandfather shook his head, bemused. "That woman."

What would it have been like to have his grandparents married in their youth and raising their daughter together? True, it would mean none of his Sullivan cousins would exist, and he kind of liked those guys. He liked them better than he liked their fathers, James and Theodore. His uncles were still a bit stuffy about their half-sister. They were stuffy about everything and made sure Jude remembered it. Not that he was likely to forget.

Jude and Grandfather returned to the fireside, and Tammy cleared the emptied plates. She brought in coffee and snickerdoodles that tasted suspiciously like Mom's recipe.

"I need your help, boy."

Finally. Jude raised his eyebrows and met the old man's gaze. "With what, sir?"

"I'm not getting any younger, and neither is Eleanor. How can I convince her to take a chance on me and let us enjoy our remaining years together?"

Whoa.

"The FBI is still on the case." Grandad pursed his lips as though he had more to say but wasn't sure if he should.

Kaci studied his face as he stared pensively into his glass of iced tea. "That's good, right? They'll get to the bottom of things."

He sighed heavily. "I believe it is good. I gave them all the information you and I found over two years ago, and there really isn't much, Kirsten."

She nodded slowly. He was right. It had mostly been snatches of cut-off conversation, not that different than parents not discussing their children's Christmas gifts in front of them. There'd been odd, unexplained absences and several phone calls where the caller had hung up, but so very little to go on. Oh, there'd also been the text.

"Where do we go from here?" It wasn't like she could just waltz into her parents' mansion and say she'd been kidnapped on her way home from work two and a half years ago, but all was well now. Not if the niggling bits amounted to anything.

"I wish I knew. The FBI's policy is that information comes in but does not go out, so I've had no updates."

Kaci lurched to her feet and paced over to the window. After so long in Montana, she was accustomed to views of nature, but as her hand shifted the sheer drapery, Grandad spoke.

"Best not be visible in case anyone is watching."

She turned slowly. "Like whom?"

Grandad shook his head. "I'm here under my own name, unlike you, but if anyone suspiciously followed me, they'd certainly recognize you."

She'd let the black hair dye and curly perm go after a few months, reverting to her natural look. Maybe she should have kept it up, but then a snoopy watcher might think her grandfather had a young mistress.

Kaci turned back to the room and studied her mother's father. He seemed to have aged a decade since she'd seen him last. He looked despondent, maybe even depressed. Creases lined his face, and he'd lost weight.

"Are you ill?" Because he looked it.

He brushed his hand to the side.

That was so not an answer. "Are you?"

"I am 80 years old, Kirsten."

"That doesn't answer my question." Wasn't Mr. Sullivan even older? He looked a whole lot spryer than Grandad did at the moment, which was a far cry from the man he'd been three years ago.

"There are always health challenges. One day I will be reunited with my beautiful Mary, but I hope to see things settled with my own daughter before that time comes."

His daughter, Lillian. Kaci's mother.

Pursue his health? Or talk about Mom? He clearly didn't want to discuss his health, and she'd be here a few more days. Maybe he'd let something slip yet. "Do you think my mother is complicit?"

"I don't know what to think." Concern etched Grandad's face. That might be all that afflicted him. "I would like to think we raised her better than this, but I can't be certain. Who is there to trust?"

"You can trust me. And you can trust God." It seemed a short list, though.

"And Walter Sullivan. Has he been good to you? I know janitorial services is beneath you. I wish we could have—"

"He's been good to me, Grandad. The job suits me fine, at least for now. It's a way I can bring order to at least part of my world. I have staff under me who do most of the labor, but I am also perfectly capable of scrubbing toilets. Someone needs to. Why not me?"

"Because you're a Moorehouse. An Atkinson."

"Makes no difference, Grandad."

Tears threatened to flood his eyes once again. "I wish I could have done a better job protecting you."

Kaci huffed a laugh. "That would have been my parents' job, not yours."

"If I'd raised my daughter better…"

She shook her head. "She made the choice to marry my father."

"But they wouldn't have met if I hadn't introduced her to the aspiring young attorney in my firm."

Kaci knelt in front of him and took his hands in hers. "Life is full of what-ifs. We make the best choices we can at the time, and then we have to move forward."

His hand brushed her cheek. "Kirsten, you are doing my heart good. I don't deserve you."

She leaned into his touch. "If Douglas Atkinson and Lillian Moorehouse had never met, I wouldn't be here." A fate she'd wished upon herself a time or two in the past few years.

"Nor would Duncan or Owen."

"We were close as kids." At least she and Owen had been. Duncan had always been Daddy's shadow with little time for a sister four years younger.

Grandad cleared his throat. "I've rewritten my will."

Panic surged. "I thought you said you were well."

"And then reminded you I'm 80."

"Which doesn't mean you're on death's door."

"You do know that it is better to have one's affairs in order well before one is facing imminent death."

Kaci blinked. "I guess that's true."

"I have named Kirsten Catriona Moorehouse-Atkinson as my only heir. If she is unable to be located within 12 months of my passing, my entire estate goes to Kaci Moore of Montana."

"But—"

He lifted his hand. "My attorney feels this is a foolproof way to manage our situation."

"Bridget Sullivan?"

"She was consulted insofar as your legal identity is concerned."

Which meant Grandad's attorney also knew Kaci's identity. Hadn't they agreed the fewer inside the circle, the better? But if anyone would have access to trustworthy legal counsel, it would be Grandad. He might have retired from his firm many years past, but he still knew people.

Kaci sat back on her heels. "I'm honored, but I'd rather have you, especially if I could see you every day… or at least every week."

"Our times are in God's hands, Kirsten. There is no guarantee of tomorrow. Not for me. Not even for you, young as you are."

He was right. She didn't want him to be, but there was no argument strong enough to keep him alive until she was ready to let go, because that would be a good 40 or 50 years in the future.

"Should something happen to me before the investigation is complete, Bridget or Walter will be in touch with you. Bridget will guide you in whether to accept as Kirsten or Kaci."

"Mother will be livid," Kaci whispered.

A grimace crossed Grandad's face. "If only I knew for sure how involved she is. Or your brothers."

She managed to get words past her clogged throat. "If they're cleared, I'll share with them. I promise."

"That is all I can ask. I trust your judgment, child."

"Thank you. Is that why you called me here?"

"It is. Also, I wanted — needed — to see you again with my own eyes."

"Maybe we can do this again. Maybe every six months or so?"

"I'd like that." He held his arms open, and Kaci fell into them.

CHAPTER NINE

The next evening, Jude sat in Uncle Theodore and Aunt Bridget's posh living room along with Uncle James and Grandfather. They'd gathered here a few times last winter, though Jude and the men had met at the country club more often. The atmosphere there was more inviting, but it didn't take much.

This house was perfect and immaculate, belonging in one of those decorating magazines he glimpsed in supermarket checkout lanes. Perfectly stark, like no one actually lived in it. How had Graham ever managed to be a kid in these surroundings?

Jude forced away the grin that wanted to spread on his face. His cousin hadn't been the kind of youngster Jude and Weston had been. Graham had been into reading and computer games and chess, not jumping corral fences on horseback, mud-wrestling his brother, and skinny dipping in the pond to get the worst of the dirt off before squooshing his way into the aptly named mudroom.

Every time Jude entered this house — or spent time

with his Chicago relatives at all — he marveled at how decently his cousins had turned out... Graham especially. Uncle James and Aunt Maribel's boys had grown up in small-town Kansas and were slightly better grounded. Money tended to mess people up.

One thing about Kaci, if she ever let him in. She was normal. She'd have fit in with the old Jude just fine.

Uncle James lifted a glass of wine. "How are things at the ranch, Jude?"

"Gearing up for a busy summer, sir."

He glanced at his father. "I can't believe you've turned that place into a paying proposition."

Grandfather nodded, a smirk toying with his mouth as his eyes twinkled. "It's been the boys more than me. Your boys." He looked between James and Theodore. "And Nadine's boys. Each of them has contributed a lot to square things up."

"Even Bryce?" James sounded dubious.

"Even Bryce." Grandfather settled deeper into his seat. "He's done miracles with the landscaping."

"I can't believe my son is a groundskeeper... and likes it."

"Grandfather is right," Jude put in. "Bryce is good at it. He has vision."

"Well, I guess I'm glad he's good for something besides messing up."

Jude cringed inwardly. His own dad had had many faults, but this kind of disparagement hadn't been part of it.

"I think Bryce has outgrown that, for the most part,"

Grandfather said mildly. "Discovering he's a father has changed him. And rediscovering his faith."

"Marriage should come before babies." Uncle James scowled at his father. "Should have for you, too."

"You're not wrong. I'm so thankful God is in the forgiving business. The redemption business."

Jude swirled his pinot noir. He wasn't much for drinking, but at least the stemmed goblet and red liquid gave his hands something to do while the conversation shifted around him. No one had ever commented when his glass returned to the kitchen nearly as full as it had been upon arrival.

"Isn't it better not to need forgiving?"

Jude shot a quick glance at his bitter uncle. Wow, that was a loaded question from a man who'd put work first and all but abandoned his family.

"We all need forgiving." Grandfather shrugged. "The Bible says none of us are good enough on our own. That's why Jesus came."

Uncle James sighed. "Of course."

Did the man have any faith of his own? Jude didn't feel he knew his uncle well enough to confront him. Confrontation wasn't likely the best tool, anyway.

Uncle Theodore and Aunt Bridget exchanged a glance, and Jude wondered what they were thinking.

Also, could this visit get any more awkward? Even though he'd endured several such evenings over the winter, he'd never relaxed, even for a few seconds.

"So, I've been talking with Jude about his grandmother."

Jude sucked in his breath. Yes, it could get more awkward.

"I'm not asking you boys for your blessing or anything like that, but I need you to know that I plan on spending much of the summer at the ranch this year with one goal in mind — to court and marry Eleanor."

Jude's uncles exchanged a horrified look. "You can't do that, Father," Theodore said.

"At your age?" James asked.

"I can, and my age has nothing to do with it, other than that none of us is getting any younger." Grandfather gave James a stern look. "And by that I mean, you should seriously consider reconciling with Maribel."

"We have been divorced for 15 years." James glowered at his father.

"I'm aware. And I regret my part in that."

The man shook his head in disbelief. "How did you cause our divorce?"

"By demanding so much of your time overseeing the hotels. By constantly summoning you to meetings and to the various establishments that needed attention."

"I could have found a different job."

"You could have." Grandfather inclined his head. "But I don't recall ever encouraging you to take weekends off or to take one of your boys to a ball game. And I'm sorry."

"It's our mother you should have begged pardon from," James retorted. "She put up with an awful lot."

"She did. We spoke of it, and she forgave me. You may recall that for the last few years of her life, I worked fewer hours. We traveled together and rarely for business."

Theodore raised his eyebrows at Jude before turning to his dad. "Did Mother ever know of your youthful fling with Eleanor?"

Grandfather looked down. "Eventually, yes. But I do want you to know I was faithful to Gladys every minute of our marriage."

"But now you want to take up with Eleanor again."

"I do. She's the mother of my daughter, and I find I truly enjoy her company. I might even love her."

Jude had never heard his grandfather speak so softly on any topic, but his heart warmed at the declaration.

"You've carried a torch for her all these years." James's tone was bitter.

"That is not true. I was wholly devoted to Gladys. Things might have been different had I known of Nadine's existence, but I didn't. Eleanor was my past, and Gladys was my entire world."

"Besides Sullivan Enterprises," Theodore amended.

Grandfather tilted his head in acknowledgment.

Was this a bad time for Jude to excuse himself to use the facilities? He had no business being here for this discussion. Maybe Mom should have been, since these were her half-brothers, but not him.

"Marriage is hard." Grandfather took his time studying each of them in the room, ending with Jude. "I'm not trying to sugarcoat it. And marriage to Eleanor in our declining years will not be all fun and games, either. Each partner must put the other's needs and desires first. Since we are selfish human beings, that is *always* a challenge. You did not put Maribel first, James."

"Neither did she."

"That may or may not be true, son, but it takes two." He turned to Theodore. "I have concerns about your marriage, too. Where there once was devotion and attention, it seems to mostly be indifferent tolerance now."

Theodore and Bridget glanced at each other but said nothing.

"And you, Jude, have yet to experience it. But know that though love is a sacrifice, it is very worthwhile."

"Yes, sir."

"Perhaps that is enough for this evening." Grandfather set his nearly full glass down and rose to his feet. "Jude, can you call Kenneth?"

Jude jumped to his feet and pulled out his phone. "I can."

The other three rose as well.

"That's it, Father?" Theodore asked. "You came to criticize your sons, to inform us of your intentions with your former mistress, and then leave?"

The old man looked utterly exhausted. "Yes."

IF IT HADN'T FELT SO unnatural to stay inside Grandad's suite for hours on end every day, Kaci would have wished this interlude would never end. Oh, how she'd needed this balm to her weary soul.

Nothing had changed. At least, not that Grandad knew, but Kaci was grateful all the same. It had nothing to do with her inheritance. Grandad was nearly as wealthy as the Sullivans. The Moorehouses had been Texas cattle barons, but her grandfather had chosen the legal world instead of ranching.

Sure, money was nice, but she'd had little to spend it on

at Sweet River. Her needs had been pared to the basic and simple.

What would she do when Grandad passed, and she inherited everything? Would she be able to accept as Kirsten? If not, would there be any way to keep hiding the identity of Kaci Moore?

And... what would Jude think when she suddenly turned up rich?

Ugh, she didn't want to think about that. She hadn't lied to him in words, but she certainly had lied many times by omission. By letting him believe whatever pictures he conjured up in his head.

Jude might have access to money now, but he'd grown up poor and still had simple tastes, not that that was a bad thing. Previously, he'd mentioned how uncomfortable his uncles' lives made him on visits to the city, so his week must have been far less pleasant than hers.

She rode in the back of a Dodge Caravan toward the airport now, having said her goodbyes to Grandad and wept a bucketload of tears. Once she walked through the doors, she needed to be over it, back to her neutral face.

Mr. Sullivan would be flying back with them, so hopefully it would be less awkward than the eastbound trip. How she hated that things with Jude were uncomfortable.

What would it be like if she could accept — encourage — his tentative advances? But she couldn't. Not until things in Texas were settled and she could be open about her identity.

The car pulled in at the private sector of the airport, where the driver jumped out and retrieved her bag. He'd been prepaid and pre-tipped, so she expressed her thanks, straightened her shoulders, and strode toward the doors. They slid open at her approach.

Kaci ducked into a restroom and changed into more comfortable jeans and a cozy Montana sweatshirt. She hadn't dared be quite this casual around her grandfather, but what had held her back? He knew where she lived and what kind of environment surrounded her. But leggings and a belted tunic had been as casual as she'd dared. Even that was much less formal than the attire she'd worn in her years as an Atkinson.

Next time, she'd show Grandad who she'd become as Kaci.

Next time, maybe there'd be answers.

She approached the waiting area, and Mr. Sullivan rose to greet her with a smile. "Is all well?"

"Yes, thank you." She'd tell him more if others weren't present in the room.

He indicated the window. "Jude's doing preflight checks."

Kaci let herself take in the sight of Jude's lithe body moving confidently around the exterior of the aircraft. "He's doing well with the whole pilot thing."

"He is."

"Were you and Jude able to accomplish what you needed him for this week?"

The old man's eyes twinkled. "I think so, but I'll tell you the truth. The trip was mostly for your sake."

"But he told me of his summons days before I knew I was coming."

"I know. These things take time to come together."

Kaci should have known. She lowered her voice. "I can't tell you how thankful I am for all you've done."

"I'm happy to do it. I can't imagine being separated from my own grandchildren indefinitely."

And yet, he had been, since he hadn't known of their existence until they were grown men in their twenties. As far as Kaci knew, there were no skeletons in her family's closets. Not that kind, anyway. Who knew what the FBI would really find as they dug into Dad's business practices? Maybe she, too, had hidden half-siblings.

She shook her head. Couldn't be.

"Any new word?" Mr. Sullivan asked.

"No. Other than he rewrote his will and cut my mother and brothers out of it."

The old man winced. "Bridget mentioned she'd been consulted on how to present you." He held up a hand. "I promise no one else in the Sullivan clan knows a thing, not even Theodore. It's not the only secret either of them is keeping."

"I'm sorry." Kaci bit her lip. "On the plus side, Grandad showed me some photos of Duncan's little boy, Tyrell. He's about the same age as Simon, Tate and Stephanie's son. I'd sure like to see him."

"I'm sure you would." Mr. Sullivan squeezed her shoulder. "The time is coming. Have faith."

Have faith. There wasn't much else she could do, was there? But she hated waiting. Two and a half years seemed much too long already.

Beyond the glass, Jude tucked his clipboard under his arm and turned toward the terminal.

"Looks like he's ready to fly," the old man remarked. "Give my boy a chance, eh?"

A chance for what?

But Kaci didn't ask, because she suspected she knew what he meant. Everyone thought she and Jude were a done deal, but didn't she have any say in the matter?

Not without using her voice, and she couldn't do that.

But if Kaci Moore could legally pay taxes and accept an inheritance, couldn't she get married?

Not without telling her husband who she really was... and she wasn't free to do that.

CHAPTER TEN

Have a good time in Chicago?" Weston drawled.

Jude had sought his brother out at the stable. Now he glared at him. "There's nothing more entertaining than hanging out with the uncles."

"What? Grandfather didn't have a plethora of meetings to make you sit through?"

"Ha. I'm not even a cog in Sullivan Enterprises. You know that. Grandfather doesn't need me for anything besides chauffeuring him around." And not even that in the city. That's what Kenneth was for.

"And other Sullivan dignitaries," Weston added.

"Very few of those," Jude muttered. "Don't get me wrong. I enjoy flying. It's fun seeing the awe on tourists' faces when they look down on the ranch and the surrounding area. But any hired pilot could have done that."

Weston studied him for a long moment. "Time for a ride. No one's been out on Pepper in too long."

Fresh air and sunshine on Jude's face did sound

welcoming. "Okay. I have a couple of hours. Are you sure you have time?"

"Yeah. Let's do it." Weston turned to Ranger's stall and began sweet-talking the gelding.

Jude fed a carrot to Pepper and started tacking her up. In just a few minutes, he and his brother trotted up the main trail where they could ride side-by-side.

"Okay, talk." Weston glanced his way.

"What about?" As if Jude didn't know. He'd returned from the short trip grumpy, and there were several reasons why.

"Grandfather. Kaci. The uncles. The tourists. Whatever you need to dump, go for it. I've got big ears and wide shoulders."

Jude urged Pepper into a canter. He didn't want to talk and sound like a whiny brat. He wanted the cobwebs out of his head. Nothing but a ride in the pure mountain air would accomplish that.

Huh. That was what was wrong with flying. The air was canned, not natural. The sunshine on his face in the cockpit had no warmth. The breeze only came from air-conditioning vents.

Maybe he'd been dumb to become a pilot. Little Jude Kline should have been satisfied with what he'd been born with. Life had been so much simpler before Mom went hunting for Grandfather, and the brothers had discovered how rich people lived. Grandfather had meant to absorb them into the family, but Jude still felt like a very separate entity surrounded by Sullivans.

Weston must feel it even more... except he, at least, had Paisley to ground him. Jude had no one. Why had he fixed his heart on the one woman who kept him firmly friend-zoned? As though he could snap his fingers and attract any *other* woman he wanted. Just because Paisley's sister had draped all over him at their siblings' wedding didn't mean Kait was representative of the female race. Jude could only hope.

Weston settled Ranger beside him and Pepper. "Talk to me."

"There's nothing to talk about."

"I might be dumb as an ox, but I know that's not true."

Jude growled under his breath.

"I heard that."

How could he have over the pounding of horses' hooves on the trail? Jude eased Pepper back into a trot. "Who am I?"

Weston scowled at him. "Is that some sort of trick question? You're Jude Michael Kline, my kid brother."

"And who's that? What difference does it make if I'm here or anywhere?"

"Should I be worried about your mental health?"

Should he? Jude pondered then shook his head. "I just don't understand what difference I make."

"Are you fishing for compliments, or what?"

"I don't think so."

"Huh." Weston stared up at the trees along the trail. "I'm no good at this stuff."

Neither was Jude. Obviously.

"Okay, so you're my brother, son of Nadine and Michael, grandson of Eleanor... and Walter."

Jude nodded. Had he truly expected Weston to provide insight?

"Created by God. Loved by God."

He knew that. Didn't seem to help.

"Paisley and I have been memorizing Psalm 139."

"Oh, yeah?" Another reminder Weston had something Jude didn't. Not only a wife, but a spiritual partner.

"O Lord, you have searched me and known me! You know when I sit down and when I rise up; you discern my thoughts from afar. You search out my path and my lying down and are acquainted with all my ways." Weston chuckled. "That's as far as I've made it. I dunno, seems comforting to me that God knows me that well. And that He cares about what He knows."

"Sure. That makes sense."

"I guess what I've learned is... when I'm feeling down, I need to get into the Word. So, if you don't know who you are, ask God... then ask Google."

Jude snorted.

"Hear me out, bro. You can search all kinds of things, but here's one for you: 'Bible verses about my identity in Christ,' then start digging into the results."

"Didn't know you were acquainted with the World Wide Web."

"Dude. It's the twenty-first century. I'm not a Neanderthal."

"Didn't say you were." Thought it, maybe.

"Okay, blame Paisley. She taught me everything I know."

Jude laughed. It felt kind of good after teetering right on the edge for the past week.

"So, now tell me why there's this current crisis of confidence."

"It's complicated."

"Life is."

Ranger veered as a squirrel darted across the path.

Jude held Pepper in check. "Well, some of it is the same as for you — the awkwardness of trying to fit into the Sullivan world and never being sure I'm doing it right." Half the time, not being sure he wanted to fit in.

Weston offered a sidelong look. "You spent months with them in their own environment."

"Hence the crisis. You've never seen Uncle Theodore's house, West. It's like this humungous museum. He and Aunt Bridget are so prim and proper he barely loosens his tie when he's at home. How do they live that way?"

"This affects you how?"

"I'm just a cowboy from the sticks. I didn't even own any pants besides Levis for the first 25 years of my life."

"Not following."

Jude sighed. "They only see rednecks when they look at us. And for good reason."

"Again, I ask. This affects you how?"

"Seriously, West! Don't you care what people think of you?"

"Not so much, no. Why do you?"

Jude opened his mouth. Closed it again. How had he expected his brother to understand? Weston had never followed the beat of any drum besides his own. "I think perception matters. We're Christians. We should want to reflect Christ well."

"Uh, yeah, but that's not what you said."

Jude blinked. "It *is* what I said."

"Bro, caring what people think of Jesus is the part that

matters. You don't want to mess up God's image. But it's not all about you."

And the difference was what?

"Giana."

The girl snapped her gum as she turned toward Kaci. "Oh, hey, you're back. How was Chicago?"

"I'm back, and I'm checking on the cottages."

Giana rolled her eyes. "And now you're going to tell me I'm doing a lousy job."

"That is exactly what I'm telling you, because it's true. You checked off cottage three, but the master bathroom floor wasn't washed."

"Did you swab it for germs?"

"I didn't need to. Not when there was a blob of goo behind the trash can."

"Who looks behind trash cans?"

"I do. And many of our guests do. Please go back and clean it properly."

"It's clean enough."

"It is not clean enough. This is your final warning, Giana. If there is any further cause for concern, you will no longer be employed by Sweet River Ranch. Nor will you get a letter of reference."

"And who will you find to clean way out here in the middle of nowhere? The pay isn't worth putting up with you and the hoity-toity *guests*."

Kaci's eyebrows shot up. "Are you quitting?"

Giana eyed her. "Then you'd have to get your hands

dirty."

"I've done it before and can do it again."

"Well, then, have at it." Giana kept eye contact as she blew a bubble with her gum then popped it.

"Is that an idle threat or are you following through?"

"You know what? I'm following through. I can get a better job somewhere else. *You* clean the unknown goo off the bathroom floor."

"I'll accompany you down to the office so we can get your paperwork finalized."

"Can't wait to get rid of me, huh?"

"You've got until then to change your mind." *And your attitude*, but Kaci kept that part to herself.

Giana stripped off her cleaning gloves and dropped them in the trash bag beside her caddy. "Let's go."

"We'll take my golf cart."

"Of course." Giana rolled her eyes then marched out and clambered into the passenger side.

Kaci drove from Dragonfly Lane to the lodge and tapped on the open office door. "Tate? Giana Norris would like her severance papers."

Tate looked up from his desk across the room and leaned back in his chair. "Giana? You're leaving us?"

"Sure am." Giana shot Kaci a dirty look.

"I'm sorry to hear that. Let me pull up your file." He tapped into his computer and confirmed her mailing address. "I'll have Graham cut your final paycheck and get your record of employment out in Wednesday's mail. You have until midnight tonight to clear your personal effects from staff housing."

Giana glared at him. "Fine."

"Have a nice day."

How Tate managed a pleasant closure to the conversation, Kaci had no idea. "I'll drop you off at your duplex. You're in 12 with Trish, right?"

"Yeah."

A slightly more subdued Giana slid off the cart on Hummingbird Lane without a word.

Kaci sped away before releasing a long breath. That girl had gotten on every one of Kaci's nerves since almost the first day. Why had she even applied to the guest ranch's housekeeping division if she didn't want to get her hands dirty?

Grr. But Kaci would need to fill in until Giana could be replaced. She pulled back in beside the office and went in.

"Thought you might be back." Tate nodded with a grin. "I've started scanning applications for someone to fill the vacancy."

"Thanks." Kaci dropped into the chair in front of his desk. "She's been a frustration since the beginning. I was going to give her another chance after screwing up today, but she decided to call it. I can't say I'm sorry."

"There are people like that in this world." He tapped around his keyboard. "Hey, look, Kait Teele applied for work here."

"Not a chance."

"Oh?" Amusement sparked in Tate's eyes. "You wouldn't want Paisley to have a chance to get to know her sister better?"

"Not here. Not on my watch."

He leaned back in his chair. "Maybe a change from Phoenix would be good for her. Their mother moved in with her boyfriend and is using again. There's not much keeping Kait there."

Drat. Tate made it sound like Kaci would be the mean person not allowing Kait a second chance, but she was done with second chances.

"She seemed pretty interested in my man Jude at the wedding." Tate smirked.

Did that require a reply? Kaci kept her expression as steady as she could.

He chuckled. "You might need to snap him up yourself, if you're going to get all hot under the collar."

"I'm not hot under the collar." Although it did seem a little warm in the office. Maybe the air conditioning wasn't working at full strength. Or, yeah, maybe it was her.

"Word of advice." Tate leaned toward her and lowered his voice, though no one else was in the room. "Don't let him get away. He's one of the good ones."

"I'm not looking for a relationship." How she wished that were not true.

"What are you looking for, Kaci Moore?" Tate glanced at his screen. "You're one of only two or three hires my grandfather put through before I took over in HR. And you're the only one without an off-site mailing address or employment history."

Kaci's blood ran cold. "I don't need an off-site mailing address. I live here now."

"Employment history?" Tate's eyebrows rose. "Education? Anything? There's no application on record."

She pulled to her feet. "If you're asking if I'm a criminal on the run, I am not. When you have a candidate or two for interviewing, please let me know. Meanwhile, it seems that I have cottages to clean. Have a good day."

"Just trying to help," she heard Tate mutter as she strode down the corridor to the exit.

Mr. Sullivan had assured her that her records were fine as they were, that no one would notice the blank spaces. Well, Tate was the acting CEO of Sweet River Ranch, and he had noticed. The big question was, was he going to push? Was he going to try to fill in the blanks? Was he going to dig into her past? Her identity?

And she'd just seen Grandad for the first time in two-and-a-half years. Was Tate suspicious because he'd had her followed in Chicago, or was this nothing to do with her recent trip?

There was no one to ask except Mr. Sullivan, and he wouldn't know. He was too busy driving into Missoula every day to see Eleanor. He might as well get a room in the city for as little as he was at the ranch.

CHAPTER ELEVEN

Jude lifted the helicopter into the air, grinning at his passengers' exclamations of awe.

"This is amazing!" the woman next to him gushed into her headset. "We came into Missoula on a jet, but this is so much more... immediate."

Immediate. That was a good word for it. Jude loved that there was so little between him and the unending views of his beloved Montana. He skimmed over trees, creeks, and slopes as he listened to the chatter. He'd wondered if the woman next to him would need an 'accidentally' malfunctioning headset, but she hadn't talked overly much. Others were able to get their two bits in.

"Did you grow up at Sweet River?" someone from the back asked.

"No," Jude replied. "On a ranch over near Seeley Lake." A ranch that had been nothing like the huge guest ranch his grandfather had bought and restored. "We ran cattle in the traditional way."

"Does Sweet River have cows? I haven't seen any around."

"We do. My stepfather is the farmer in charge of that part of ranch operations."

"All in the family, huh?" The man laughed.

"You could say that." Somehow, Mom had had little trouble integrating into the Sullivan clan. Marrying Keith Ralston soon after the Kansas farmer's arrival in Montana only solidified her standing. She was completely at home on Sweet River and more contented than her sons had ever seen her.

Unlike Jude. He had one foot in the past, one foot in the high-flying world of aircraft, and one foot in daily life at the ranch. Yeah, yeah, he knew that was one foot too many, but it was still how he felt. Like he was torn in pieces and didn't quite know where he belonged. Or, like he'd said to Weston the other day, exactly who he was.

Wasn't he too old for an identity crisis? But maybe he could be excused. Not every guy had his entire world tipped end-over-end in his mid 20s.

And then fallen in love with a woman who refused to entertain future options.

Love? Jude sucked in a sharp breath, and his hands tightened on the controls. *Steady.* While flying was not the time to let his mind slip into the existential, especially with tourists onboard.

"What's that over there?" The man across the cockpit asked, pointing.

Jude veered the chopper in that direction, scanning the steep mountainside. "Mountain goats. We can get a bit closer safely."

The woman between them clasped her hands eagerly but remained silent as she leaned for a better view.

"Pass me the binoculars," someone said in the back. Then, a moment later, "Oh! Here, have a look." Cameras clicked.

Several pairs of bins were in use as Jude hovered the whirlybird just far enough away not to stress the half dozen mammals on the cliff face. He'd seen mountain goats several other times on trail rides from both the Circle K and, more recently, Sweet River, but this was the closest he'd ever been to them. While the magnification of the bins would bring the details in closer, the naked eye would have to be good enough for him. He had everyone's safety in his hands, after all.

"My Jeremy would have loved seeing this." The woman beside him swiped beneath her eye. "He was always so interested in nature."

What was Jude supposed to say to that? He didn't know this woman — let alone her Jeremy — from Adam. "God's creation is amazing."

"It is." She glanced at him. "He was about your age when he died."

Her husband? She looked to be maybe a decade older than Jude, give or take. "I'm sorry. Death is hard."

Just thinking the word reminded him of Dad. His passing had been difficult, but so had life. Michael Kline had not been an easy man to live with. Weston had fought with him like two stallions in one pen. Their clashes had been fierce and unending, while Jude tried to duck out of sight.

Had he wondered who he was even then? Because he

hadn't always wanted to be known as Michael's son around Seeley Lake. People knew what a hothead Dad was. Knew what a poor land manager he was. Knew that his wife needed to work off the ranch as a caterer to keep cash flowing.

Dad had just snarled at the universe for his poor luck. It was always someone else's fault, not his. And, while they couldn't control the weather or the price of calves, Dad wasn't big on managing the things he could.

Anything Jude could do to prove he was the opposite of the man who sired him, he'd do. Even though Mom said Dad had his good sides, Jude couldn't remember what they were.

Everything had flipped after Dad died, they'd lost the ranch, and Mom had found her own father, Walter Sullivan.

Was it any wonder Jude didn't know who he was?

Child of God.

Yes, but besides that.

Did anything else matter?

They'd had their fill watching the mountain goats, and Jude sent the helicopter further aloft again. They'd flown north today and weren't too far from the Circle K. What would his old stomping grounds look like from the air? A quick flyover would not be amiss.

ONCE EVENINGS like this had been something Kaci looked forward to. In the early days, the gang had often crowded into one of the duplexes for game or movie nights. Over the slow months, they took over the lodge's great room. Now that Stephanie and Tate had their own home nearby — and two boys to put to bed early — they often hosted R&R nights.

Kaci hadn't questioned her inclusion at the beginning. They'd been a bunch of singles who had a ton of fun laughing together, but over the past two years, pairing had begun. Stephanie and Tate had been an item almost from the first moment. Then had come Cadence and Graham, then Paisley and Weston. Eryn and Maxwell had been next, now Madison and Bryce.

Kaci tapped on Stephanie's door and let herself in. She missed Madison living at the ranch, but she and her toddler were still in a basement suite down in Jewel Lake while she and Bryce tried to decide where they were going to live after their marriage.

And now the only remaining singles were her and Jude... and everyone had been shipping them since the beginning.

Kaci pulled her hoodie over her head. Would being a couple with Jude be so horrible? Not even a tiny bit. He was gentle, caring, and kind, all the things Dad and Duncan and Owen didn't seem to be.

"Hey, Kaci! Come on in!" Madison called. "We brought a raft of chicken wings from the Golden Grill. Get 'em while they're hot."

"Madison!" Kaci launched at her friend. "I wasn't expecting to see you. Where's Everly?"

"We got a sitter tonight." Madison squeezed her in return. "Sometimes we need a night out, you know?"

"Well, I'm so glad to spend your night out with you! I've missed you tons."

"You know you're welcome to visit anytime." Madison linked their arms and dragged her toward the kitchen, where the hum of voices and laughter came from.

"I do know. It's just been busy." There'd been her trip to Chicago, plus the angst of trying to figure out if she should just go for it with Jude and let the chips land where they may. They'd definitely land at some point was the problem. But might the risk be worth it?

She waved as she entered the kitchen. "Hey, everyone. Mmm, wings! My fave."

Stephanie laughed. "There's lots of other stuff, too. See? Chips and dip and a veggie platter because Paisley thinks we need that. Apples and grapes. Help yourself."

Kaci managed not to make eye contact with Jude as she circled the island, piling her plate high. So, she wasn't quite prepared when his low voice spoke at her side.

"Hey, haven't seen much of you lately. It's about time we had a games night, huh?"

She shot a smile somewhere near his shoulder. "For sure! What's up tonight?" Hopefully not charades or Pictionary. She was over both of those, though she had to admit they were suitable for large groups.

He leaned closer, and she inhaled the outdoorsy musk of him. "I don't think anyone knows what we're doing."

Wasn't that a basic life truth? None of them knew what they were doing, Kaci least of all.

She reached for a handful of broccoli, partly to get away from Jude's proximity. "A movie sounds good."

Jude groaned. "Like this crew can decide on anything to watch. Graham would go for horror—"

"I wouldn't believe that if I hadn't seen it for myself." Kaci moved forward to add chips to her plate. "That doesn't suit his personality at all."

"I know, right?" Jude laughed. "Weston thinks all movies should be westerns starring Tom Selleck and Sam Elliot as the Sackett brothers. Bryce is looking for satire... and all you girls want to watch is romance."

Kaci took a huge step away from the island as her gaze snagged with Jude's. "Action adventure is a thing." But the words came out almost a croak.

He grinned, his eyes practically boring holes in hers. "If it has a romantic subplot."

"Romance makes the world go round."

He shifted closer. "Does it? I wouldn't know."

The kitchen was suddenly very quiet. Maybe everyone had gone into the family room. Kaci forced her gaze away from Jude's. Nope. They were all attentively tuned in to her conversation with Jude.

What were they thinking?

Madison and Eryn elbowed each other.

Kaci glowered at the two of them, and they smirked and turned away. Great. Everyone thought they were experts. They always had, and Kaci had done her share of teasing the others when they were tipping over the precipice of romance. They thought the same thing was happening now to her and Jude.

Little did they know what was holding Kaci back.

Because she hadn't told anyone.

Because her own safety was at risk. Not that Dad would

come after her — probably — but if he were working for the mob, danger could come from anywhere. She couldn't be too careful.

Guarding her privacy was getting to be more than a nuisance, though. She'd listened to Cadence's betrayal as a jilted bride. To Paisley's trauma after meeting her birth father. To Eryn's tearful tale of her twin's rejection. To Madison's angst over whether or not to tell Bryce that Everly was his daughter.

But when her friends asked innocent questions about her own past, Kaci had no choice but to clam up or change the subject. At first, they hadn't seemed to be aware, but as their friendships had deepened and lengthened, they'd noticed.

"So... a movie tonight?" Kaci broke into the silence. "*The Princess Bride* is always good for a repeat. It's got enough action and enough romance to suit us all, right?" Did her smile look forced? Probably.

"As you wish." Tate laughed.

She made a face at his lame quote. "Nice one."

"I try." Tate winked at Jude as he turned away.

"I brought my guitar," Madison said to Kaci.

"You did? Are you going to sing for us after the movie?"

"Not exactly. I'm still a bit out of practice, but we could all sing together."

Kaci gave her friend a one-armed hug and steered her toward the family room. "I can't wait. We don't even have to watch a movie. I was just trying—"

Madison glanced over Kaci's shoulder and lowered her voice. "You were just trying to get away from Jude."

"Shh."

"So, it's true and not just my imagination?"

There were still too many of their friends lingering nearby. "Not now," Kaci whispered.

"Will you come clean with me later? Promise?"

How much could she divulge and still keep her core secrets? "Maybe?"

Madison sighed and turned away.

"Madison…"

"What?" She glanced back, face full of sadness.

"It's not like that."

"I have no idea what isn't like that, since you never say a thing."

"I have reasons." Which might be the most she'd ever divulged so plainly.

"And you have friends who have your back. See?" Madison gestured around the room in front of them. "And who have Jude's back."

Maybe it was a mistake to have come at all. Jude's interest was more obvious. Their friends were more determined to meddle. And things in Dallas were no closer to a wrap-up.

Kaci pivoted toward the kitchen. "I can't do this." She set her plate down, snagged her hoodie, and headed out the door. She'd order wings next time she was in town.

She didn't realize she hadn't seen Jude in a few minutes until she rammed into him on the back steps.

"I thought you might run away."

Kaci burst into tears.

CHAPTER TWELVE

hoa. Jude didn't know what he'd expected by confronting Kaci outside, but it wasn't an explosion of waterworks. And he hadn't meant it to be a confrontation, either, but here they were.

He reached toward her, but she wrenched sideways to avoid his hand. "Don't."

"Don't what?"

"Don't… touch me. Don't care about me. Just don't."

His heart shattered, and he shoved his hands into his jeans pockets. "I didn't mean to."

Didn't mean to what? Didn't mean to fall for her. It had just happened, but how could a guy fall for a girl who kept so much hidden away?

She bolted down the steps, her shoulders still quaking.

"Let me give you a ride. I've got a golf cart." And she almost certainly hadn't driven over.

"I can walk." Her voice caught.

"Kaci…"

She stopped, her back still to him. "What?"

So, her words, her reactions, did not reveal her true heart. He knew that, but now he saw it. "Are you married?"

"*What?*" She pivoted to face him, eyes wild. "Where did you get that harebrained idea?"

Jude jogged down the steps and stopped a couple of feet away from her. "What am I supposed to think? You..." No, he really shouldn't push her. Not when her emotions were raw like this from whatever she and Madison had been whispering about. He'd seen the challenge in Madison's eyes, noticed Kaci's shoulders hunch defensively. It hadn't taken a shrink to figure she'd make a run for it.

She stuffed her hands into the kangaroo pouch of her hoodie, her hair nearly occluding her face in the dim light. "No, Jude, I'm not married. I'm also not a fugitive from the law or an illegal immigrant. I'm just a person who values her privacy."

She said it so calmly that he almost believed her, but her actions and evasions over the past two years spoke louder than her current words.

"There's privacy and then there's paranoia."

"Your point?" Her voice chilled in warning.

A wise man would back off and pretend nothing was going on, but it had been a bit since anyone had called Jude wise. "My point is..." This would be so much easier if she weren't poised to flee, if she seemed the least bit receptive to hear him out. To actually reciprocate.

He took a deep breath. He felt how he felt, and it wasn't some teen hormonal impulse. He was a grown man, and he'd known her for over two years. "My point is, I'm falling for you, Kaci. And I'm pretty sure you have feelings for me, as well, but you're pushing me away, and I'm just trying to understand why."

Falling for her? Ha! He was long past that stage. He'd tumbled headlong all the way into love, but that might be a declaration best suited for another time… if she ever gave him the chance to speak again. Would she? Or was this it?

Panic made him bolder. Her silence and stillness emboldened him. Jude stepped closer and rested his hands on her hips. He'd have reached for her hands if they weren't buried in her pouch. His palms warmed against her body, even through all the layers. "Please, Kaci. I know you care."

A tear wended its way down her cheek, the trail glistening in the faint light.

Jude lifted one hand and gently wiped the tear away. "Kaci," he whispered.

"Jude, I…" Her voice caught in a sob.

This time, he couldn't resist but tugged her closer and wrapped both arms around her, snugging her body against his own, though her hands still fisted between them. He laid his cheek against her smooth hair, closed his eyes, and breathed. If this was going to be the only time he ever got to hold her close, he wanted to remember every single sensation. The way she felt in his arms, the way her faint floral perfume swirled in his nostrils, the way a tiny sigh preceded a slight relaxation in her shoulders.

Jude's eyes sprang open at the realization. He could only hope she couldn't feel his response to the way she sort of eased against him, or she'd lock up again.

"Kaci." His voice sounded rough, even to him, and all he

wanted to do was tip her head back enough to kiss her, to feel her lips respond to his.

Warning bells clanged in his head. She wasn't there yet. She might never be there. Even though the temptation to test her response was great, he managed to hold back from following through. Yes, even if it meant he'd never get to taste her lips, he couldn't — wouldn't — pressure her in a moment of vulnerability.

"I can't, Jude," she whispered.

He matched her tone. "Please tell me why."

"There's so much about me you don't know…"

"I'm ready to listen."

"But I can't tell you. No, I'm not married or a criminal, but that's all I can say right now. There are… dangers."

He could almost see her biting her lip to stop her words. "What kind of dangers?"

"I can't tell you."

"What does this have to do with your trip to Chicago?"

Kaci shook her head against his chest. "I can't say."

Frustration nearly made him growl. "Trust me, Kaci. Whatever it is, let me help you. I'll keep your confidence. You don't need to face this alone."

She stepped back out of his arms, which dropped to his sides. He felt chilled where she no longer warmed him. Jude flexed his hands, but the moment — whatever it had been — had vanished.

All his fault. He'd pushed. But how else could he get her to face that whatever stood between them didn't need to be there?

"Tell me you don't care for me the way I care for you."

Her shoulders hunched forward as her head bowed. "I can't tell you that, either."

"Because you do care."

"Jude... I can't."

He barely heard her whisper. So many emotions swirled in his gut and flooded his mind. "All those things don't matter, Kaci. You don't ever have to tell me what you're hiding. Let me be here for you, today." The words sounded reckless, even to him. How could any relationship thrive with secrets like the ones she seemed to shield with her very life?

"That's not fair," she whispered.

And she was right. It definitely wasn't fair. But he'd said the words, and he couldn't unsay them. Didn't really want to. Whatever part of her life Kaci would allow him into was better than no part.

Did he really believe that?

Yes, he did. Oh, probably there would be doubts later — he wasn't so swept up in the moment that he couldn't realize how foolish this was — but he'd stand by them.

Because Kaci shouldn't have to shoulder her burdens alone.

"It's okay, sweetheart. I'm here for you. In whatever way you let me."

KACI STARED at the man silhouetted against the glow of the porch light. He couldn't possibly mean those words. No doubt, he thought he did, but when push came to shove —

if Dad's goons found her before the FBI solidified their case — Jude might be in danger he'd never have guessed.

So, tell him. Give him that head's up.

No. She couldn't endanger him. But how much peril was she really in? There'd been the cut-off conversations, the glimpse of Dad's computer, the late hours, the lines etched on his face, the response to her first tentative questions. Oh, and the text.

Something was wrong. She knew there was. She'd gone to Grandad, the only person she felt she could trust. He'd believed her. The two of them couldn't have imagined everything.

Could they?

But Walter Sullivan had taken them seriously, too. His attorney daughter-in-law had provided a new identity for Kirsten Catriona Moorehouse-Atkinson. She was Kaci Moore now, though maybe the name was still too close. Hadn't Duncan sometimes called her KC when they were kids in that snooty voice of his? And Moore. Why hadn't she decided to become Jen Smith or something so common a million women had the name? A name not remotely connected to her own identity?

Her gaze remained riveted on Jude even as her brain spun. He took a couple of steps forward, once again close enough to touch.

Kaci wanted to touch him. That moment he'd held her in his arms? She wanted that again. Longer. She wanted it often. She wanted Jude Kline in a forever sort of way.

"Do you mean that?" she whispered.

No. She should keep going as she'd begun, back to the

duplex she shared with Emma Cavanagh, back to a life where she let no one close for any reason.

"Trust me, Kaci." His voice was low.

The battle inside her was bitter. She hadn't felt as safe for two and a half years as she'd felt those few seconds in his arms. But what could Jude really do to protect her if things ended badly?

Nothing, if he weren't prepared.

He stretched both hands toward her, palms up. She couldn't make out his features, but she could imagine the hopeful expression. Or perhaps wary, expecting rejection once again.

She shifted closer only to make out his countenance. That was all. Right? She couldn't have expected Jude to take that movement as acquiescence. And since she'd taken one step, why not two? Why not feel that glorious sensation one more time? The touch of a loving human, someone who cared deeply about her.

And she stepped right into Jude's waiting embrace. This time her arms wrapped around his back as his did around hers. This time she held him just as tightly, just as fervently, as he did her. She rested her cheek against his chest, feeling the smooth texture of the T-shirt he wore beneath an open denim jacket. Feeling his heartbeat.

This was what home felt like.

More than home. She couldn't remember ever feeling this depth of security before. Growing up, perfection had been expected and rewarded. Duncan, Kirsten, and Owen had been birthed to make Douglas and Lillian proud. Duncan had succeeded. Owen probably would.

Kirsten never had. Her interest in nursing instead of law had not helped.

But Kaci was free of Kirsten. Free of the Atkinson expectations. She didn't need to feel unworthy anymore. She was a child of God, far from Texas, in the arms of a caring, kind man.

Would it be so bad to let him into her mess?

Instantly, her resolve firmed along with her spine. She couldn't jeopardize the FBI's probe, but she hadn't promised never to fall in love. Now she tensed for that second reason, for that realization.

She loved Jude Kline.

His hands soothed her back, and she slowly relaxed against him. The future would have to take care of itself. So would the investigation.

Kaci was a woman, and she craved this man. He'd been her friend through thick and thin over the past two years. They'd ridden together, played games together, watched movies together, ribbed each other, laughed together, hung out together.

But did she dare take it one step further? All it would take was looking up at Jude, filling her gaze with him, and he'd do the rest.

She wanted his kiss more than anything.

Almost more than anything, but conditioning was overwhelmingly strong. The alarm bells in her head clanged too loud.

Okay, so no kissing. Not tonight, anyway. This whole thing was way too new for that.

Except they'd been good friends for two years. That wasn't new.

No, but accepting that he cared was like two *minutes* old.

She held on for dear life for another heartbeat or two. Maybe five. Who was counting? Not her.

Finally, she eased away from him. The chill of the late spring evening filtered onto her overheated skin cells.

Jude caught her hands before she pulled out of reach. The contact felt nice. More than nice. It was almost enough to make her rethink the decision she'd just made.

"Thanks for the hug," she said in a low voice.

"Any time." Jude huffed an awkward chuckle. "Really, truly, any time."

"I appreciate that more than I can say." Kaci winced. Why was she back to referencing hidden things, untalked of things? But maybe this was different. It felt different.

"Want to go back inside and watch the movie?"

Did she? She shook her head. Later would be soon enough to face all their friends and Jude's family. Besides, she couldn't quantify the shift between her and Jude. Their ever-so-helpful group would sense something in two seconds flat, and how would they reply?

"Yeah, me neither. They're all too curious in there."

"Aren't they, though?" But Kaci wasn't quite ready to separate from Jude, for all she knew keeping him at arm's length would be the wiser decision. "Hey, want to take a couple of kayaks out?"

"Sure. Sounds fun."

When Jude reached for her hand, she let her fingers wrap around his.

CHAPTER THIRTEEN

Jude reveled in the sensation of Kaci's palm pressed against his, their fingers intertwined as they strolled toward the lodge and the lake beyond it. He never wanted to forget this night, this very moment, and the heady joy of a new, deeper connection with Kaci.

Words weren't needed. In light of the fact that he'd kind of promised not to press her for things she refused to speak of, words could easily get in the way. Was walking on eggshells, weighing every word out of his mouth, worth it? Yes. He squeezed her hand lightly. A thousand times yes.

She bumped against his elbow, and Jude yearned to put his arm around her. Yearned to hold her again and, this time, kiss her.

He kept walking.

They took the walkway around the perimeter of the lodge. Just as they came abreast of the back deck, Jude froze, and he pulled on Kaci's hand. She looked questioningly up at him, and he pressed his finger across his lips.

"I heard something," he whispered.

Kaci tilted her head in a listening mode.

The porch swing on the deck creaked. Someone was out here. Did Jude care if that someone saw him and Kaci together? He held back a scoffing sound. They'd been seen together a thousand times. It wouldn't seem unusual.

But they hadn't been holding hands then.

He could let go, but he didn't want to. Didn't want to break the moment. The rack of kayaks stood as a dark blemish against the starlit night not far away, but the path was here. Over there was a rock wall and a steep slope. They could stumble.

"Walter, I'm not sure this is a good idea."

Every muscle in Jude's body tensed as he heard Nana's voice.

"But I love you, Eleanor."

Grandfather had better not say he'd pined for Nana all these years. He'd been married to Gladys for decades in between and, by all accounts, they'd been happy together. Mostly.

Nana sighed. "We're too old for this kind of nonsense."

Way to break a man's heart, Nana.

"If *I'm* not too old, then you're not. I've got five years on you." Grandfather's voice sounded light, but the tone didn't fool Jude. He knew what rejection felt like, and it wasn't easy to take when you'd put your heart on the line.

"Nadine desperately wanted to know her father. I'm thankful for the closure for her sake."

Not for Nana's own sake? Still, it was a start.

"I am, too, but my feelings aren't based on our daughter. A lot of years have gone by — water under the bridge, so to speak — but I appreciate what time has done for you. You are a beautiful, wise woman, and I love you."

Kaci's fingers all but strangled Jude's.

This was a private moment, and they shouldn't be eavesdropping. Jude allowed himself a look of longing toward the kayak rack then took a careful step backward, pulling Kaci with him.

"I don't fit into your life, Walter."

Nana's voice was fainter now, but Jude could still hear. He backed up again, his heel colliding with a rock bordering the walkway. "Oof."

He froze again, as did Kaci, who still clung to his hand. Had Nana or Grandfather heard him?

The swing creaked mightily. Footsteps crossed the deck.

Jude glanced around. Though they were in shadow and Grandfather's vision probably not quite as sharp as it had once been, Jude didn't think there was any cover they could dive for and remain undetected.

Maybe Grandfather — or was it Nana coming? — could be fooled into thinking they'd never gotten close enough to overhear.

Having regained his balance, Jude pulled Kaci into his arms, making sure her back was toward the lake so he could keep an eye over her head.

But when she slid her hands up around his neck, all thoughts of the elderly couple's problems whizzed right out of his head like startled ducks fleeing a lake.

He looked into Kaci's eyes, but it was too dark to read any expression.

"Who goes there?" Grandfather called out.

"Kiss me," she whispered.

"Are you sure?" But he was already dipping toward her. The instant his lips brushed hers, everything else was forgotten. Kaci Moore was everything: his senses, his breath, his very existence.

"Jude?" Grandfather's voice sounded incredulous. "Kaci?"

Go away. But Jude's mouth was too busy to speak out loud.

"Well, I never." Amusement, this time. Grandfather's footsteps receded.

"What's going on?" Nana.

Grandfather's reply was too low to hear, but Jude heard the chuckle. Then he blocked everything else and poured all his focus into kissing Kaci. It wasn't hard. It was one of the most beautiful moments of his entire life, one that superseded his first horseback ride, his first flight as a passenger, his first flight behind the controls. It was almost in the same vein as the intense exhilaration that flooded him when he emerged from the waters of baptism. Not quite. But almost.

Kaci eased away before he was ready. Long before. "We've been found out," she whispered.

Found out? Jude's brain scrambled to reorient itself to anything but the bliss of her kiss.

Right. Grandfather. Nana.

But Kaci had been the initiator. His heart soared again at the realization. Sure, she'd done it to deflect his grandparents, but that wasn't something she'd ever have done in the past.

In previous summers, they'd have been running, not holding hands but jostling elbows, chattering at each other and laughing like the friends they were — or had been — and likely been totally oblivious to the elderly pair on the porch as they launched a pair of kayaks in the dark.

There would have been no need for a deflective kiss.

But surely it meant more to Kaci than that? She had to realize what it meant to him. He gripped her hands. "Kaci."

"Still want to paddle?"

Not really. He wanted to explore this amazing turn of events. Repeat it. "Do you?"

"Absolutely. Race you to the kayak rack."

"No…"

But she'd already ripped out of his grasp and begun sprinting toward the lake.

Did he have any choice but to follow?

Not if he didn't want to stop and explain his life to his grandparents.

Jude dashed after her.

KACI PAUSED to grab a personal floatation device and a paddle then heaved a kayak off the rack in an effort to launch before Jude caught up with her.

What on earth had she been thinking, kissing him like that? Heat flushed her face despite the cool air. Not even running into the cold water in the dark to float the kayak before jumping in counterbalanced the heat.

She'd worked so blasted hard for two full years to build

a solid, unromantic relationship with Jude Kline. He was an amazing friend, and didn't everyone need friends, even people who were trying to hide their identities?

Kaci should have stuck with the girlfriends, but everyone had hung out in a larger, mixed group from the beginning. Before the pairing off began, leaving it starkly apparent that she was avoiding that sort of relationship with Jude.

Oh, Jude.

That kiss.

The kayak wobbled as she clambered aboard. Immediately, she began paddling, her ears tuned behind her to the sounds of Jude's kayak hitting the rocky shore. The scrape as he dragged it to the water's edge. He'd catch up in a few seconds.

This made everything so awkward. She absolutely shouldn't have kissed him. Whatever his grandparents might have wondered about her and Jude rushing past to launch kayaks was nothing to what they now knew.

Would they tell?

Was this the kind of secret that should be kept? Yes... but could it? Not that the elderly couple were blabbers. Mr. Sullivan had kept Kaci's confidence for two and a half years.

She could hear Jude gaining on her, his much stronger arms propelling his watercraft faster than she could hope to. And what was the purpose of trying to outmaneuver him? Habit. Were they beyond that now?

"Hey, you're hard to catch."

If that wasn't loaded with a multitude of meanings, Kaci would eat her paddle. "I needed a workout."

"About that…"

"Sound travels on water."

Jude's sigh certainly did. He lowered his voice, not that it would be enough. "We need to talk."

She tried for lightness. "Do we?"

"Kaci…"

"Not now."

He groaned in frustration. "What's going on here?"

"Sound travels on water," she repeated.

His paddle pointed to the cove not far away on the south side of the lake. "Not so much around corners."

They'd have to talk. She knew that. But now, while his phantom lips still caressed hers? While every nerve ending in her body still stood on alert and jangled for more?

She didn't reply, but she did turn her kayak in the direction he pointed. They'd stay in their boats, and there'd be no repeats of that kiss.

She wanted a repeat.

No, she didn't. It wasn't wise. Not with everything else going on. Just because she'd finally acknowledged that she was even hiding anything to begin with didn't mean that she should have gone hog-wild and kissed this guy.

It was all her fault. She knew that. Kicked herself for it or would if she could reach her own backside. As it was, paddling fiercely enough to give her shoulders a burning ache would have to do as self-punishment.

She zipped around the rocky point until the lights of the lodge were no longer visible behind the bushes and trees. A stream burbled in not far away, and she could smell the fragrance of the sweetgrass that the river and the ranch were named for.

Sweetgrass, revered by the indigenous people for the way it spilled its fragrance when crushed, the lesson being people should do the same by offering a pleasant aroma to those who'd wronged them.

Jude hadn't wronged her. She'd wronged him.

Kaci let out a long breath as Jude's kayak came up beside hers. "I'm sorry."

"For?"

"Taking advantage. For using you to escape questions." Would the questions have been as bad as the evasion? No.

"Kaci, you didn't take advantage of me. In case you didn't notice, I was a very willing participant."

"I know." She knew, all right. Her lips still tingled. "But I led you to believe I could give you more than I can. All previous disclaimers still apply."

"Kace? Look at me."

She didn't want to, but something in his imploring tone made her slowly lift her gaze to meet his. Her pupils must have become attuned to the darkness, or the starlight reflecting in his eyes must be stronger than she'd suspected, because she could see the love — no, no, not love. Just affection — glinting there. "What?" she managed to croak out.

"I'm in it for whatever you can offer. I meant that before kissing was on the table, and I totally don't feel taken advantage of now. Instead, I am honored that you trust me this much."

"I… thank you." What else could she say? Really?

"I do have a question."

Of course, he did. Kaci herself had about 843 of them. "Yeah?"

"So, my grandparents know we've shifted beyond just friends. I don't think they'll tell anyone, but... does this need to remain a secret from everyone else?"

Kaci weighed his words. How she'd love to stuff everything back in Pandora's box and throw away the key. No, what she'd really prefer would be for Kirsten to be here with nothing to hide. She and Jude would likely have been a couple at least a year ago.

She wasn't Kirsten anymore but Kaci, and the secrets must be kept. But Kaci was a separate person with all the legal rights of any American citizen. Kaci could turn her back on Kirsten once and for all.

She couldn't abandon Grandad. Or justice.

Jude turned away. "I guess that's your answer."

She studied his profile as his jaw tightened. "For now?"

"You think no one will notice we're different?"

"Why would they?"

"Oh, come on." He sounded impatient. "Don't you remember how we all eyed the others as they fell in love? We all saw things they claimed not to see, that they denied even existed."

She shoved the words 'fell in love' right out of her head, not that they'd stay evicted. "We'll see less of each other. I won't go to any more of your family's parties."

"Kaci." His voice pleaded. "I want to shout to the whole world what Kaci Moore means to me. I don't want to pretend otherwise. It feels like lying, and that doesn't sit well."

Welcome to my life, buddy. Everything in it is a lie.

No, not all. She did honest work for an honest paycheck. She had real friends... even if they didn't know she wasn't who she said she was. But in this moment, the lies felt less like they were protecting her and more like they were strangling her. And her growing affection — she would *not* call it love — for Jude Kline was definitely not a lie.

CHAPTER FOURTEEN

Hey, what happened last night?"

Jude froze. So much for his game plan of being first in line at breakfast and first out the door again. Then he'd been waylaid by excited passengers who couldn't stop asking questions about their upcoming flight. If only his metabolism didn't scream for breakfast, he'd have skipped the dining hall altogether.

He'd been *this* close to freedom. Now he glared at his brother who blocked the steps of the lodge. "What do you mean?"

Weston rolled his eyes. "Seriously? You're trying to pull that over on me?"

"Pull what over?" Hey, Jude could stick to his own party line.

"Dude." Weston cocked one eyebrow in a way Jude had never been able to mimic. "You slid out of Tate's place seconds before Kaci skedaddled like the house was on fire. Neither of you came back, and you're pretending that was a coincidence? You didn't see each other outside? Nothing happened?"

Jude made a show of checking his watch. "I don't have time for this."

"Simple question." Weston leaned closer and lowered his voice. "Did you finally make a move and kiss her?"

Jude's jaw dropped. No doubt, guilt was pouring out of his eyes, evident for any passerby to see.

Weston smirked and slugged Jude's arm hard enough it would likely leave a bruise. "Way to go, bro."

"It wasn't like that." Jude rubbed his arm.

"You didn't kiss her? I may not be the world's best at reading body language, but yours is screaming loud and clear. Want to tell your big brother all about it?" Sarcasm dripped from Weston's voice.

"Not really. Thanks, anyway. I need to do my preflight checks before I take tourists up this morning."

"You hate lying, and I can't help noticing you're not answering my question. So, you did kiss her."

"Not exactly." Kaci had kissed him. That was different, right? Although, he'd certainly kissed her back, so the point was muddied.

Weston shook his head with a chuckle. "You made your move, and she shot you down again? Sorry, bro. I know I shouldn't laugh, but you guys are more fun to watch than the posturing of a pair of sandhill cranes."

Whose elaborate dance was for mating purposes, but Jude wasn't going to fill in the blank Weston had left open. "Did I not mention I need to get down to the helipad?"

Weston pointed two fingers at his own eyes then at

Jude's in an *I see you* gesture. "Don't think we're done with this conversation."

"You might not be, but I am."

"You wound me." Weston pressed his hand over his heart. "You and me gotta stick together in this Sullivan tribe. If you can't dump your woes on me, who can you? I've got your back, bro."

"Uh, thanks." *I think.* "Gotta go." Jude jogged down the steps and climbed onto a golf cart for the drive down to the helicopter.

His brother's questions were only the first ones. Jude had made it in and out of the dining hall before any of the Sullivan cousins had shown up for the meal, but they'd be in his face, too. Bryce and Maxwell would, for sure.

Why didn't Kaci want anyone to know they'd changed their relationship status? They weren't kids. He was 28 years old, and he was ready to declare his love, marry her, and start a family.

He nearly swerved off the ranch road at that realization. *Whoa, Jude. Rein in that there stallion a tad or you'll get bucked to the ground and trampled.*

But it was true. He'd propose marriage in a heartbeat if she gave him the slightest hope she'd accept. Still, they'd made progress, right?

That kiss.

He'd relived it a dozen times in his dreams through the night… when he wasn't reliving it while staring wide-eyed at the dark ceiling. By the time they'd finished their night-time paddle, Grandfather and Nana had gone inside. They'd parted ways — kissless — outside the duplex Kaci shared with Emma before Jude went into his own place.

That one kiss had changed everything and yet nothing. Frustration welled up inside him. He wanted to shout his love for Kaci from the mountaintop. Well, nothing was stopping him. He could always drop the helicopter on the butte by the mountain lake, clamber out, and bellow to his heart's content. But that wasn't going to solve anything. He didn't want to avoid his grandparents. Didn't want to fib to his brother — okay, he'd pretty much lied, and that didn't sit well. He'd made a thing about valuing honesty and truthfulness, and this whole situation with Kaci had his principles tipping over the edge.

He parked the golf cart beside the fuel shed. Thankfully, none of the tourists had arrived before him, so he had another moment to gather himself.

There were two options that he could think of. Tell everyone he and Kaci were a couple against her express request or tell her they couldn't be a couple if she wasn't ready to openly commit. Either way, their revised relationship would be over before it even began, and he'd lose their two-year-old friendship in the bargain.

He shouldn't have kissed her back.

It was awfully hard to regret, though.

Was there no other way?

The other possibility was her agreeing to date him with no strings attached. He'd already asked, and then they'd kissed for the first and — according to Kaci — last time. So much for no strings.

Jude bowed his head over the steering wheel and scrubbed his hands through his hair. "God? I could really use some help here. I don't know the best way to handle this situation. I love her, Lord."

His fingertips dug into his temples.

The growl of an approaching vehicle dragged a sigh from deep inside. He glanced up at the blue sky where only a few puffy clouds floated. "To be continued, Lord. I'm listening for Your answer. Or, at least, I'm honestly trying to."

Jude pulled out his checklist and approached the helicopter. He'd thought he wanted nothing more in this lifetime than to fly.

He'd been wrong. Flying was second place, behind winning Kaci.

No. Both were behind his love for God and his commitment to clarity and honesty.

How could this possibly end well?

THE ONE GOOD thing about Giana's defection was that Kaci had a lot of physical work to keep her hands and mind occupied. Should she stop by the office and see if Tate had any prospects lined up for interviews?

Yeah, no. Tate had been witness to Kaci's escape the other night. No doubt, he'd also noted Jude's absence. Would Tate be able to keep his questions to himself? She doubted it.

Tate Sullivan had never experienced a moment of self-doubt in his life, from what Kaci could figure out. He'd been the golden second son of Maribel and James, and had stepped into his older brother's role when Wally died, both with parenting Wally's son, Jamie, and with Sullivan Enterprises. He'd won Stephanie's love in a blink... no, he couldn't possibly understand how difficult all these things might be for someone else.

Tate would let her know when he had someone for her to consider hiring. In the meantime, it was best simply to avoid running into any of the gang. If that meant Kaci was surviving on outdated granola bars and potato chips, so be it.

She gathered the soiled linens from all the beds in Firefly Lane's cottage five, hauled them out to the laundry bin on her golf cart, and lifted a stack of clean ones.

Another golf cart rounded the corner, and Kaci glanced up to see who was arriving.

Eryn Ralston. Kaci's gut clenched. There was no reason for Eryn to be in the guest cottages unless she were looking for Kaci, not when the resort gift shop was now open for the season.

Pretending she hadn't noticed Eryn wasn't an option, so Kaci pasted on a smile and waited, arms full of clean sheets, their lavender fragrance not in the least stress-relieving. "Hey!"

"Hey." Eryn turned off her vehicle and jumped off. "Can I give you a hand?"

This was even worse than Kaci had first thought. "Don't you have a job of your own?"

"The gift shop doesn't open until 10:30. I've got an hour."

Yikes. That long?

Eryn grinned. "I know you're short-staffed."

No denying that, not that Eryn's help for an hour made a significant difference. But how could Kaci refuse her friend? She should, though. There was only one reason

Eryn would be here, and it wasn't so Kaci wouldn't be overworked.

She sighed. "Sure. I'm nearly done in this one. Just making up the beds again then moving over to Dragonfly three, as they also checked out this morning."

Eryn smiled. "I can help."

That was what Kaci was afraid of. "Grab that stack of towels then."

"You've got it." Eryn followed Kaci inside and up to the loft. She set the towels in the bathroom then grabbed the other side of the sheet Kaci flipped across the king-size bed. "Hey, remember that day we all went to Jewel Lake with Madison when she was running away from Bryce?"

Kaci eyed her friend. "Yeah?" The two of them and Paisley had known Madison needed friends. Needed people in her corner to support her while she worked out things with Bryce. Oh, and with God.

"That's what friends do, right? I mean, I had very few of them growing up — they all belonged to my twin sister — but that's how I understand friendship."

In her memory, Kaci could hear her own voice speaking to Madison. *The biggest mistake would be cutting all of us out at the same time, and we're not going to let that happen. You need us.*

Now, she gave the sheet an extra flip, which caused Eryn to fumble it for a second before regaining control and tucking it in. "Your point?" But Kaci knew.

"I don't know what's going on, Kaci, because you are very careful to make sure no one knows any details. But I'm your friend, and I'm still here for you, because everyone needs their community."

"I kissed him." Kaci slapped her hand over her mouth as her wide eyes stared at Eryn. Why on earth had she blurted that out?

A slow smile spread over Eryn's face. "I'm glad. But why are you now avoiding each other like one of you has the plague? Or, at least, cooties."

Kaci pressed her lips tight. "It was a mistake."

"Why?"

She waved her hands. "All the reasons."

"All the same ones you keep all of us in the dark about, like everything in your life before you came to Sweet River? Secrets aren't good, Kaci. They eat away at your insides. Even if you did horrible things, embarrassing things, admitting it is freeing." Eryn stuffed a pillow into its case. "Ask me how I know."

"If only," Kaci muttered.

"You can tell me, you know. I promise it won't go any farther unless you spread it yourself. I can keep secrets... but I think it would do you a world of good to have someone to talk to. If not me, how about Paisley?"

Jude's sister-in-law? Sure, she'd been one of Kaci's closest friends here all along, but her marriage to Weston had changed that. Now Paisley's loyalties were divided. Just as Eryn's were, since she was engaged to Jude's cousin Maxwell.

So, Kaci didn't answer. She just zipped up the bottom of the duvet cover.

"I can't make you talk."

Nice of Eryn to notice.

"But I want you to know I'm praying for you, and I'm here whenever you're ready."

"Thanks."

"Although I'm dying to know about the kiss."

"Nothing to report."

Eryn chuckled. "Well, you can fill me in later then. Hey, did you hear Madison and Bryce are taking a vacation to visit her family?"

Kaci eyed her friend. "They're what? But it's the busy season here at the ranch."

"Bryce has staff who can keep the landscaping in check for a few days."

And Madison worked as a medical transcriptionist from her suite in town, not at the ranch at all. Her hours were likely flexible.

"Everly will be happy to see everyone." The couple's 20-month-old daughter missed her cousins and grandparents back in Pittsburgh. "That's nice for them."

"They'll probably be making wedding plans with Madison's family." Eryn reached for another pillow and case. "They haven't set a firm date yet."

"Have you?"

Eryn got a faraway smile on her face.

Kaci should have steered the conversation here from the beginning.

"Second Saturday of September. It can't come soon enough for me."

"You and Maxwell are so cute together."

"You and Jude would be, too."

And here they were, back around again.

CHAPTER FIFTEEN

Hey, Emma."

The kitchen worker paused on the steps of the duplex she shared with Kaci. "Hi."

Jude put on his most winning smile. "Have you seen Kaci today?"

"Not since this morning. Why?"

"She's been awfully hard to catch." And Jude meant that in every possible way. He gestured to the duplex door. "I was wondering if she was home."

"Did you knock? Text her?" Emma eyed him suspiciously.

Did she know anything? Had Kaci confided in her roommate? Jude had never seen the two of them hanging out, but that didn't mean they didn't share confidences after hours.

"Uh… I just got here." And that was a lie. "I mean, I did knock, but no one answered, and then I saw you coming, so I thought I'd check with you." That was better.

"Look, I don't know what's going on with Kaci. I

don't know how she feels about you. She barely mentions what she thinks of the weather, okay? So, please don't assume I'm your ticket to the inner workings of Kaci Moore, because she's the most tight-lipped person I've ever met, let alone roomed with. You're on your own, Jude Kline."

He'd kind of figured, but it was nice to have confirmation. Not really nice — part of him had hoped there was someone at the ranch she shared with — but at least he hadn't been completely wrong about her.

"Look, if she's home, can you tell her I'm outside and would like to talk?"

Emma rolled her eyes. "Sure, lover boy."

"We're just friends."

She lowered her gaze at him, eyebrows tipped up. "Tell yourself what you need to hear. I've got six older brothers, and every single one of them was totally delusional when they were trying to deny their fixations on the women they ended up marrying. My twin and I figured out the signs long before any of them did. You can't fool me with that 'we're just friends' talk. I've seen through that for over a year."

Doubtful. That was longer than Jude had known it himself, but he wasn't here to argue with Emma. He needed her on his side. "What are you seeing from her?"

"I already told you. She doesn't talk. Not about anything in her past or any of her hopes for the future. If it isn't about *today*, it doesn't exist."

Jude opened his mouth and closed it again. Kaci was hiding something big. She'd admitted as much. And it had something to do with her trip to Chicago last week. She'd been nervous on the flight east, but that didn't hold a candle to the nerves radiating off her on the return trip.

She'd told him she had secrets she needed to keep, but it still hurt like the dickens that she didn't trust him with them. He'd help her in any way he could. Kaci had to know that about him. He wasn't fickle. He was devoted to their friendship.

Devoted to more with her. And that's what seemed to be scaring her away.

Except she'd kissed him.

What a conundrum.

The door closed behind Emma, and Jude hadn't even noticed her movement. He needed to pay better attention... to everything.

"Hey, Jude!" Maxwell called out. "How goes it?"

"Fine, thank you!" Jude managed a bright smile, not that his cousin would be fooled. Max, like everyone else, had witnessed his and Kaci's escape from Tate's. And now Maxwell wasn't dumb enough not to notice that Jude was hanging out in front of Kaci's home like some lovestruck Romeo.

There was an idea. He should serenade Kaci at her bedroom window. If only he had a decent singing voice. If only it wouldn't make him look like a fool. If only it would make a difference.

"She's still not talking to you?"

Oh. Maxwell was still present. Jude's life was nothing but a documentary for everyone else to watch and comment on. It certainly wasn't a rom com.

Jude scratched his jaw. He didn't want to confide in his cousin. Or anyone, for that matter. "Uh..."

"Look me up if you need a shoulder." Maxwell lowered his voice. "Eryn talked to Kaci this morning."

Jude took an involuntary step toward his cousin.

Maxwell grinned like he knew. "Your call."

Tempting... but then the door opened, and Kaci stood framed in it. "Hi."

"Later." Maxwell chuckled, and the sound of his footsteps on the gravel drive faded.

"Kaci." Jude filled his eyes with her. She leaned on the jamb looking exhausted, her hair slipping out of its ponytail. "Come for a walk?" He nearly held his hand out to her, but this was too public a place.

She hesitated.

"A bit of fresh air will do us both good. Or we could go for a ride if you have an hour."

She studied him as she bit her lip. "Okay. A bit of time on Nutmeg sounds good."

"Yeah, I don't exercise Pepper as much as she'd like. Let's do it."

"Meet you at the stable in a few minutes. I need to change and tie up a couple of loose ends." She closed the door.

So, that's how it was going to be? She didn't want to be seen walking or driving to the stable with him. Probably horseback riding sounded like it would help her keep a safer distance than going for a walk. She wasn't completely wrong about that. He'd certainly had thoughts of sort of accidentally bumping against her arm then twining his fingers with hers while they walked.

Beggars couldn't be choosers.

She'd agreed to a ride, so he'd scoot on over and saddle

both horses. Getting Nutmeg ready was the least he could do for Kaci.

KACI IGNORED Emma's smirk on her way out the door. She hopped on her golf cart to get over to the stable — the day had already been exhausting. She was feeling the effects of doing Giana's job plus her own for over a week now. Eryn's brief help hadn't offset the labor but had added to the tension because of her probing questions.

Everyone had questions.

No one had answers except Dad, and probably Mom and Duncan.

Who needed answers? Kaci did, along with Grandad and the FBI. Why was everything taking so long?

She pulled to a stop beside the corral. Nutmeg already stood hitched to the post beside the gate as Jude led Pepper out.

He shot her a grin. Were there tension lines around his eyes? Of course, there were. She'd briefly reversed her position before strengthening it again. Poor guy was probably getting whiplash.

Kaci opened the gate then gathered Nutmeg's reins and led her out, Jude with Pepper right behind her.

He reached for the gate as she began to swing it shut. "I've got it."

Wasn't that her line? But he was being helpful and kind, typically Jude. He didn't deserve her defensiveness.

"Thanks." She swung up on Nutmeg's back, and the mare pricked her ears as she shifted eagerly under Kaci's weight. Kaci smoothed her shoulder. "Ready for a run, girl?"

Nutmeg tossed her mane, and Kaci laughed. "Me, too, girl. Me, too."

"Which trail?" Jude mounted up.

Kaci pointed to the lake trail and pressed her knees into Nutmeg's sides. The horse shot forward, and Kaci reveled in the feel of the power beneath her and the cool breeze on her face. A ride was much better than a walk for so many reasons, not the least of which was keeping Jude out of reach.

She heard Pepper's hoofbeats closing in and leaned over Nutmeg's shoulder, urging her on. Nutmeg stretched into a smooth canter.

This was the life. If only everything ran this swift and this smooth. But all too soon, Nutmeg slowed to a trot, and Kaci adjusted to accommodate the more jolting gait.

Jude brought Pepper up beside her and glanced over with a wide grin. "Wow, she was in a mood to run."

That had all been Kaci, though Nutmeg had been eager, as well. "I'm sure Weston doesn't allow most of the tourists to stretch the horses like that."

"No, you're right. Too many inexperienced city slickers in the bunch."

It was two years too late for Kaci to pretend she hadn't ridden since childhood. That had been the one good thing about her parents moving out to the estate. Kaci and Owen had begged for horses long enough for Dad to relent. Duncan, of course, had been too cool to ride.

Somehow, he'd won over Deena and married her. Kaci would have liked Deena better if she hadn't fallen for

Duncan, but no such luck. Their wedding was one of the last family events Kaci had attended after her graduation from nursing school.

Man, she wished she could pick up where she'd left off. She'd been eying a position in the emergency department when she'd been forced to face the mess her family was in. Everything had gone off the rails very quickly after that.

Of course, if her life hadn't been derailed, she'd never have met Jude... but wouldn't it have been better not to know him than to know him but need to keep her distance?

That kiss.

Kaci sighed deeply.

"A penny for your thoughts?" Jude asked lightly.

She jolted, and Nutmeg shifted sideways. Kaci kept her seat, but her face flushed. She needed to do a much better job of remembering where she was and whom she was with. No more traipses down memory lane unless she were lying on her bed at night.

"My thoughts aren't worth the paper they're printed on." She tried to match his tone.

"I beg to differ. Isn't it in the psalms where it says that God knows our words even before we utter them? That doesn't sound worthless to me."

"Ah, Psalm 139. One of my favorites." Kaci latched onto the potential for a change of subject. She'd leaned heavily into verses four and five in the early days: *If I take the wings of the morning and dwell in the uttermost parts of the sea, even there your hand shall lead me, and your right hand shall hold me.* It had been such a comfort to know God was with her no matter where she found herself.

She'd also been a little too fond — perhaps — of praying verse 19: *If only you, God, would slay the wicked! Away from me, you who are bloodthirsty!*

"Search me, God, and know my heart," Jude mused. "Test me, and know my anxious thoughts. See if there is any offensive way in me, and lead me in the way everlasting."

Did Jude have anxious thoughts? Probably every one of them had been caused by Kaci. No, he was a complete human being apart from their non-relationship. Of course, he had other concerns.

"It's a great psalm from beginning to end." Seemed safe enough to say.

Jude glanced over at her, his face inscrutable. "It is an amazing statement of the worth of each of us as individuals."

Kaci squirmed in the saddle.

Jude sighed. "I don't want things to be weird between us, Kaci. I thought we'd maybe turned a corner the other night — not just kissing, but talking. But your signals are all over the place, or maybe it's me. Maybe I'm just terrible at interpretation."

So much for dodging difficult topics. Kaci chewed on her lip. This guy was too precious to mess with, and that's all she'd been doing. She'd tried to avoid him, tried to set him free, but he was nothing if not persistent. He was all in, and nothing was diverting him from his pursuit.

She was honored. She was thrilled. She was so uneasy she couldn't figure out which direction was up. She couldn't let Jude in.

But... why not? Why not swear him to secrecy and

dump the entire load on his broad shoulders? She glanced over at him.

He wore his Levis like a second skin, his scuffed cowboy boots resting in his stirrups. A white T-shirt peeked out of his red-and-blue plaid snap-front shirt. His hair was mostly covered by his brown Stetson, and his jaw was lined with a five o'clock shadow she longed to touch.

Jude didn't deserve the weight of the Moorehouse-Atkinson problems. And then there was the one-in-a-billion chance he'd say the wrong thing to the wrong person and blow Kaci's cover. He absolutely wouldn't do it on purpose, but the guy was so upright he wouldn't be able to lie for her without something showing.

Wasn't that a quality worth preserving? Absolutely. She valued honesty even though her life had become a warren of pretenses and half-truths interspersed with a few outright lies. All that was for a greater good.

Right?

Grandad agreed. He believed her. More importantly, he believed *in* her.

The FBI were on the case.

Patience, Kirsten Catriona. Patience.

CHAPTER SIXTEEN

She was a stubborn one.

Try as he might, Jude had been unable to get a real conversation out of Kaci during their ride. Looking back, she'd always deflected personal questions and comments, but he hadn't really noticed at the time until all the pieces stacked up so high they obscured everything else in his line of vision.

Tonight, she'd chatted on-and-on about the trials of running the ranch's housekeeping short-staffed. Did he care that she felt overworked and stretched too thin? Absolutely. But there were other topics of conversation.

When she switched to questions about his flights over the past couple of days, he'd seen it as the diverting tactic it was. Great. She refused to talk about her past, and also about them as a couple.

They weren't a couple. How could he have mistaken that kiss for anything but a distraction from admitting to his grandparents that they'd overheard a conversation not meant for their ears?

Even Jude's 82-year-old grandfather had more game than Jude did. Huh, and he also knew what it was like to be shot down by the woman he'd been pursuing for two years.

Now, as they approached the stable, Kaci raved about the beauty of the sunset.

She was right. The western sky was totally lit with an orange and pink glow, but who cared?

Not Jude. Not anymore. Not when Kaci refused to share her heart with him.

He should back off completely and protect himself, but wasn't it much too late for that? Besides, that wasn't what real love did. He'd been reminded of 1 Corinthians 13 at Weston's wedding to Paisley not long ago.

Love... is not self-seeking, it is not eagerly angered, it keeps no record of wrongs... It always protects, always trusts, always hopes, always perseveres. Love never fails.

"You're sure quiet tonight." Kaci dismounted beside the corral and glanced his way.

Jude scoffed under his breath. "There's not much to say if your companion isn't willing to talk."

"I talked."

"Not about anything important."

Kaci's grip tightened on Nutmeg's bridle as she narrowed her gaze at him. "The fact that housekeeping is short-staffed doesn't matter?"

He grunted. "You know what I meant, and you're doing it again."

"Jude, I can't give you what you want."

"A normal conversation?" Man, he should have bit those words off before they came out. Or managed to make them sound less testy... not that it would have been possible.

"That's what you're after? A normal conversation? I'm here to tell you, buster, that normal conversations include things like, 'how was your day at work?' 'Terrible, thank you for asking.' 'I'm sorry to hear that.' Etcetera."

"That's a normal conversation between acquaintances, but it's only a starting point for communication between actual friends. And when a guy is led to believe there might be more than friendship possible, sticking to surface chat as though one's life depended on it is inane."

"Did it ever occur to you that someone's life *might* depend on it?" Kaci's eyes grew wide, and she pivoted away to lead Nutmeg into the stable.

"Hey, what did you mean by that?" Jude hollered after her. No reply. Of course, no reply. What had he expected?

Pepper nuzzled Jude's shoulder, and he dug in his pocket and absentmindedly fed her a carrot. What had Kaci admitted the other night? That her reasons for secrecy were not because she was married or a criminal. What other possibilities were there that might threaten a life?

He snapped his fingers as realization hit him. He hurried into the stable and stopped in front of Nutmeg's stall, where Kaci was already lifting the saddle off. "Did you observe a violent crime? Are you in witness protection?"

Her back was to him. "What is this, 20 questions?"

Another non-answer. "I can come up with 18 more if you force me to."

"Jude, stop it. I've already told you I can't talk about it, so leave me alone."

"Kaci, I..."

She whirled to face him. Were those tears on her cheeks? They were. "Jude, no."

"Then what good is this?" He gestured between the two of them. "How can anything solid be built without a foundation?"

"It can't! That's what I've been trying to tell you!"

"Kaci..."

She wrapped her arms around the mare's neck with her back to Jude.

For better or for worse, he was on a roll now. "You're unbelievably stubborn. I care about you. I'm here for you, but all you do is shove me away." Not all. There'd been that kiss the other night. It might have been the only almost-real moment they'd ever shared. And so what if his frustration showed? Frustration was honest.

"It's for your own good!" she snarled back.

Oooo-kay. She was being real for a moment again. Not the kind of real he wanted, but at least he'd gotten through her facade. Was that all he wanted? He groaned. No! A thousand times, no. What he wanted, more than anything, was for her to melt against him, tell him everything, and allow him to take care of her. Wasn't that what love did?

Oh. First Corinthians 13 again. *Love is patient... it is not self-seeking.*

Jude was an absolute failure at showing love. Did that mean what he felt for Kaci wasn't love at all? That couldn't be it. More likely, he was just too stinking human for his own good. There was only so much a guy could take standing up.

"I'm sorry." His apology was so quiet he wasn't sure

she'd hear him, but by the tensing of her shoulder muscles, he figured she had. "I need to get something off my chest."

She stayed rigid with her back to him.

"I love you, Kaci, but I can't play this game. When you're ready to talk to me — real, honest talk — you know where to find me. In the meantime, I'll pray for you. Pray for us both, that God will do His thing in our lives. But this superficial dance is tearing me apart, and I'm reacting poorly. Real love takes openness and trust from both sides."

Did it, though? "That doesn't mean I'll stop loving you without it. It's not something I can turn on and off at will." Wouldn't that be a great preventative for deeper pain? He gulped a deep breath. "It does mean I'm done playing this game."

Pepper shoved his shoulder with her nose, but he dug his heels in and refused to be pushed by a horse. But then again, what did it matter if Kaci rejected him now?

"I love you, Kaci." Then he led Pepper down the corridor to her own stall. He removed her tack and brushed her coat for a long time, until he heard the whisper of the stable door and knew Kaci was gone.

This isn't fair!

Kaci wanted to scream the words into the dusk sky, but what good would it do? None, that's what.

An image from her childhood sprang into her memory. Gran Moorehouse had loved to cross-stitch before her vision declined, and one poem, surrounded by stitched wildflowers had hung in an ornate frame in their front hall. How had the words gone?

God hath not promised skies always blue, flower-strewn pathways all our lives through; God hath not promised sun without rain, joy without sorrow, peace without pain. But God hath promised strength for the day, rest for the labor, light for the way, grace for the trials, help from above, unfailing sympathy, undying love.

Gran had explained what the pretty, stitched words meant, and even as a little girl, Kirsten had been fascinated by the lyrical rhythm and by the juxtaposition of the poetry's two sides. After that, she'd always practiced reading the poem out loud when she entered her grandparents' home. Not that she could apply the meaning to any life situations back then.

Because the takeaway had been lost on a child of privilege. Kaci understood it far better now. Life wasn't meant to be fair, because growth came in hard times. *Because* of hard times. But hadn't Kaci had more than her share of difficulties?

Get a grip, girl. Not when there were believers dying for their faith in far-off lands. Not when people were enslaved or starving or hiding from missiles. Her life was easy. She had an okay job in a beautiful environment surrounded by good people. Really, really good people like Mr. Sullivan watched out for her.

Jude loved her.

At least, he loved the person he thought she was. Wasn't that the real Kaci? Sort of... but it wasn't the real Kirsten.

Frustration had rolled off him in waves and battered against her defenses. Her heart cried out to give up, give in, give him everything he asked for. If she didn't think her own life was fair, Jude must feel it quadruple-fold.

Tell him. Just sit him down and tell him.

While she wasn't officially in a witness-protection program — how had he slid so close to the truth? — she might as well be. Many of the same rules and cautions applied.

It wasn't only her own safety at stake. It was Grandad's. It was the possibility of an entire crime ring either going to prison or going free, even if that included Dad. Justice was required. Wasn't that a higher calling than hormonal emotions? Wasn't it the prophet Amos who'd said, *Let justice roll on like a river, righteousness like a never-failing stream?*

It was. She and Grandad had searched the scriptures and spent time in prayer as they tried to determine what to do two-and-a-half years ago. They'd done more of that last week in Chicago. They'd been certain God meant for them to uphold integrity and not turn a blind eye.

No, she'd made her choice. She couldn't change course now... even if it meant giving up any hope of a future with Jude.

It might be best to contact Bridget Sullivan and see about relocation. Surely the attorney had other ideas besides the family ranch in rural Montana. Didn't the Sullivans own an entire hotel empire? She could work at any of them.

Yeah, and those were all in urban centers and major tourist destinations. They'd be the sorts of accommodations men like Douglas Atkinson would frequent on their travels. She was only safe at Sweet River Ranch because

Dad wasn't a fan of smelly horses. He'd sold their two horses the minute Owen left for college. Even keeping a groom on staff was too close to horseflesh for her pristine father. Too bad he hadn't been as concerned about keeping his morals upstanding as he was about keeping his hands clean.

The light was still on in the duplex loft, which meant her roommate was still up. Yes, Emma would respect her privacy, but she'd be curious. She'd see Kaci's tear-stained cheeks.

Kaci wandered down the back trail from staff housing to the lake and settled on a boulder at the water's edge. Lights glowed from the lodge windows a few hundred yards away. More of them lit the deck and the beach. Soft music played from somewhere over there. Around the far side of the lake sat the well-lit bathhouses in the campground section. LED lights surrounded the awnings of numerous RVs.

Jesus claimed to be the light of the world. He'd told his followers to be lamps not hidden under bowls or in corners. People yearned for light... unless their deeds were evil. Then they were afraid they'd be exposed.

Kaci had been called to flip on a floodlight. She had a duty to perform, and she would carry on.

All she could do was pray that it would all be over before Jude gave up waiting on her forever.

CHAPTER SEVENTEEN

I t was Sunday morning when Jude spotted his grandfather ahead of him in the breakfast line. Might this be his chance to at least touch base? He watched as Grandfather carried his tray over to a vacant table near the windows. As early as they were, a lot of tables were empty.

Jude loaded his tray as quickly as he could — oatmeal, check; yogurt, check; fruit salad, check — and hurried over to where the old man was removing items from his. "Can I take your tray and get you a coffee?"

Grandfather raised his eyebrows and grinned. "Sure, boy. Just black."

"You've got it." Jude was back in a flash with two cups of coffee. The old guy might like his untainted, but Jude needed a splash of flavored creamer in his. "Here you go."

"Thank you." Grandfather took a sip. "A man would almost think you've got something on your mind."

"Besides being helpful?" Jude tried for a casual smile.

"Besides that."

Why hedge? Grandfather was right, and the longer Jude waited, the more likely it was that someone would join them. "I was wondering if you had any plans for this afternoon."

"Well… your aunt Melinda invited me to lunch after church."

Jude blinked and sat back in his chair. "Aunt Melinda and Uncle Reggie?" Didn't they hate all things Sullivan? They couldn't seem to stop being snide to Mom about defecting from the Evans family in favor of the Sullivans. Weston and Jude were no better in the Evans's eyes. Except Mom hadn't been born into their family, which they also always noted. They simply hadn't expected their illegitimate half-sister to come out ahead.

Grandfather seemed amused that he'd stunned Jude right out of words. "It's a shock to me, as well. I'm thinking they have ulterior motives but, hey. I can handle them."

"Are they looking for a handout?" Jude wouldn't put it past them.

The old man shrugged and dug his spoon into his bowl of oatmeal. "Most likely."

"You don't owe them anything." Heat surged up Jude's neck. "Well, you didn't owe West or me anything, either." And he hadn't always been grateful for it.

"You're my family," Grandfather said simply. "It's not a matter of obligation. But your nana… I wronged her all those years ago. There's not much I wouldn't do to make up for it. Not that it's even possible."

A shadow fell across the table as Maxwell and Eryn joined them. Grandfather greeted them then turned back to Jude. "Any particular reason for asking? I'm sorry I got sidetracked."

"Uh…" Jude glanced at his cousin and lowered his voice. "Just wanted a chance to talk in private. Maybe some other time."

"How about this evening, if you don't have plans?"

Ha. As if Jude had a life.

"I'll be back from Missoula by seven or so. You see my car, come on up to my rooms. If you want."

Jude had only been in the penthouse suite a couple of times before, and then only briefly. "Sounds good, sir."

"What are you up to this afternoon?" Maxwell asked in a near mimic of Jude's earlier question.

"No particular plans." Now that Grandfather had put him off until evening, anyway. "What about you?"

Eryn buttered her toast. "There's the Pot of Gold kickoff rally at the church this afternoon. We thought we'd check that out and see if it seems something that could fit into our schedules."

Jude frowned. "That's geocaching, right? I've heard a bit about it the past couple of summers. Town is a long way to go to participate in something like that."

"Here's a concept." Maxwell leaned forward on the table, meeting Jude's eyes. "At least, I think it might be a real thing. Apparently not everyone who signs up is trying to win the event. Radical, huh?"

For a competitive bunch like the Sullivan-Kline bunch, it definitely was.

Maxwell smirked. "A lot of people do it just for the fun of it. They log a few geocaches? Great. Meanwhile, they're forging friendships and getting out into nature. Win, win."

"Since when are you a nature boy?" Jude hadn't meant for the words to come out sharp, but somehow they did.

"Since moving to the backside of beyond here at Sweet River. Since Eryn agreed to marry me and we decided to make Montana our permanent home. We've bought a lot in the Agate Bay subdivision on the outskirts of Jewel Lake, and I'll start building in the fall when things slow down around here a little." Maxwell tipped his eyebrows toward their grandfather. "If the boss man stops thinking up new projects every five minutes, that is."

Jude blinked. "You bought property?" How was he the last to know? Or maybe he wasn't. Not that it mattered.

Grandfather cleared his throat. "I thought maybe we'd start on that staff apartment complex this fall. Should keep you plenty busy all winter and beyond."

Maxwell stared at his grandfather.

The old man stared back. Then winked.

Winked? Jude shook his head. Sometimes he forgot how well his cousins knew their grandfather. Jude had missed out through no fault of his own. Only Nana could have changed the course of history, and she'd chosen not to. She'd thought she was doing what was best for everyone. Nearsighted, but honest.

Water under the bridge. Jude needed to let it go, once and for all.

"I've got an idea for you, boy." Grandfather eyed Maxwell. "Got your house plans all drawn up yet, or is there room for some input?"

Maxwell studied him. "We're still sketching. What do you have in mind?"

"How is the property zoned? Might there be a place for

a grandparent suite? Maybe accessible by elevator over the triple garage, or something like that?"

Eryn's spoon clattered to the table. She wasn't the only one staring at the old man.

Maxwell found words first. "You thinking of settling out here permanently? You've already got rooms at the lodge." He nodded toward the ceiling. "Plus your place in Chicago."

Grandfather's gaze slid to Jude then back to Maxwell. "It's a strong possibility. If things work out."

Eryn cleared her throat. "You're getting on in years, sir, and the medical facilities in Chicago are better equipped than Missoula. Not that you wouldn't be welcome. It's just that... never mind. I shouldn't have said anything."

Jude had seen Eryn embarrassed before, but the depth of crimson flooding her face was impressive.

Grandfather waved a hand. "Health care here is solid, and when it's my time to meet my Lord and Savior face to face, I'll be ready. Meanwhile, I expect to have a lot of life left to live."

Would he win Nana over? Jude couldn't help hoping so, and it wasn't only because it was a love story decades in the making. If Grandfather could win over a reluctant woman, maybe Jude could do the same.

Where there was life, there was hope, and Jude had fifty-plus more potential years than his grandparents did.

KACI'S PHONE dinged then dinged again. Then an absolute barrage of notifications followed. Her gut froze. Had Dad or Duncan found out her new number? What was going on?

She eyed her phone on her nightstand. Call her a coward, but she'd skipped Sunday lunch at the Golden Grill with the gang in favor of a deli sandwich from Super One and an afternoon holed up in her bedroom with a new mystery novel that was failing to rivet her attention.

Several more notifications chimed.

She picked up the device and keyed in her password. No facial recognition for this girl. Not a chance.

A new text conversation showed only the last few responses.

Weston: *Sly dog!*

Stephanie: *I'm so happy for you guys! [heart-eyes emoji]*

Maxwell: *Congrats, you two! Welcome to the family.*

Tate: *Do our parents know? I don't see them on this list.*

Paisley: *Hey!!! What about the wedding plans we talked about????*

Say what? Kaci scrolled up and up to the beginning of the convo.

Madison: *Bryce and I got married! We're heading off on our honeymoon, and Everly is staying with Lacey and Bill for a few days. We'll all be back next weekend. TTFN!*

Whoa. No wonder the airwaves were blowing up. How had no one seen this coming?

Kaci hadn't expected to be asked to be a bridesmaid, not when Madison had a close sister and was tight with all the women at Sweet River. Kaci shouldn't be disappointed to not be included, especially since Paisley and Eryn hadn't been, either. And Paisley, at least, sounded even more shocked than Kaci felt.

Madison had eloped with Bryce. Or was it eloping when likely her family had been in attendance? It was Bryce's family that had been excluded. Oh, and probably Madison's mother, who lived in Chicago, not Pittsburgh, and had her nose stuck in the air.

Kaci: *Congrats! Where are you going for your honeymoon?*

Not that she expected an answer. Hopefully, the newly-weds were smart enough to have turned their phones off to focus on each other.

The other thing Kaci hadn't expected was the searing jealousy. Definitely not jealousy regarding Bryce. And not that she wished his and Madison's struggles on herself, not in the least.

Madison's solo pregnancy and birth, Bryce blocking his ex and not even knowing he had a daughter... the whole situation had not been easy for them.

Kaci knew that. But look! There'd been a few hiccups and growing moments, they'd reconciled, and — poof! — they were now one happy little family, neatly tied up with a red bow and heart eyes.

While Kaci had no choice but to keep pushing Jude away.

Okay, fine, she had a choice, but it was an impossible one. None of the women whose friendships she'd come to treasure over the past couple of years had been hiding from their own families the way Kaci needed to. None of them suspected their parents of working for the mob. Cadence's mother had a gambling addiction, true, but that wasn't the same thing at all. Paisley's mom was a druggie shacked up with Paisley's dad... again. Also not ideal, but probably not criminal.

No, it was just Kaci. She had all the nasty luck.

Also, she was likely PMSing, but whatever. Her ovaries only accentuated what was already true.

Emma was spending the day at Rockstead, her family's nearby ranch. No one was going to notice if Kaci ate her weight in cookie dough ice cream. There were a couple of cartons in the freezer, because a girl who suspected she'd need comfort had stocked up.

This group text tipped the scale in ice cream's direction. Notifications flew on as Kaci peeked out of her room to make sure the coast was clear before heading into the tiny kitchenette. Yep, her stash was safely tucked at the back of the freezer, beside Emma's peanut butter chocolate swirl.

Who needed a bowl? It would only require washing. Kaci grabbed a spoon from the drawer and settled on the loveseat with the full carton. Mmm. She felt better already as cold, creamy, sweetness slid over her tongue.

Someone pounded on her door.

Kaci eyed it. Who could that be? She wasn't about to open up. No one could prove she was home. She'd locked the door, right?

Oh, no. She probably hadn't. Emma hated fishing for her keys when she knew Kaci was inside... but that wasn't Emma.

Jude wouldn't pound like that, either.

"Kaci! I know you're in there!"

Paisley. The woman should be in her own home with her own husband, not roaming the ranch looking for someone to intrude on.

"Kaci!" Knock, knock, knock.

Kaci peeked at her phone, but there were so many

notification bubbles stacked on top of each other she couldn't make sense of any of them without opening the text app again. And she'd seen enough of that.

"Kaci!" The knob clicked. The door flew open, and the knob bashed against the wall. Paisley stood poised in the doorway. "I knew you were home! Why didn't you answer?" Then her gaze fell to the carton in Kaci's hand. "Oh, boy. What's going on?"

Kaci scrambled to her feet. "It's not what it looks like." It was totally what it looked like.

"Oh, you're not eating your feelings?" Sarcasm dripped from Paisley's words.

"No?"

"Got another spoon?"

Kaci blinked. "Sure... but why?"

"I know you saw the text, because you responded."

Kaci should have waited until tomorrow to tap a reply. "Why is it bothering you so much?"

Paisley plucked the spoon out of Kaci's hand and waved it. "I might ask you the same thing."

Yeah. Complicated. "I asked first." Kaci snagged it back then grabbed one for Paisley from the drawer. "Here."

Paisley dug a large spoonful from the carton then moaned as the sugar rush hit her. "I needed that."

"Why?"

"Did you know they were going to elope?"

"No. It doesn't sound like anyone did." Yeah, yeah, she'd scanned the texts above her own reply.

"I had no clue. Madison let me go on and on *and on* about planning their wedding. We talked about dates, about venues, about themes, about how many attendants...

everything! And all along, she probably knew she wasn't going to do any of it. She was likely laughing at me behind my back the whole time."

"Maybe Bryce surprised her?"

Paisley eyed her. "You think that's what happened?"

"Could be. Only they know for sure."

"Huh." Paisley took a big scoop of ice cream and popped it in her mouth.

"Though she might have known before they left for Pittsburgh a few days ago."

"There's a three-day waiting period in Pennsylvania." Paisley licked her spoon before plunging it back into the carton. "I looked it up."

They'd left Montana with enough time for that. Maybe they'd even applied before the trip. But Paisley was right. The likelihood Madison and Bryce had made an instantaneous decision was approximately zero.

Having their wedding in Pittsburgh near her family made sense, especially for Everly's sake. The little girl was comfortable with the Woodrow side of her family, and who wanted to take a 20-month-old on a honeymoon?

No one, that's who.

"I'm happy for them," Kaci said flatly as she nudged Paisley's spoon out of the way inside the carton.

"Me, too." Paisley knocked the ice cream off Kaci's spoon.

"Hey! That means war."

"Bring it." Paisley's grin was feral.

Maybe Kaci wasn't the only one with PMS. Or something.

CHAPTER EIGHTEEN

Jude rapped on his grandfather's door that evening.
"Come."

He entered the suite's living room to see the old man seated in a wing chair beside the lit fireplace. The last vestiges of daylight glowed on the lake beyond the wide windows, and the whole atmosphere was Montana lodge, a long way from any Sullivans' spartan Chicago residences.

Grandfather gestured to the sideboard. "I brought a carafe of tea up from the kitchen if you'd like a cup."

"Thank you." Jude poured a mug — smelled like chamomile — and added a splash of creamer before taking a seat across from the old man. "I suppose you knew about Bryce and Madison's elopement beforehand."

Grandfather grinned. "I hardly think it qualifies as an elopement when it's preplanned and several family members are there."

So, he *had* known. "But none of the Sullivan clan."

"No, but I can hardly blame Bryce for that. James won't

speak to Maribel unless forced to, and Bryce could hardly invite his brothers without his parents. Never mind that would have required opening up to everyone at Sweet River. Suddenly, it wouldn't have been a small, private affair."

"Don't you wish you could have gone?" Jude knew their grandfather had applied a lot of pressure to Bryce over the years.

"Of course. But I attended Wally's wedding and Tate's and Graham's and Weston's. I expect to be at Maxwell's in September." Grandfather sipped his tea and eyed Jude. "And, one day, yours."

Jude forced a chuckle. "Not any time soon."

"It might be sooner than you expect."

That was a cryptic comment. What did he mean? "Do you know something I don't know?"

Grandfather laughed. "I'm 82 years old, and you're what, the reverse of that? Of course, there are many, many things I know that you don't. When you get to be my age, you'll understand."

Which was not at all what Jude had asked. Once again, Jude was reminded that Grandfather had not only been behind his trip to Chicago a few weeks ago, but seemingly also behind Kaci's. And way back, over two years ago, wasn't it the old man who'd hired Kaci before Tate had taken over HR?

Yeah. Grandfather knew things and didn't intend to talk about them. Heads of enormous companies like Sullivan Enterprises needed to know how to keep their secrets, but wasn't this a time to be a little more open?

Grandfather stared straight at Jude over the rim of his

teacup.

Jude wasn't getting anything out of him that Grandfather didn't choose to give. And, while Jude would certainly appreciate the revelation, he'd settle for the other topic.

He leaned his elbows on his knees. "You said you planned to pursue my grandmother. I imagine that would be with marriage in mind."

"Yes on both counts."

"But she seems unwilling. How will you win her over? What's your game plan?"

"Are we still talking about Eleanor and me?"

Of course. Who else might we be talking about? "Mostly?"

"Or are we talking about you and Kaci?"

Jude heaved a sigh. "Both, I think." How pathetic was it that he had to go to his elderly grandparent for advice? Maybe he should talk to his more familiar grandmother instead of the grandfather he barely knew. Would Nana offer any insight to the workings of the female mind?

"I'll tell you my game plan." Grandfather leaned forward suddenly.

"I'd like to hear it."

"It goes like this. Apologize from the heart, which I have done."

Jude nodded. As far as he knew, this wasn't one of his own steps.

"Genuinely listen to the hurts I've caused, and don't try to minimize them as being so far in the past that they no longer matter. They remain relevant."

Still not on Jude's page. This visit might have been a mistake or, at least, unhelpful.

"Work on simply being a friend moment by moment. This is where I've been for the past two years."

As had Jude.

"Step up the action." Grandfather's eyes twinkled. "Let her know that friendship isn't the end game... then give her time to become accustomed to that concept."

"How much time?" Gah, those words should have stayed inside.

"I cannot answer that question. I wish I could, but it leads into my next step."

"Which is?"

"Pray," Grandfather said simply. "Pray about her, pray for her, pray with her."

"I've been praying." But had he been genuinely asking for God's wisdom and patience, or had he only been begging God to make Kaci see that they were meant for each other?

"And then waiting some more. Not pressuring, but not backing off, either. Being a constant fixture in her life while allowing God to do His thing."

"What if... what if reuniting with Nana is not God's idea?"

"I sincerely hope that is not true, but part of the praying step is asking God for His will, not mine, to be done. Truly focusing on aligning my wants with God's, and asking Him to remove my desires if they are not His."

Jude nodded slowly. "I thought I was being patient."

"Just imagine how two years feels when you're over 80. You've got time, boy. God's clock is not the same as ours."

What if time runs out? But that wasn't a question Jude

could ask. "Has Nana said what her holdup is?" Not that it was any of his business. Probably.

"Mostly Reggie and Melinda, I think. This afternoon was full of how much they've done for Eleanor, how they invited her into their home and cared for her selflessly. They could be making money on leasing out that little suite, after all."

Jude sighed. His aunt and uncle had always nitpicked every penny to death. "So, then, they should be glad if you take Nana off their hands and they can find renters."

"But then it looks like she's spurned their benevolence."

A snort came out before Jude could stop it. "Benevolence?"

"That's how they see it, like she'd be choosing Nadine's family over theirs. Oh, they'd never flat-out punish her for it, or they'd never see a penny of her estate when she passes, but that jealousy is still at the root. I might be wrong, but all evidence points in that direction. I speak to you in confidence, boy. This isn't gossip. You asked a specific question about your family."

"Would it help if I talked to Nana?"

Grandfather's eyebrows tipped up. "That is between you and God. All I know is she hasn't listened to your mother, since Nadine is clearly biased by all the years of begging for answers Eleanor refused to give."

How could Nana have clutched her secrets close for over five decades? Which wasn't the slightest bit reassuring, since Kaci seemed bent on the same course. Did Kaci have a child she was hiding, too, like Eleanor and Madison had?

The thought was ludicrous.

But there was definitely something big. What if she never divulged the truth? Jude eyed his grandfather. "How long have you known Kaci?"

"I don't believe the answer to that will help you in your quest."

Which totally meant Grandfather knew there was more to Kaci's situation than met the eye... which Jude had already figured out.

"Boy?"

Jude looked away long enough to try to wipe the frustration and yes, maybe anger, from his expression. "Yes, sir?"

"Let's pray together, right here, right now."

TATE: *I've got a couple of interviews lined up for this afternoon for the housekeeping position. Please come to the office at 2:00.*

Kaci blinked at Tate's text. Finally! The last ten days had been exhausting in all the ways; physical and emotional topped the list.

Kaci: *I'll be there. Thank you!*

She stretched and looked around Dragonfly three. These guests had left the place so immaculate it almost didn't need cleaning. The beds had been stripped and the linens folded. The towels lay in a pile in the shower. Otherwise?

If she were Giana, she'd do a quick swipe and call it good.

Kaci wasn't Giana. Anything worth doing was worth doing well, and Sweet River's reputation depended on perfection in every minuscule detail. Lack of attention was not going to be found in any area over which Kaci held jurisdiction.

Her personal life was already a total, uncontrollable disaster. Her professional life? Was in control, or it would be when she wasn't doing two people's jobs. Trish and Kylie had helped out some to cover the deficit, but Kaci didn't feel she could ask too much of them. Instead, she'd taken the entire burden on herself.

Typical of Kirsten Catriona.

Why did she do this to herself? Kaci heaved the still mostly crisp sheets into the laundry bin on the golf cart.

"Hey, there!" The guest from four waved frantically. "We need our towels refreshed. The kids have been in and out of the lake a dozen times, and we don't have a single dry towel in the place."

Wow, that drawl threw Kaci back to Texas. "Sure." She lifted the pile that had been destined for #3 and carried them over. "You do know you can request more at the front desk anytime, right?"

"But that's way over there, and you're right here." The woman took them with an indignant glare at Kaci.

"Of course. I'm happy to help." Or she normally would be, but today? Everything was an irritant, and this meant an extra trip to the laundry herself. *Tate has help lined up,* she reminded herself. Right, then she'd have more time and bandwidth to obsess endlessly over Jude. There was no winning.

"What do I do with the damp ones?"

Kaci managed a smile, though it likely didn't look

authentic. "Feel free to place them in here." She patted the laundry bin.

"Isn't that your job?"

She gritted her teeth. *Keep smiling, Kaci.* "You might recall that daily guest services are not part of your cottage rental. Your privacy and autonomy are important to us."

The woman huffed. "Fine. I'll send one of the kids out with them."

"Sounds good. Is there anything else?"

"Not at the moment."

"Then have a good day." Kaci pivoted and marched back into the cottage she'd been cleaning. How could entitled people not even notice how demeaning their attitudes and words came across? Housekeeping staff were right there with restaurant servers and parking attendants. So unappreciated.

Her parents were like that. Only people with influence, which meant people with money, were important enough to be deferred to. No wonder her choice to become a nurse had seemed ludicrous to them. Purposefully choosing to work with sick and injured people? Expose herself to germs and blood and all the nasty stuff?

And here she was, cleaning cottages instead of caring for the needy, while her father continued to manipulate his clients back in Texas. The guest's accent had thrown her. Not that many Texans sought out Montanan guest ranches. They had enough of those back home, apparently bigger and better than anything Montana could offer. But Kaci needed to stay on guard, remembering that anyone could travel wherever they wanted.

She was early to the lunch line, knowing Jude's flight

schedule would put him coming in toward the end. Was she avoiding him? Yes, yes, she was. Why? Because how did you interact casually with the guy whom you'd grabbed by the shirt collar and passionately kissed a few nights ago after being adamant there could be nothing between the two of you?

She started another cottage after lunch and made it back to her duplex by 1:30, where she changed her clothes, brushed her hair into a fresh ponytail, and swiped on a touch of makeup. She entered the office wing of the lodge with five minutes to spare.

Tate looked up and smiled at her. "We've got two candidates coming in. I wouldn't be opposed to hiring both if you think they'll be a good fit, and we can do a little more rotation. On the other hand, we have quite a few multi-day reservations over the summer, which limits the needs for housekeeping services. What do you think?"

She took a seat. "Hmm. Let's meet with the applicants and go from there. Who have we got?"

Tate tapped a few keys on his keyboard. "First, we have an older woman from Jewel Lake, Jane Mitchell. After her, Candy Masterson from Flower Mound, Tex…"

But the buzzing of an entire hive of bees swarmed through Kaci's head at the second name so that she barely heard the rest of Tate's words. There was literally no way Candy wouldn't recognize her. The Mastersons and the Atkinsons had been best friends for years.

She surged back to her feet. "You'll have to do the interviews yourself. I'm suddenly not feeling well at all."

Tate studied her with concern. "You can use the office restroom if you're going to be sick."

"I need to leave. I mean, I need to lie down at my place. I'm sorry." She pivoted for the door and bolted into the corridor just as a middle-aged woman raised her hand to knock.

"Excuse me, please." Kaci dodged past her and out the door. A car pulled into the parking lot. Probably Candy. Kaci turned away, sprinted to the golf cart, then peeled toward the duplex without a backward glance

How could she warn Tate without raising suspicion? Ha. He had to know something was up. But if he employed Candy, Kaci had no choice but to leave before her start date. Either way, things were going to look suspicious. Her house of cards was crashing down around her.

Her fingers trembled as she pulled out her phone and opened her text app, then her recent convo with Tate.

Kaci: *please do not hire Candy Masterson. Just don't. I have a bad feeling.*

And if he asked for more? What would she tell him?

Heaven only knew.

CHAPTER NINETEEN

I t had been two days since Jude had seen Kaci from a distance, let alone close up. How was it even possible for her to avoid the dining hall while he was there unless she were fixing her own meals?

He could ask her roommate. That had worked so well last time.

Jude eyed Emma across the serving counter as he loaded his dinner tray, but she seemed distracted. Either that, or she was purposefully avoiding eye contact because she knew something. Wasn't that laughable? Kaci let no one in, not even an inch. Her roommate wasn't a likely candidate for that level of confidentiality, although... who knew? Because the friend group that included Jude was so tight — or it used to be — and everyone else was paired off now, which would probably make such confidences harder to keep.

Not that Jude could do more than guess whether married couples kept those sorts of secrets or told each other everything. He was not-so-blissfully unaware.

Tate waved at him from near the back corner. Jude nodded at his cousin, filled a glass with iced tea, and carried his tray to the table Tate shared with his wife and two little boys.

Three-year-old Jamie beamed at him. "Hi, Unca Dude."

Jude's heart warmed as he ruffled the little guy's hair. "Hey, squirt."

"I not a squirt. I James Walter Suwwivan, and I Mommy's boy."

Tate choked on a sip of water and turned away, obviously trying his best not to laugh.

Jamie studied his dad before looking back at Jude with a frown. "Simon Mommy's boy too."

"Is Daddy Mommy's boy?" Jude couldn't help asking.

"No! That silly."

The three adults burst into laughter while Jamie scowled at each of them in turn.

Simon took that opportunity to fling his spoon, which nearly winged the head of a tourist at the next table before clattering to the floor over ten feet away.

"I'll get Simon another spoon." Stephanie sighed, got up, and retrieved the one on the floor.

"Kid's got a future in baseball." Jude settled into his seat. He might be torn up at not seeing Kaci, but this moment with his cousin's family was doing his heart good.

Tate leaned in. "Hey, while we've got a couple of seconds, do you know anything about Candy Masterson from Flower Mound, Texas?"

Jude blinked. "No? I've never heard the name, that I recall."

"I interviewed her today. Kaci was supposed to do

interviews with me. She even arrived, but when I told her who was coming in, she turned white as a sheet and bailed. Then she texted me not to hire Candy, which honestly is kind of a bummer, because she's experienced and eager. I think she'd be an asset."

Jude stared at Tate blankly, though his brain was churning. "I have no idea." Over near the counter, Stephanie stood chatting with Paisley.

"It was a long shot." Tate shook his head. "I told both women I'd get back to them, but I really wanted to hire on the spot and have one or both start tomorrow. And Kaci's not replying to texts."

"Masterson?"

Tate brightened. "You got something?"

"Not Candy, for sure. Way back — like 12 years ago — I went on a mission trip to Mexico. Our church in Seeley Lake partnered with a larger church in Dallas. They sent some teens, too. I think our pastor had been mentored by theirs or something..."

"Masterson," Tate prompted, glancing over at Stephanie, who'd stopped to chat with someone else.

"There were these two guys, Duncan Atkinson and Joe Masterson that were tight as thieves trying to get the rest of us to do their work for them. I never figured out why they would have even bothered going on a missions trip. Probably just to get a vacation without their families? But that's got nothing to do with a girl named Candy. How old is she?"

"Twenty-two according to her application. Like I said, long shot. I know you're not from Texas—" Tate glanced around and lowered his voice even more "—but Kaci is, and I just wondered if she'd ever mentioned any names from down there."

"You're kidding me, right? I've never met anyone more tight-lipped about their personal history. I don't know anything at all except a few things I've picked up, like she was comfortable on horseback and had been up in a helicopter enough times that she didn't need instruction."

"Here, Simon." Stephanie handed a spoon to the toddler, who chortled and banged it incessantly on the highchair tray. "Need help cutting up your meat, Jamie? Daddy can help you."

"Sure can, shorty." But Tate's gaze didn't slide from Jude to Jamie very quickly, even as he leaned over the little boy's plate.

Jude took a bite of his own slice of pork roast. An overreaction like Tate mentioned was uncharacteristic for Kaci. She'd deflected conversations away from herself so subtly it had taken more than a year for anyone to notice.

"It's wild that Bryce and Madison eloped, hey, Jude?" Stephanie asked. "I did *not* see that coming."

"Grandfather said it's not eloping if it's preplanned and there's family present."

"You talked to him about it?" Tate angled a look at Jude.

Jude shrugged. "We speak about a variety of topics."

Stephanie smirked. "You keep practicing, and you'll be nearly as good as Kaci at hiding things and turning conversations."

Jude exchanged a glance with Tate.

"Wait, what? Did I miss something?" Stephanie glanced between them. "What are you not telling me?"

"Not now, honey."

Her eyes widened. "So there *is* something going on. Jude, when are you going to pin that girl down?"

"We're just friends."

Tate and Stephanie laughed. Jamie giggled. Simon threw his spoon and clapped his hands.

Okay, so once upon a time, Jude had sounded more convincing saying that line. He'd even managed to fool himself for over a year.

"Simon!" Stephanie scolded. "No throwing!"

"I'll get him a fresh one." Tate excused himself.

"You're still reciting that old line, Jude?"

No one had ever accused Stephanie of being sensitive or tactful for one main reason. She wasn't.

Jude shrugged. "It's the best I can do."

"She's still shutting you down, huh? I thought maybe the other night...?" Her question trailed off suggestively.

He had thought so, too.

KACI: *I'm sorry I bailed on you. How did the interviews go?*

Tate: *They went well. I hope you're feeling better.*

Kaci eyed the text conversation. She was only feeling better if Tate had taken her advice — call it a plea if not an order — and told Candy she wasn't hired. But how could she ask without showing her hand?

Kaci: *Somewhat better. My gut was churning like crazy earlier.*

Still was, and it wasn't from anything she'd eaten or any bug she'd caught.

Tate: *Can we talk?*

Ugh. The whirlpool increased. She stared at the phone until the screen blanked out.

There was only one person at Sweet River who knew the truth, and that was Walter Sullivan. Would he call Tate off if she asked him to? But Tate's suspicions were already aroused, and that would only intensify his curiosity.

What if Tate asked Candy if she knew Kaci Moore? Candy's no would only last as long as they didn't meet in person, and with Candy assigned to housekeeping, that was obviously impossible. Even if she were hired as a stable hand, it couldn't work. There weren't so many staff members onsite that anyone could be avoided.

Tate: *Kaci, are you there? I can meet with you this evening. You can come over to the house, or I can meet you at the office at 7:30pm. You tell me which place.*

It was face her boss… or pack up her stuff and drive off the ranch in the next half hour. She'd leave everyone in the lurch with no head of housekeeping. She'd be cutting ties with all the friends she'd made in the past couple of years.

How could she leave Jude without so much as a good-bye? But she'd have to do that. Only her attorney, Bridget, could be trusted with her whereabouts. And Mr. Sullivan — he'd done absolutely nothing to tip her hand. She couldn't thumb her nose at all he'd done to give his old friend's granddaughter a job and keep her identity hidden.

Wouldn't she be far less safe elsewhere?

She didn't want to leave Sweet River Ranch. Didn't want to leave Jude. Was there no other way through this?

You could pray.

Hadn't she been? She had. She'd dumped all her woes on God more times than she could ever count.

But it had all been about her. Her protection. Her fears. Her needs. Had she truly trusted God with all the details?

Tate: *Kaci?*

She'd have to change her number again if she left. She'd be on her own, never able to trust anyone, forever looking over her shoulder.

Or she could swear Tate to secrecy and tell him everything. How would he respond?

The duplex's door creaked as someone entered, spiking Kaci's fears. Emma called out from the other room. "Hey, Kaci? You here? Are you okay? I didn't see you at dinner."

Of course, it couldn't have been Candy, anyway. There was no way her family acquaintance was here to track her down. It was coincidence, plain and simple.

"I'm here. Not feeling great." Hopefully that would keep Emma at a distance.

"Can I get you anything? I brought a plate of leftovers, but maybe pork roast is too heavy if your gut is queasy. I could run back and get a jar of chicken soup from the pantry. Would that help?"

Tears prickled Kaci's eyes. Her roommate was too sweet. There were so many awesome people here at the ranch. "I'm okay, thanks." But her voice caught on the words.

"You don't sound okay."

"I will be. Promise." Somehow.

"Okay, if you're sure. I'm heading over to Janessa and Tina's, so I'll stick your plate in the fridge. If you need anything, shoot me a text."

"Thanks."

Kaci listened to Emma move around the duplex then

head out again. She jiggled her phone and stared at Tate's last text.

Kaci: *Office at 7:30 is fine.* That way, she wouldn't get sucked into chatting with Stephanie.

Tate: *Great. See you there.*

Maybe. Probably. But Kaci hadn't completely ruled out throwing her stuff in her Benz and driving away. She glanced at the clock. Forty-five minutes wasn't very long to figure out what she was going to do.

She could pray… but what good would that do? She needed a reply like two seconds ago, and God was noted for being kind of slow in answering. She'd been waiting two-and-a-half years for closure on the thing with her father and, as far as she could tell, God was taking that whole 'one day is like a thousand years, and a thousand years like one day' thing to its limits.

She could call Walter Sullivan and ask for advice, since he was even at Sweet River at the moment. He might be on a date with Jude's grandmother… but it was worth a shot.

Kaci: *I'm in a bit of a pickle. Do you have a few minutes to give advice?*

WJS: *Would you like to chat on the phone, or do you want to come up to my place?*

Right. He might know how to text, but he was old-fashioned enough to prefer vocal conversation. She needed to head to the lodge to meet Tate soon, anyway… unless she decided to make a run for it. Man, that temptation was strong.

Kaci: *I can come up. Is now good?*

She chewed her lip while she watched the three dots dance, disappear, then dance again.

WJS: *That would be fine.*

She whooshed out a breath she hadn't realized she'd been holding. Okay, so her first move was not running away, after all. It was getting some wise counsel such as Grandad would give.

A tsunami of homesickness rolled over her, and those dratted tears threatened to gush once more. Oh, God, when would this end? Could she ever freely love Jude? When would justice be served and her exile ended? When could she become her whole, true self again?

See? That was a prayer, right? That meant she was praying.

Really, Kaci? That was whining in God's direction, not a prayer.

CHAPTER TWENTY

K aci tapped on Mr. Sullivan's door on the lodge's top level. She could have her car loaded by now if she'd chosen that route. She could be on her way to places unknown in just a few minutes. That would probably have been the best move.

"Come."

She squeezed her eyes shut, breathed another frantic prayer, and entered the upscale suite.

Mr. Sullivan sat in a wing chair next to the lit fireplace and gestured to the sideboard. "I brought a carafe of tea up from the kitchen if you'd like to pour yourself a cup."

"Thank you. Would you like one, as well?"

"I already have one. Thank you."

"Okay." She poured a mug of tea with trembling hands and added a large dollop of honey before sniffing the brew. Chamomile? Was calm even a remote option? Then she turned to face the elderly man who'd become another grandfather figure to her.

"What can I do for you, Kirsten?"

Her heart hammered at hearing her true name. "Has Tate talked to you about the hiring process for a new chambermaid to replace the one who quit the other day?"

The old man blinked and pulled back. Clearly, this wasn't what he expected their topic of discussion to be. "No. Have a seat, and tell me more."

Kaci perched on the edge of the other wing chair and clutched the mug between her hands. She inhaled the sweet aroma. Shouldn't she be feeling soothed already? How long did it take for this stuff to work?

She studied the old man, whose bushy eyebrows had pulled together. "He had two interviews this afternoon and invited me to participate."

Mr. Sullivan nodded. "As he should."

"True." Imagine if he'd hired Candy without consulting Kaci at all first? They'd have first met in a housekeeping staff meeting. "The thing is, one of the interviewees was the daughter of my parents' closest friends. We've gone on more vacations together than I can count."

He leaned closer. "You're telling me your cover has been blown?"

"Not exactly. Not yet. Tate mentioned the names ahead of time, and I abruptly told him I was sick, and he had to do the interviews without me. Then I texted him not to hire Candy. Needless to say, he's suspicious and wants to meet with me in half an hour."

"I see."

"Should I... should I leave the ranch?"

"What? No!"

"I don't know what to say to Tate."

"He may need to know the complete story."

"But…"

"You have two choices: leave, or stay. Leaving is not a good option. It involves a lot of uncertainty and extra risk of exposure. For you to stay and be safe looks like it requires us to bring Tate into confidence. I trust my grandson implicitly."

"Don't married people tell each other everything?" She should *not* have blurted that out.

A twinkle returned to the old man's eyes. "You're thinking he'll tell Stephanie? I'm sure she's equally as trust-worthy as Tate, but he won't talk to her if we ask him not to."

If any of this generation of Sullivans knew her story, she wished it were Jude, not Tate. It didn't seem right for Jude's cousin to have information he didn't have. He was going to be upset when that came out… if it ever did.

Hmm. It sounded like her subconscious had already decided to follow Mr. Sullivan's advice. "I don't know what to tell Tate. Does he need to know all the details?" Kaci glanced at her watch. She was meeting him in 15 minutes.

"Why don't we invite him here? I can handle the disclo-sures if you prefer."

Relief gushed through her heart. "Oh, would you?"

"You're welcome to speak for yourself, if you prefer. I'm not trying to intrude or control the narrative."

"No. I appreciate the offer." She swiped at moisture in her eyes.

He reached for his phone. "I'll call Tate."

"Let me text him. That way it's less likely for Stephanie to be alerted."

Mr. Sullivan nodded, leaving his device on his side table.

Kaci: *Change of venue! I'm at your grandfather's suite. Please meet me here.*

Tate: *Right-o.*

She gave Mr. Sullivan a smile, but it hurt and felt wobbly. "Now we wait."

"Now we pray," he corrected as he leaned forward, resting his elbows on his knees and clasping his hands. "Precious Father, we come to You this evening for guidance."

The longer Mr. Sullivan prayed, the more peace settled in Kaci's soul. By the time Tate's knock sounded on the door, she was ready.

JUDE COULDN'T RECALL the last time he'd been invited to Uncle Reggie and Aunt Melinda's home in Missoula. He nearly declined the invitation now, but what was he doing that was so important on a Tuesday evening? Nothing at all, especially since Kaci was still on full evasion mode, and Jude felt helpless to break the impasse.

Besides, Weston and Paisley were going, so Jude might as well join them, even if that meant riding in the backseat of West's pickup like a little kid.

"Any clue what's going on?" Jude asked, not for the first time.

Weston shook his head, but Paisley turned to face Jude. "Is this unusual?"

"Very. We've never been particularly close, but Uncle Reg has barely spoken to us since Mom found Grandfather. We're some sort of gold-diggers to have aligned with the Sullivans when the Evans family should have been good enough for us." Sometimes Jude felt like that was true.

"But... you *are* Sullivans." Paisley frowned. "That's your heritage."

"I know, but they feel we're traitors or something."

"That doesn't even make sense."

"It does to them." Jude shifted in the seat. "This is going to be awkward."

"Yeah." Weston met his gaze in the rearview mirror. "I notice Mom and Keith weren't invited."

"Ugh. I hadn't even thought of that."

"Because your head is stuck on Kaci." Paisley smirked.

Jude shook his head, not that he'd convince anyone. "I've only seen her at a distance for the past few days."

"Same." Paisley scowled. Her facial changes would be entertaining if it wasn't for the seriousness of the topic. There was something major going on with Kaci. Jude knew it in his bones. "I've hardly seen her, either. We used to be so close, but now it's like she's a stranger."

"Because you're married to Jude's brother," Weston remarked.

Paisley turned her narrowed gaze on him.

"Come up with plausible denial."

"I hate that you're likely right. I'm now in the enemy camp. What did you do to make her so skittish, Jude?" She giggled.

I kissed her back when she kissed me. Not that Jude was

about to share those events with anyone, least of all with his curious, chatty sister-in-law.

Jude turned the conversation to some of their recent tourists. A few had flown with him, ridden with Weston, and participated in some of the family activities Paisley led daily.

Soon enough, they pulled onto Uncle Reggie's street, but several vehicles already filled the driveway.

Who all had been invited? What was going on? This must be a bigger deal than Jude had suspected at first. Knots twisted, like he needed more of a mess going on in his gut.

"Hi, cousins!" Reggie's daughter, Daniella, opened the door wide. "Long time no see."

Since Weston and Paisley's wedding less than two months back, not very long in the grand scheme of things.

"Hi, Daniella!" Paisley stepped forward to hug the woman. "May I call you Dani?"

"Um, no. It's Daniella. Full name."

"Aw, okay. Dani is such a cute name, though." Paisley linked arms with Daniella and stepped into the foyer.

Jude caught the smirk Weston sent him as they followed. For a guy as socially awkward as Weston, it must be nice to have a wife who had no fear in any situation. Paisley waltzed right on in and made herself at home where angels feared to tread.

Nana came around the corner and smiled at them. "It's so good to see you boys."

"We're happy to be here, Nana." Jude squeezed his grandmother. "Is this your party or Aunt Melinda's?"

"Both?" She turned to embrace Weston.

That wasn't as reassuring as it might seem.

"We're honored." At least, he hoped they were. "Who all is here?"

"Kenneth and Lisa came in from Butte this afternoon. All your cousins are here."

All the *Evans* cousins. The Sullivans wouldn't be welcome. "Practically a family reunion. It's too bad my mother couldn't make it."

And, yeah, he knew for a fact Mom and Keith hadn't been invited. Weston said he'd outright asked her.

Nana pursed her lips. "Be that as it may."

Jude sincerely hoped she wasn't going to make him or his brother choose one side of the family over the other. He also sincerely hoped she would give Grandfather a real chance. Nana had much more to gain than to lose by accepting his advances, gains that had nothing to do with financial security. Even if they never married, Jude couldn't see Grandfather allowing Nana to be in need. He'd find a way to support her whether she encouraged him or not.

Like he'd do for Kaci if she allowed it.

They were swept into conversation with their uncles, aunts, and five Evans cousins. It didn't feel like they had much in common anymore, even though Kenneth's son Keon was between them in age and worked at the Mustang Mountain Ranch near Saddle Springs and was as single as the day was long.

Jude couldn't help waiting and watching for the other boot to drop all the way through dinner, because something was obviously going on. His uncles shared grumpy expressions even Weston at his worst might be hard to supersede. Jude's grandmother didn't look all that comfortable, either, and his aunts kept talking over each other as though to prove which of them had the better life.

Jude was surprised to realize he found the Sullivans refreshing by comparison. They were confident of who they were and didn't feel the need for posturing. Was it because they had all the money they could ever want or need? Didn't hurt, but Jude doubted that was all of it. Even with James and Maribel's broken marriage, everyone just seemed so much more settled. At least, now that Bryce had come around.

"What do you think, Jude?"

He blinked and turned to Uncle Reggie. "Pardon me?"

"You can't think she'd be better off with that scoundrel than with her true family."

"Uh... back up?"

Reggie glared at him. "Weren't you listening to a word I said?"

"There's a lot going on in here, and I wasn't aware you were addressing me."

"You've been bought by those highfalutin' rich people. How does it feel to have them own your soul?"

Somehow Jude managed to keep his voice even. "Only Jesus owns my soul."

"Jesus didn't buy you a helicopter. That's not a normal birthday present in our world, boy."

So much to unpack, starting with Jude vastly preferring the way Grandfather called him 'boy.' It didn't sound demeaning like it did from his uncle.

"The helicopter I fly belongs to Sweet River Ranch. It's not mine, and it definitely wasn't a birthday gift."

"Semantics."

"Not really. I received training paid for by the company I work for, same as many people do. And the tools to do my job are also provided by the company I work for."

"You think you're better than the rest of us now."

"I believe you know, deep down, that isn't so." Jude didn't dare say more on that subject. "Now, what were you saying earlier?"

"Your grandmother wants everyone to weigh in about whether she should consider Walter Sullivan's offer. Of course, it's ludicrous, and I have no idea why she thinks making a change like that at her age is appropriate."

Jude's heart leaped. He hadn't realized things had progressed to this level so quickly. Hadn't it only been a few days since Grandfather had confided in him? Now, he leaned closer to his uncle. "You want my opinion?"

"Sure." And the look on Uncle Reggie's face told Jude exactly what the correct answer ought to be.

"I think she's old enough to make up her own mind about what makes her happy."

Did that go for Kaci, too?

"I should have known they'd have brainwashed you as well as your mother."

Jude pushed out a chuckle. "So that's why you didn't invite her tonight? Because you knew her response, but you hoped you could still sway Weston and me?"

"Not at all."

Right. That was why Reggie's eyes shifted away.

"It's just that we've done so much for your grandmother, and we feel she is too frail to make such a major decision. There've been a few signs of forgetfulness—"

"Reginald!" Nana to the rescue. "Like you haven't forgotten anything. Just last week you forgot what Melinda sent you to the store for. You don't get to call me senile."

"I didn't use that word, Mother."

"You meant it." Nana pulled herself to her whole five-and-a-half-foot height and glared at her oldest son. "I asked for this gathering this evening to make sure all my children and grandchildren understood where I'm at right now." She cast a glance at Jude. "Nadine and I have spoken."

Jude nodded and willed his lips to stay zipped.

Nana turned to the group, which had fallen strangely silent during her tirade on Uncle Reggie. "You may feel as though I'm simply trying to live out my last years in the lap of luxury by encouraging Walter's attention. You all know how much Nadine and I argued over this whole situation with her father. I knew that if I came face-to-face with Walter again, it would be hard to hold onto the grudges I'd clung to for so many years. He was a good man then — contrary to evidence — and he is a good man now. He married a lovely woman, Gladys, and they had a good life together."

Jude dared a quick peek around the room. At least everyone was listening.

"I never wished ill on Walter. The mistakes we made in our youth were as much mine as his. It seemed that nothing good could possibly come from facing those days." Nana pursed her lips. "I was wrong."

"Mother—" Uncle Reggie protested.

She held up a hand, and her son quieted. "The give and take of apology and forgiveness is a valuable commodity. You should try it sometime." She skewered Reggie with a look. "And I find that the man I once knew is now a much better man."

"You mean richer," Reggie mumbled.

"His bank account has nothing to do with anything," Nana retorted. "Walter is a man with a genuine relationship with his Heavenly Father. It's been a privilege and joy to see how he steers his company, his sons, and his grandsons with prayer and clear thinking."

"You've already made up your mind." Reggie sighed.

But, had she? And why hadn't Grandfather known it if she had?

CHAPTER TWENTY-ONE

J ude didn't have a chance to talk to his grandfather before lunch, and he could only hope to run into the old man then. He had taken two groups of tourists up in the air for an overview of Sweet River Ranch and the surrounding area. There would be more flights this afternoon, so he would most likely meet the goal he had set for how many trips he'd fly this first summer.

He scanned the dining hall, not missing the fact that Kaci was nowhere to be found. He'd almost given up hope of running into her casually by this point, since it had been several days since he'd seen her at all. He'd texted her a time or two, but there had been nothing but a lot of silence interspersed by a few cursory replies.

Now he gathered his lunch tray, fixing himself a sandwich on his mother's amazing sourdough bread.

"Who's that?" Maxwell said from beside him.

Jude looked around and noted a young woman surveying the area. "One of the tourists?" It wasn't like there was a shortage of people he didn't know in the dining hall on any given day, but most of their skimpy clothing consisted of swimsuits and coverups. This woman's attire was more of the consciously provocative kind. "Why? Do you think you know her from somewhere?"

"She was here a couple of days ago for a job interview, I think. I thought Tate hadn't hired her, but maybe I'm wrong and she's here to report for duty. Strange outfit for work, though. Someone needs to get her a staff T-shirt."

And Jude was supposed to care why? He glanced over at the woman again. Nope, still not familiar. Which basically meant that she hadn't been on any of his flights in the last week or two.

She must have been looking for Tate, because she scanned the room then headed his direction.

"Must not have been too happy to not be hired," Maxwell muttered. "Let's sit where we can overhear."

Jude wasn't into eavesdropping. It kind of seemed like gossip, honestly. But hadn't Kaci gone off the rails a couple of days ago, when Tate had been interviewing possibilities for the housekeeping position that Giana had left behind? Maybe a little eavesdropping would be in order. The dining room was a public space, after all.

He followed Maxwell to the table next to Tate's just as the woman braced her hands on the chair back across the table from Tate. "Your employment page on your website says you are still looking for someone for the house-keeping position," she said a little more loudly than would be required.

Hmm. This was interesting.

The woman went on. "I have two summers of experience working at a resort in Galveston. If you bothered to check with my previous employers, you would see that they have no problem recommending me. So, why didn't I get the job?"

Tate stared at the woman so long that Jude became uncomfortable on his behalf. What was going on? If this woman was qualified, why hadn't Tate hired her?

Oh... Jude remembered Tate asking him if he knew a woman named Candy Masterson. Why on earth he should have known her, he had no idea, though Tate seemed to have assumed that Kaci talked to him occasionally. Ha. Once upon a time, maybe. Recently? Not so much, and never any name-dropping from her past.

"Are you just slow at updating the website?" the woman Jude assumed was Candy demanded. "Because I'm also available for web work. I have skills in a lot of areas."

"I chose not to hire you," Tate said slowly. "I'm not required to give you a reason."

"But you still need someone."

"We're managing."

Candy pulled out the chair and sat, tucking her short skirt beneath her tanned thigh before leaning forward on the table. Was she seriously angling her low neckline in Tate's direction? "I can help you."

"I made the decision two days ago not to hire you, and I stand by the choice today."

She hooked long blond hair behind her ear. "I influence people. I can write a bad review about your hiring practices. I'm a Masterson."

Wow, did that line, in that tone of voice, take Jude back to Mexico or what? There had to be thousands of Mastersons in Texas. What was the likelihood Candy was related to the only other one Jude had ever met? But... she had to be spouting the family line just the way Joey had done. The guy had figured everyone should cater to him because of his name.

Tate's eyebrows angled up as he leaned back in his chair. "Are you seriously threatening me, right here in public? Dozens of people are listening to this conversation right now. I nearly hired you on Monday, but I would likely have had to fire you by now if this is the attitude you're going with."

"I would have worked hard."

"We'll never find out, will we?"

Candy's gaze flicked around the room.

Jude averted his eyes and focused on taking a big bite of his ham sandwich. "Mmm, good," he mumbled to Maxwell in the sudden silence.

He wasn't the only one pretending not to listen, as a low murmur of voices rose slightly. He focused on watching Candy in his periphery. If Tate needed someone to escort this woman to her car, Jude would be ready.

What had Tate said the other day? *When I told Kaci who was coming in, she turned white as a sheet and bailed. Then she texted me not to hire Candy...*

Reality slammed into Jude's chest. Kaci knew Candy from before. Was Candy here to blow Kaci's cover, or was her arrival coincidental? How did they know each other? Tate said Candy was 22. Kaci was 24... at least, if she'd been telling the truth about her age. Why wouldn't she, though?

Who the heck knew? Because there was so much she'd

left out, it was impossible to know if she'd also told a lie or two.

Being honest and truthful was vital to a child of God. Jude had made it his mission to remain focused on truth, even when it was uncomfortable. Could he ever believe it was better to lie than to tell the truth? How could that even be?

But there were stories in the Bible like when Rahab lied to protect the Israelite spies from being caught when the leaders of her walled city, Jericho, were seeking to kill them. It even sounded like Rahab had been honored for it.

Why that story flicked through his mind in that quick moment, he had no idea. Was he trying to justify any lies Kaci might have told? Because if she hadn't outright lied, she'd certainly done so by omission.

"Do you have something against Texans? Do you have any currently working here?"

Jude exchanged an incredulous look with Maxwell. The girl was still egging Tate on?

"Nothing against Texans at all, and I don't see that I need to give you any information about our staff demographics. Would you care to have lunch before heading back to Jewel Lake... or to Texas... or wherever you're heading to today?"

There was something about the expression on Tate's face that caught Jude's attention. Kaci and Candy had known each other, but Tate had information, too. Something Jude didn't know, the list of which seemed longer by the minute. And here he'd thought he'd known the real Kaci beneath all the silence and evasion.

He didn't know her. Not at all. Even *Tate* knew more

than he did, and Jude was supposed to be Kaci's best friend. Even, briefly, maybe, her boyfriend.

Jude's hunger fled, and he pushed the sandwich away. How had he been so duped to think she'd come to him first when she was ready to divulge her secrets?

He'd likely be the last to know. The kiss had only been some pent-up emotion, some signal he couldn't hope to understand. He was just a country boy from western Montana with no college degree. Fine, he now had his PPL — private pilot's license — but that didn't mean he had smarts in any other area.

Obviously not people smarts.

"I'm out of here," he mumbled to Maxwell as he shoved his chair back.

"You okay, cuz?"

He shrugged. There was no way to answer that without lying. Ha. He dumped the remains of his lunch in the compost bin — the ranch chickens would eat well — and strode for the door, nearly colliding with Kaci on her way into the dining room.

Jude glared at her for a few long seconds then crossed his arms. "There's someone here to see you."

KACI DIDN'T MISS the way Jude managed to completely avoid touching her even while he nearly ran her over. She didn't miss the ice in his eyes or the hostile body language of his crossed arms. Yes, she'd been a horrible person and sent him mixed signals, but why was he so... angry?

Wait. What had he said? Someone here to see her? No one knew—

Her gaze shot past Jude's shoulder and across the dining hall to where Tate sat facing her, making a shooing motion. What? Why?

Then the blond woman who'd been sitting with her back to the door turned, spied Kaci, and rose with a feral smile.

Candy Masterson.

Kaci backed up two steps and pivoted, but Jude's hand caught her elbow before she could bolt. Running wouldn't help now, anyway. Candy had spotted her. Candy had known she'd be here.

What was taking the FBI so long in sorting evidence and deciding whether to arrest Dad or vindicate him? Because no one was supposed to locate Kaci until the FBI summoned her home.

"Kirsten Atkinson! Fancy meeting you here!"

"Who?" Jude sounded incredulous as his grip loosened.

Kaci yanked out of his grasp, but he caught her hand before she'd made good her escape.

"What's going on, Kaci?"

"Not the time or place, Jude," she hissed, trying to pull free, but it was too late.

Tate and Candy stood right in front of her now. "Let's take this to my office." Tate jerked his head in the direction of the office wing.

Why did it feel like Jude was her jailer? He was supposed to be on her side! He loved her! Or, at least, he was her best friend.

A best friend she'd treated poorly. No wonder he was

invested in answers. If he didn't care, he would have disappeared already, leaving her to her fate.

Oh, Lord, what am I supposed to do now? Kaci's mind raced the whole two minutes it took to walk to the office wing.

Tate closed the door and arranged three chairs in front of his desk before taking his own seat. He leaned forward, hands clasped on the polished work surface, before looking each of them in the eye. "Who wants to go first?"

Not Kaci, that was for sure. Just on the very slim chance Candy had no clue what she'd stumbled into.

No such luck. Candy gave her a long look across Jude before turning to Tate. "How is it that Kirsten Atkinson is not on your employee list, yet she works here?"

"If you're referring to the other woman in the room, her name is Kaci Moore."

Kaci gulped back fear, even while she was thankful Tate had learned the entire truth the other evening.

Candy scoffed. "That's not her real name. Her name is Kirsten Catriona Moorehouse-Atkinson. Get it? Her initials are K.C., and Moore is only part of her surname."

"I know who she is," Tate said evenly. "What I'd like to know is why you are here."

"My brother has been looking for Kirsten."

Joey Masterson. Duncan's best friend.

"We've all just been so worried about her since she vanished two and a half years ago. We wanted to make sure she was *safe*."

Kaci didn't miss the slight inflection on that final word, even while the whole speech sounded so pretentious, so condescending.

"Who are you reporting to?" Tate asked.

"Reporting?" Candy tossed her hair back. "Don't be so dramatic. This isn't an episode of *Tracker*."

"Isn't it?"

Candy rolled her eyes.

Jude rose to his feet from the middle seat. "Tate, do you need Kaci and me here for anything?"

Tate shook his head. "I don't think so."

"You can't just leave." Candy's eyes flashed.

Jude held his hand to Kaci, who grabbed it like a lifeline and let him pull her upright. "But we are."

"I'll let Joe and Duncan know where you are."

The threat was real, but this time, Jude's hand was comforting rather than accusing. What had caused the change? And would he help her get away?

He closed the office door behind them before dropping her hand and leaning against the corridor wall. "Kirsten?"

"I can explain." She was going to have to, now.

"I'm waiting."

"Not here. Not now. Not with her ten feet away."

"Fair enough. We're going for a flight."

"Don't you have one this afternoon?"

"I'll get Cadence to cancel it. You're coming with me."

Threat or promise? Kaci wasn't sure.

CHAPTER TWENTY-TWO

The rotors were too loud to have a decent conversation while they were aloft, but Jude was a patient man. Mostly. There was a reason he'd chosen to whisk Kaci away via helicopter rather than via horseback or truck. This was his element... and a place she couldn't escape from as easily.

He shot her a sideways look. She sat like a statue, stiffly staring straight out the windshield. Was she even seeing the mountains, the cloudy sky, the thunderheads gathering in the distance?

How desperate would a woman need to be to leap from a whirlybird? Very desperate, like death would be preferred over any other outcome.

That wasn't the Kaci he knew, but what about — what name had Candy given? — Kirsten something-with-a-C Atkinson.

Masterson and Atkinson. If that surname combo didn't take him back to the village in Mexico, nothing would. His random impression looked about to be proved correct. He'd once known Kaci's brother... and hadn't much liked the spoiled brat.

Jude banked over the mountain lake before settling the helicopter on the butte. He powered the engines and rotors down and waited until all systems were at rest. Then he removed his headset and turned to Kaci. "Want to talk here or down by the lake?"

"Lake." She didn't look at him.

"Okay." He pulled a backpack from beneath the seat.

Kaci cast a glance in its direction. "What's that?"

"Emergency rations. You didn't get any lunch, and I've got fire starter as well."

"I'm not hungry."

Jude shrugged and opened the door. "When you are, I have food." He jumped out and reached for her hand. No surprise, she ignored it.

Kaci scrambled down the butte as though the helicopter were about to explode.

He followed her, but when she disappeared in the direction of one of the latrines, he gathered some of the split logs stacked in a sheltered area and began to light a campfire. Not that it was particularly chilly, but the clouds had closed in, and the breeze strengthened. He had a popup shelter in case rains descended, but hopefully it wouldn't come to that. Or they could retreat into the chopper... but not lift off as long as the storm lingered.

The threat of a thunderstorm would have been enough to cancel this afternoon's sightseeing flights, so he didn't need to feel badly about bailing out on the tourists. By the same token, flying in or near a storm was completely unadvised. He'd certainly never been this close to it in his limited experience.

The tinder flared then caught the kindling. Soon, he had a nice little blaze going, but where was Kaci? He glanced around the clearing to spot her sitting on the rocks overlooking the lake.

Wasn't that just like a woman? A guy creates a safe environment, and she goes off somewhere else. Well, the fire would be waiting.

Jude clambered over the boulders and lowered himself beside her. He'd channel their best-friends relationship and resist the urge to touch her. "Looks like we're in for a storm."

"We might be stranded here until it blows over."

He couldn't resist bumping her shoulder. "Worse things could happen."

Kaci let out a long shuddering breath. "They could."

Silence, while the waves on the lake built. A few rolled over into whitecaps.

"I guess I owe you an explanation."

You think? But Jude kept his natural response locked up tight. "Whatever you're ready to share."

"So… the Mastersons were friends of my family for as long as I can remember. Mr. Masterson is a lawyer like my own father."

Jude chomped down on his lip in an effort to keep quiet.

"Their son, Joe, is a friend of my older brother. Lily was my age, and Candy is about the age of my younger brother."

Was this the time to mention that he'd met those older

brothers years ago? But Kaci was still speaking.

"My birth name is Kirsten Catriona Moorehouse-Atkinson, just like Candy said. However, Kaci Moore is now my legal name. My lawyer handled my change of identity—" She threw her head back and stared up at the sky. "This is hard."

"What did your lawyer say? Is he trustworthy?"

"It's not what my lawyer said. And I sincerely hope *she* is trustworthy, because so much rests in her hands."

Female lawyer. Okay. He shouldn't have assumed.

"Jude, your aunt is my lawyer."

"My... aunt?" Jude pivoted to stare at Kaci. *"Aunt Bridget?"* Pieces fell into place. "Did you consult with her in Chicago on that trip?"

"I did. She came over to the hotel and met with my grandfather and me."

"Wait! What? Who is your grandfather?" Man, Jude might have wanted answers, but now that they flowed, his head spun.

"Frederick Moorehouse of Dallas, Texas. He knew your grandfather many years ago, and they stayed loosely in touch. When it became necessary for me... to leave Texas... they worked things out between them."

"That's why my grandfather offered you a job and entered your files without consulting with Tate or anyone else."

Kaci nodded, still staring into the distance.

"Wow. That's a lot." Jude braced his arms behind him on the rock.

"There's more."

Of course, there was more. She'd had an entire childhood he knew nothing about, including her teen and adult years before her arrival at Sweet River Ranch.

Lightning zigzagged to hit a tree across the water, the crack of thunder simultaneous.

Jude surged off the rock and reached for Kaci. This time her hand found his as they dashed for the meager shelter of the trees. Rain pummeled them. The campfire they hadn't even enjoyed would fizzle out in no time.

Lightning struck again, closer this time, the thunderclap deafening as it ricocheted around them.

Jude hadn't feared weather in years, but being here in the eye of this sudden, fierce storm with no shelter nearby caused his heart to pick up speed. They could make a dash for the cockpit, but they'd be exposed on the climb. And wasn't the helicopter perched atop the highest point on this side of the lake?

What if lightning struck it while they were inside it?

What if lightning struck it anyway?

Jude pulled Kaci against his chest. She buried her face into his hoodie and clung to him. He pressed his cheek against her damp hair. There wasn't anything he could do about the lightning. That was all in God's hands. Just as everything always was.

God knew Kaci Moore. He knew Kirsten Atkinson. None of this was a surprise to Him. He had everything under control.

Jude's heart and mind gripped his faith even while his arms gripped Kaci.

THE STORM CRASHED all around them, but Kaci had never felt safer than she did right then and there in Jude Kline's arms. Yes, the wind and rain had found them within the negligible shelter of the forest. She was soaked to the skin, as was Jude, but they were drenched together.

Together was the keyword. She'd longed for this — not the exposure, not the storm — for over two years, and now they were having their moment. Would Jude stick around when he knew the rest of the truth? She'd lied so many times. All in good cause, but still her heart ached with all the things she'd led him to believe that weren't true.

It seemed forever and yet all too soon before the storm made its grumbling, angry path away from their spot. The rain eased in intensity but still fell.

No way was Kaci going to be first to let go. She clung to Jude with all the strength in her arms.

He shifted slightly, his hands roaming her back and catching in her low ponytail. Then he kissed the top of her head.

Kaci could get behind kissing. She tilted her head and looked up at the questioning expression in his eyes. He must have recognized her answer, because his lips gently pressed against hers.

This was coming home. The Moorehouses and the Atkinsons were not home. Jude was everything that provided shelter for her heart.

But realities still lay just outside this perfect bubble. Perfect if they weren't shivering from being soaked to the skin in the sudden cold.

All too soon, Jude murmured against her lips. "We can't fly until the storm is entirely gone."

Color her giddy at the thought of being stranded here a little longer. She kissed him again. Too bad this rain didn't dissolve the threat or wash away the memory of Candy's shrill voice in the dining hall where everyone could overhear.

Kaci shivered.

"Too cold? Do you want me to rebuild that fire, or should we go back to the chopper?"

"Will we get back to the ranch tonight?" Because the sky wasn't as bright as it had been. How much of that was cloud cover? It couldn't be dusk yet, could it?

Thunder grumbled in the distance. "We should be able to leave soon." Jude squeezed her tightly. "Not that I want to."

"Thanks for whisking me away, but it didn't settle anything. I can only imagine what Candy's been saying about me in the meanwhile."

"I'll check with my grandfather when we get back. Or, you say Tate knows everything?"

Kaci winced at the slight edge to Jude's voice. "Only for a few days since he mentioned the names of the people coming for interviews, and I freaked out. I still don't know whether it's coincidence or if she knew I was here."

"Hopefully, he and Grandfather have figured that out by now. Will they have contacted Aunt Bridget?"

Maybe the quick getaway had bought enough time. "I'm sure they have. She's the one who created my new identity."

Jude pulled back enough to see her face. His gentle fingers brushed her damp hair aside from her forehead. "I still don't know why all this was necessary. Are you in a witness protection program?"

"Not exactly?" Kaci searched Jude's face. "It's similar, though. I found some... irregularities in my father's legal firm that led me to wonder if he was on the side of justice. Or not." It still killed her to think of him as a possible criminal. Likely criminal. "I did a little poking around then took my findings to my grandfather, who took me seriously. After that, it didn't take long for him to believe I wasn't safe. He made the arrangements with your grandfather and your aunt."

"Your dad is an attorney?"

She nodded. "My older brother, Duncan, is a partner in his firm. And my younger brother is in law school." Wait. She studied Jude's face, which had frozen into an expression too blank to be real. "What?"

Jude shook his head.

"Seriously. What is it?" She had to know.

"Did your brother go on a missions trip to Mexico about 12 years ago?"

They'd been so many places that it was hard to recall. "Why?"

"I did." Jude let out a long breath, met her eyes, and looked away again. "My church in Seeley Lake partnered with one in Dallas to send a team to build a house for a missionary couple."

"That sounds familiar. Duncan and Joey went on a trip like that once. I was jealous, but I was also too young to go."

"I remember them." Jude's face was stony.

"Not good memories, I take it."

"Not so much, no. They were rude — entitled — treated the rest of the team like their personal servants."

"Sounds like teenage Dunc." Also, the Duncan of today. "I'm sorry."

"Is he still like that?"

"He and I have never been close. He always trotted at the heels of our father. He seemed to operate by the slogan of not caring who he stepped on on his way to the top, because he wasn't coming back down. No one could touch him."

"Is he guilty of breaking the law? Is your dad?"

"I don't know. It seems like it. There were just too many irregularities to ignore. The FBI is on the case now."

"So, Candy discovering your whereabouts and your *new name*—" she didn't miss the edge in his voice at that "— could jeopardize everything the FBI is doing."

Kaci shuddered. "It really could. I wish they'd hurry up. I never dreamed I'd still be hiding two and a half years later. I just want to be me again."

"Kirsten?"

"The name doesn't matter. I kind of like being Kaci. But I wish they could merge into one person with both a past and a present."

"And a future…"

Jude's voice was so quiet she wasn't sure she'd heard those three words, but her heart hiccupped as though she had.

"Okay, I have a plan, but first we need to get back to Sweet River. Do you trust me?"

Kaci looked Jude in the eye. "I trust you."

"Any other big secrets I should take into account?"

"No. I think we've covered the basics."

"All right. Time for an adventure."

Hadn't they already been having one?

CHAPTER TWENTY-THREE

Jude gently set the helicopter down in a clearing beside the old farmhouse where his mom lived with her new husband. The two of them ran out of the house as Jude went through the shutdown sequence.

"Here?" Kaci glanced over, clearly confused.

"The helipad is too obvious." After all, his truck sat beside it. Wouldn't that be where he'd be expected to return? He had to assume Candy was a real threat and act accordingly. "Besides, I have an idea." He jumped out of the aircraft. This time when he reached for Kaci's hand, she took it.

Win.

Mom rushed forward and crushed him with a hug. "I'm so glad to see you."

Jude hugged her back one-armed. He wasn't letting go of Kaci anytime soon. "We're okay. Cleared some air."

"Good." Mom hugged Kaci then leaned back and looked

her in the eye. "My father gathered a few of us and told us the basics. And we came up with a plan."

Wasn't that Jude's department? "I have a plan of my own, if Grandfather allows. We'll pop over to Missoula, take the company jet, and..."

But his mother talked over him. "We think you should take Keith's truck and head for Kansas."

Kansas? Jude's surprise must have shown. "But that's a long drive. Like 20 hours! We could be there — or anywhere else — much more quickly if we flew."

"And then you need to land at airports to fuel up. You're too easy to track."

Huh. He hadn't thought of that. With Kaci's safety in his hands, he needed to do better. "Kansas? Why there?"

"Two reasons. Keith knows people in Gilead, and your aunt Maribel Sullivan lives there. I'm sure she'd put you up for a week or two until this blows over."

Jude shook his head to clear it. "Why Keith's truck?"

"Because it's not linked to you in any way. Your grandfather brought over enough cash for your travels. If you use cards, they might be able to trace you, and we need you both safe."

Now he was also a fugitive? It made sense... and it wasn't like he was about to abandon Kaci to fight this alone. "I was thinking of flying to Texas and taking the bull by the horns."

Kaci's grip tightened around his hand enough to cut off circulation.

Mom shook her head. "Too soon. Your grandfather has been in touch with Bridget and they've called the FBI to update them. You both need to lie low for a bit, but this breach may have been enough to break things open."

"Did Candy know I was here, or was her arrival a coincidence?"

"She left the ranch right after you did, and there's no record of her staying in a hotel nearby, so we don't know. And that's also disconcerting. Where did she come from? Why?"

These were questions that could haunt Jude for a while. He eyed his stepfather. "Kansas."

Keith nodded. "Gilead, to be more precise. It's a long way from here, as you mentioned, and not a likely place for anyone to look."

"Except for Aunt Maribel."

"Who would think you were close to her?"

Maybe Mom and Keith weren't taking this seriously enough. "Is this Grandfather's advice? Aunt Bridget's?"

Keith slipped his arm around Mom's shoulder. "Yes. We all discussed it while you were away and believe this is the best recourse." He gestured to his pickup truck, a newish model he'd picked up after moving to Montana last fall. "I fueled it up for you. It's ready to roll."

"I took the liberty of packing up a few clothes for you, Jude. And Paisley packed some of yours, Kaci. Or should we call you Kirsten now?"

"Kaci, please. But what if I don't want to leave?"

"You're leaving *with Jude.*" Mom smirked as she eyed their joined hands. "And your legal counsel advises it."

"But the housekeeping..."

Plus, all the booked tourism flights. Jude winced.

"I tucked a picnic basket in the truck. Your grandfather tossed in a couple of burner phones, as well." Mom slipped out from beneath Keith's arm and squeezed Jude so tightly he thought his back might break. "Go with God. Be safe."

"Do we have a choice?" Jude held Kaci's gaze for a few seconds. Was she on board with this? Because he'd do whatever she wanted, whether it was the official recommendation or not.

"There's always a choice," Keith said quietly. "But maybe you should consider any alternatives while you drive. The keys are in the ignition."

Jude hated feeling torn in so many directions, but one thing he knew for sure. This man, this stepfather of his whom he barely knew, was giving up something big for him. Yeah, okay. In the grand Sullivan scheme of things, a truck wasn't a big deal, but Keith had scraped and saved and done without in an effort to save his Kansas farm. It hadn't been enough. He'd been forced to sell and give up everything he'd ever known after losing his wife and one of his daughters.

If Keith could venture into the unknown on the say-so of Jude's cousin Maxwell, whom he'd only just met, couldn't Jude take a leap of faith on the advice of Kaci's legal counsel?

He gave a firm nod. "Kansas it is. Ready to go, Kaci?"

"After I use the restroom."

Not a bad idea, all things considered. And then? They'd be bound southeast.

"I've never driven a pickup truck before." Kaci flexed her hands on the steering wheel and eyed the dashboard a few hours later.

They'd fueled up in Billings just as dusk fell, and Jude had pulled several twenties out of the stash under the seat — a plenteous trove.

Jude adjusted the passenger seat for his longer frame. "We can nap for an hour or two at the next rest area instead. Then I can keep driving."

"Noooo. I'm good." She moved the seat forward then up a smidge. "This will be fun."

"If you say so." He grinned.

Kaci maneuvered the truck back onto I-90. "So, I was thinking…"

"Sounds dangerous."

She loved that he'd adjusted so quickly and not forgotten their previous camaraderie. The awkwardness from the past few months had dissipated.

Kissing helped.

Kaci cleared her throat. "Can I start with being thankful your grandfather happened to have a couple of *decent* cell phones on hand? When your mother mentioned burners, I was afraid they'd be super basic."

"Me, too. Also thankful they thought to include a list of family phone numbers, since who memorizes those anymore? Just tap the person's name, and bam."

"Right? So far, I can't think of anything they forgot."

"Which makes me nervous that you've been thinking."

"I was looking at a map." She glanced at him.

"Uh huh?"

"If we were driving to Dallas, Gilead wouldn't be far out of the way."

Jude stiffened. "We're not driving to Dallas."

"But we could. You mentioned flying there, but now we have a truck."

"Kaci. Mom and Keith explained the reasons. The FBI is trying to keep you safely out of the way. Which is not in the center of action."

"I only meant when the time comes."

"Maybe I shouldn't have shown you how to drive this truck."

She chuckled. "I'm not going to steal your stepdad's vehicle... or anyone else's. It was an observation only."

Jude leaned his right shoulder against the window and fixed his attention on her. "Once I thought I knew what you were thinking."

"Two years ago, when you assumed my thoughts were superficial, and you didn't know I was hiding my identity."

"I guess. Tell me more about Kirsten Atkinson: the missing years."

"You make my life sound like a documentary." She glanced over to see his eyebrows tip up.

"To me, it is. I want to know everything about you."

Kaci stared out the windshield for a long moment as the interstate streamed by. "Grandad Moorehouse told me in May that he has listed me as his only beneficiary."

"That's why he wanted to see you?"

She bit her lip and nodded. "And he missed me. I was hoping he'd be able to tell me the FBI had made conclusions, but nope."

"Is your inheritance... significant?" He sounded cautious.

"You could say that."

"On par with the Sullivans?"

Kaci needed to remember Jude had grown up with very little. Her hands tightened on the wheel. "I'm not sure exactly how much your family is worth, but probably similar, yes." She wouldn't mention it was likely because the Sullivan wealth would be spread between multiple heirs. For the Mooreshouses? It was just her.

"Oof." He closed his eyes and leaned back into the seat.

What was that supposed to mean? It wasn't like she had earned it herself or stolen it... like maybe Dad had done. But the Moorehouse estate was separate from the Atkinsons.

Finally, Jude shook his head. "Two years in, and I'm still not used to money."

Two years in, and Kaci still wasn't used to *not* having any. Their spheres had alternated realities.

"This truck..." Jude ran his hand over the supple leather seat. "It's almost all Keith has left of the sale of his family farm. Did you know we lost our ranch, too, after my father died?"

Kaci bit her lip. "I've heard that."

"I spent the winter in Chicago and had a front row seat to how arrogant wealth can make people."

"Your uncles and aunt?"

"Yeah. Like your brother and his friend, when they were teens."

Was the air in here chilling, or was it her imagination? "Duncan was conceited then and still is."

"Sometimes I think about getting on Pepper and riding away from it all."

His voice was so low it took a few seconds for the words to register. "You'd walk away from everything your grandfather has given you?"

"It's tempting."

"But... why? How? You can't be serious."

"I said, *sometimes* I think. I didn't say I was doing it."

Her inheritance would be plenty enough for her and Jude and any kids they might have, but his words hadn't included her. He'd lumped her in with the others.

Did she deserve to be there?

Maybe? She'd certainly never expected to be permanently cut off from her family funds. When the dust settled, she'd assumed she'd be an equal heir in whatever was left. Grandad had made sure she'd be taken care of, either way.

It wasn't that she thought she was better than anyone else. After all, didn't she clean cottage bathrooms for a living? Hadn't she trained to be a nurse like many ordinary young women?

She didn't think she was a cut above!

"Money goes to people's heads."

"Not everyone's."

"Name me someone. Even my grandfather plays God in his little world. My mother has changed... I think Nana has the right of it. Steer clear."

"Jude..."

"Aunt Maribel lives in this ginormous house in an ordinary small town. Yes, it was her home when she was married to Uncle James and they were raising four kids, but Gilead is no place for a mansion like that. No one needs a house that size. It's... pretentious. She hardly has any friends because she's too busy being a Sullivan. Even divorce didn't change that."

What could Kaci say? She'd met the woman several times but never had a personal conversation with her. As a chambermaid, she was beneath notice... and that's what Jude was saying.

"I can't help who I am, Jude."

"I can't help who I am, either." He stared ahead out the windshield. "I was a nobody with no prospects. I didn't ask for money. Sure, as a kid, I dreamed of being rich. Who doesn't?"

Kaci lifted her hand off the steering wheel. "Me?"

"Because you already had it all. You know what I thought about you these past two years?"

Maybe? She glanced over.

"I thought you were a housekeeper. That I could maybe provide for you and we could be happy together. We wouldn't need much."

I'm sorry?

The apology nearly came out, but how could she be sorry? It hadn't been her choice to be born an Atkinson or that her mother had insisted on the hyphenated surname for herself and her daughter. She hadn't chosen to be born to wealth.

All she'd chosen was not to turn a blind eye to what seemed like very suspicious activity. She'd chosen to forego her identity so justice could be served. It had been for her safety... but also for integrity.

Should she have stayed put, defiantly trying to expose

Dad on the spot? Was she a coward to have hidden? Grandad didn't think so, nor did Bridget or Walter Sullivan.

Either way, it was the choice she'd made two and a half years back. She couldn't undo it.

Who was she, really? Kirsten Catriona Moorehouse-Atkinson? Kaci Moore? Or someone else?

Kaci chewed on her lip in the lingering silence as the miles flew by.

Jude might be satisfied to sulk in his own thoughts, but Kaci wasn't. She reached over and turned the radio on. They'd been listening to K-Love as they approached Billings earlier, so the same station filtered into the cab.

Chris Tomlin sang "You're a Good, Good Father," the words piercing Kaci in a deeper way than ever before. She was a Christian. Of course, she knew God was good. That was His identity, perfect in all of His ways. But the song also spoke to who *she* was, and that was the piece she'd been struggling with for so long.

The only part of her identity that mattered at all was her relationship to her good Father. She was loved by Him.

She soaked in that thought until the last line drifted away.

God loved her so much more than her inattentive parents did. Than Grandad did. More than Jude, who'd told her he loved her while telling her he couldn't handle their relationship. Would he say those words again, for real this time? As grumpy as he was right now, he might never.

Kaci's heart pinched. Her identity wasn't found in the love of any human, not even someone as amazing as Jude was… usually. She needed to cut him some slack. This day had exploded his ordered world, and suddenly he was on the run with her.

Only what God thought of her mattered, and what was that? She'd once memorized the beginning of First John 3: *See what great love the Father has lavished on us, that we should be called children of God! And that is what we are!*

For right now, that was going to have to be sufficient. Truth? It already was.

CHAPTER TWENTY-FOUR

J ude paced Aunt Maribel's house, her Chihuahua clickety-clacking behind him on the polished wood floors until the dog's presence nearly drove him batty.

His aunt had embraced her role of protector with gusto. She and Kaci were holed up in the kitchen with Dominica planning meals for the next few days. And that was another thing. What one-person household needed to have a full-time cook?

Two days of being cooped up. He needed to feel the wind on his face in the worst way. Maybe because Aunt Maribel had gently but firmly assured him he was safer inside. Who knew him in Gilead? Absolutely no one. His cousins may have grown up here, but he didn't particularly resemble them, and he certainly hadn't ever visited as a child. As an adult, he'd been Maribel's chauffeur rather than a nephew.

Which was only because he'd asked Grandfather for the chance to get his PPL. Guilt over that still bothered him.

He'd made a big deal to Kaci about how privileged people lived, but at the first opportunity, he'd taken advantage of the perks for himself.

He was two-faced.

Also bored beyond belief. He'd kind of liked their plan of taking the fight head-on to Kaci's family. And yeah, he could see why it didn't make sense. Safety, blah, blah, blah.

When had a Kline ever backed down from potential pain?

Jude pivoted at the garage door and began the long march back to the West Wing, where his rooms were. Tate thought the nickname was hilarious. Tate had been born to money and power. To Jude, the moniker screamed of elitism.

Click, clack went Princess's claws. The dog probably hadn't had this much exercise in years.

Jude snapped. Hadn't Maxwell mentioned a nearby ranch? Maybe he could wrangle a horseback ride. He'd be happy to muck out a stable. Anything to get out of this house.

He strode over to the kitchen door where the three women were discussing the merits of sous vide egg bites. Whatever those were.

Kaci glanced at him, but her smile looked cautious.

As it should. He'd been grumpy lately, and he knew it. This whole situation was ridiculous. Yes, serious, but also not something the average cowboy from rural Montana would ever be involved in. Only people with money had problems like extortion and hit men and hidden heiresses.

He'd fallen for housekeeper Kaci, not pampered, rich Kirsten. And right now, all he could see was Kirsten in an environment that likely wasn't dissimilar to the home she'd left.

Remember the winter the power company turned off electricity at the Circle K because your dad drank all the money away?

That was where he'd come from, not anything like this.

"Jude? Are you all right?" Aunt Maribel floated toward him, deep concern on her face.

He'd gotten lost in his own head. Again. "I…" His gaze darted to Kaci then back to his aunt. "I'm headed out for a while."

"Now, honey, we talked about that."

"With all due respect, I'm going out. There's that ranch near town, Walker Ridge? Gonna see if I can find a horse to ride for a bit. I need to see something bigger than four walls." Even if these four walls were vastly larger than his staff housing at the ranch.

Maribel's smile seemed forced, but didn't it always? "We would prefer—"

"I'm going. Kaci, want to come?"

Her eyes widened as she looked between him and his aunt. "I'd love to, but—"

"Never mind. You don't need to explain. I'll be back in a few hours. You know how to reach me."

The low Kansas hills couldn't possibly block cell signals like the Montana mountains did. No place could be out of range.

Aunt Maribel's protest bounced off Jude's back as he headed to his room. Mom had been smart enough to toss in his Tony Lama boots, and he practically lived in his jeans and cowboy hat. It didn't take long to grab his boots and head out the door.

The truck's GPS directed him to Walker Ridge, and he soon pulled into the ranch yard.

An older man came toward him with an outstretched hand. "Jeb Walker. What can I do for you?"

Jude hesitated. Should he be hiding his name? He scoffed under his breath. This was ridiculous. "I'm Jude, from Montana, looking for a horse to ride. Have any rentals?"

"Montana?" The man looked at him closely. "Only folks around here who've got Montana ties are the Sullivans. Know them?"

"We've met." Jude tugged down his cowboy hat as he scanned the area. "Do you rent by the hour, or what?"

"Know your way around horseflesh then?"

"Yes, sir." Practically born on the back of a horse. He could outride nearly anyone he knew besides Weston... well, Weston and actual rodeo cowboys like Adam Cavanagh.

"Trigger's the big black over there. He needs a good stretch."

The tall horse's head came up, and he tossed his mane.

"Looks good."

"There's trails laid out back of the corral. Not that you can get lost iffen you keep in mind that the river runs through town." He pointed and tugged his Wranglers up before turning back to Jude with a smirk. "Besides, Trigger knows the way home."

"I bet he does." Pepper sure did.

"Just need you to fill in some paperwork before we get you on your way."

Jude stilled. So much for flying under the radar if he put his local contact down in case of emergency. Naw. He'd put his brother's name and number. Weston knew how to contact Aunt Maribel if the need should arise. Not that any two-bit Kansas horse could toss a Montana cowboy like him.

Darn if he didn't have his own share of prideful ways.

"WHAT'S WITH JUDE?" Maribel asked as the door closed behind him. Keith's truck revved in the driveway.

"Not a clue." Kaci had wracked her brain over the switch in his attitude way back before they'd left Big Sky Country in the rearview mirror. He'd been grumpy ever since he'd realized her family had money.

"Those boys." Maribel shook her head. "I always thought Jude had a more level head on his shoulders than Weston but, at the moment, I'm not so sure. Poor things."

Kaci frowned. "Poor things?"

"You know, raised in poverty and such. All this can be a bit much for someone unaccustomed."

"It's not their fault."

"I didn't say it was. Well, now that Mr. Thundercloud is out of the house, what shall you and I do? There's not much for shopping around here."

"I thought we were supposed to lie low." That's why she was frustrated with Jude. It was like he didn't even care who saw him. What if someone had traced them? Followed them? Guessed they'd go to Jude's relatives?

Maribel fluttered jewel-encrusted fingers. "I'm sure it will be fine. Gilead is a sleepy little town."

"I was told to stay put." The personality trait that had caused all this trouble to start with raised its head. She was a rule follower and expected the same of others. Starting with Dad. Then, Jude, and now, Maribel, who'd only put up a token protest at Jude's choice to leave the house.

Her hostess sighed. "There isn't much I can offer for entertainment within this house."

"I don't need entertaining." Hopefully Kaci's smile would remove any sting from the words. "It was a long trip, and neither of us got much sleep since we alternated driving. Maybe I'll catch a nap."

"As you wish. I should probably log into the Sullivan servers and see what tasks Walter has for me today."

"I forgot you worked remotely for the company."

"Well, I couldn't let James have all the fun! Not when I have useful skills of my own. Thankfully, Walter saw it my way even when James couldn't."

Kaci didn't want the details of Maribel and James's decades-old divorce. She'd heard enough from their sons Tate, Bryce, and Maxwell. "I'll leave you to it, then." She feigned a yawn that suddenly felt real.

Not that sleep would be possible. Not when she felt the distance between her and Jude so acutely. Not only the fact that he was miles away riding someone else's horse, but the emotional distance since he'd blurted out how he felt about generational wealth.

What would he say if she offered to turn down

Grandad's legacy for him? It was a ridiculous thought, because Jude would have to do the same and reject the Sullivan roots his mother had worked so hard to discover. When Nadine started on her journey through DNA sites, she had no idea she would discover a wealthy family. She could as easily have found a deadbeat like Paisley's father.

Why couldn't Jude accept his newfound lot in life? It wasn't like he hadn't benefited from it. His grandfather had paid for private pilot lessons and then bought a helicopter, all because Jude had dreamed of flying.

A tap sounded on Kaci's door.

"Kirsten? Walter wishes to speak with you. He's on vid."

Dread clenched her belly. "Coming." But maybe it was good news. Right? It could be.

She followed Maribel into the expansive home office and took the seat at the desk her hostess indicated.

Mr. Sullivan's face filled the screen. "Kaci! You are well?"

"I'm fine. Thank you."

"Where's Jude?"

"He... went horseback riding."

The old man scowled. "What part of staying out of sight did he miss?"

"I'm not sure, sir. Do you have any news?"

"I do. I was talking to Frederick, and he indicated it might soon be time for you to come home. Things are about to go down."

Kaci's heart skipped a beat. "What does that even mean?"

"The FBI are in position in Dallas."

She closed her eyes. Good thing she was sitting down,

because she suddenly felt lightheaded. "They're going to arrest my father." She should feel more glad about that. About justice being served.

Mr. Sullivan cleared his throat. "Frederick seemed a bit vague on exactly what he expects to transpire. He was surprised to learn you're in Kansas, not Montana."

They'd agreed to keep her and Jude's whereabouts on a need-to-know basis, so that wasn't surprising, but Kaci felt better that her grandfather was up to date. "What do I do now?"

"Besides get Jude back in line?"

"With all due respect, sir, he's his own person. I'm not his keeper."

The old man studied her. "I thought you two were on a kissing basis."

"We were." Hadn't been since early in the journey. "I can have all the good intentions in the world, but that still doesn't make me his keeper."

"Maybe that's Eleanor's problem."

Surely, she hadn't heard correctly. "Pardon me, sir?"

"She feels the need to keep her independence." He scrubbed his white hair. "But causing her to rely on me is not my motive. I only want to love her. Yes, I want to meet her needs, but only to ease her life, not to control her."

"To be honest, sir, only God can meet needs."

His bushy eyebrows peaked. "True. When did you get so wise?"

Kaci huffed a laugh. "About five minutes ago, I think. So, what do you think I should do next? Sit tight and wait?" Man, she was tired of patience.

"Be ready to drive to Texas as soon as you get the go-ahead. You're what, about six hours out of Dallas?"

"Roughly." Oh, how homesick she was for the flatlands of eastern Texas. The hilly terrain of western Montana was gorgeous, no doubt about it, but it was so different from home.

Home.

Was it still home if Dad was convicted of criminal behavior? Her heart cringed.

"I'll confirm with Frederick. If not tomorrow, most likely the next day."

"I'll await your word."

"Thank you. Now, where did Maribel go?"

"She's right here, sir. I'll talk to you later."

"Yes, yes."

Kaci knew a dismissal when she heard one. She escaped back to the guest room she'd been assigned. What she'd told her boss was true. No one could meet all of another person's needs, and yet partnership in marriage was a thing. She'd seen evidence from her friends lately. From Jude's cousins and even his brother.

Both partners needed to rely on God first. Then each other.

Where did money come into it? Third... or maybe further down the list than that.

She was nearing a crossroads. Presumably, she could make her home in Texas. She could rebuild her friendships — at least, if her peers weren't too freaked out about her father's indictment. She could apply for work as a nurse, which had been her dream since childhood. Which meant that Tate would need to hire not only a chambermaid or two, but a head housekeeper. It was early in a summer season that promised to be very busy. She wasn't conceited enough to think she was irreplaceable, but her resignation would cause a temporary bind for the ranch.

In that scenario, she'd leave Kaci Moore behind and embrace life as Kirsten Moorehouse-Atkinson.

She'd also leave Jude and Sweet River Ranch behind.

It all sounded good — welcoming, plausible, even — until she got to that part. But whether Jude wanted it or not, he now owned a big piece of her heart. Maybe all of it.

She'd throw everything else away without a second thought if he twitched his pinky finger in her direction.

But he had to decide if he could love the real her.

Whoever that was.

CHAPTER TWENTY-FIVE

Jeb Walker had been correct. Trigger wanted — needed — a good canter. The tall gelding had a long, even stride, and riding him was like flying along the ground.

Jude could be tempted to make Jeb an offer on the big boy, but Pepper had a few good years left in her, and a huge chunk of Jude's time was already taken up with actual flying. He didn't have time for two horses.

And he was obviously trying to distract himself from the real question of the day, which was Kaci, who had led him to believe a lie for two and a half years. Who was a pampered, rich—

He was wealthy, too. While it was great not to have to scrabble to pay his bills — and flying was a definite perk — he didn't feel any different than the Jude Kline of several years ago.

Maybe money was just an exterior thing, like a comfortable jacket.

It wasn't, though. It seemed to live on the inside of his uncles and aunts, if not his cousins.

Money changed people. Remember Rayna? Weston's girlfriend had bailed on him when Mom had to sell the Circle K to get out of debt. Rayna resurfaced last year when she heard that Weston had rich relatives.

Money hadn't changed Rayna. The loss and hope of it had only demonstrated who she already was inside.

And Kaci... she'd had good reasons for not telling the whole truth. She hadn't really lied about anything. At least nothing Jude had figured out yet. She'd been evasive, but she hadn't lied. She was still the same woman he'd called his best friend for a couple of years.

The problem was in Jude's own head. He wanted to be the special one. The one she trusted with the truth when no one else made the cut. It was small consolation that the rest of their friend group had remained in the dark along with him. Tate had only found out a couple of days before Jude, when Kaci's cover looked to be blown.

Grandfather had known all along. So had Aunt Bridget. Probably Uncle Theodore, though Jude wouldn't be surprised to learn they kept secrets from each other, and Kaci's situation likely merited professional confidentiality.

Jude reined in at the top of a knoll and looked around. A guy could see for miles in every direction. Gilead lay nestled along the river with the Bible college anchoring the town's east end. Everything seemed green, but then it was early June, and moisture was still prevalent. Jude had flown here often enough to know that later in the summer, the only greenbelt would be right along the river.

While it wasn't his beloved Montana, there was a certain beauty to the landscape here.

"I lift up my eyes to the mountains — where does my help come from? My help comes from the Lord, the Maker of heaven and earth."

Trigger's ears twitched at the spoken words, and Jude patted the gelding's shoulder. "Sorry, boy. I guess I've been caught up in my own thoughts."

But how did he get out? If this were a roundabout, he'd been stuck circling the central island for a couple of days now. A lane or two over were multiple opportunities to veer off, but choosing his exit lane then crossing over to it seemed fraught with danger.

What if he chose the wrong one or got schmucked crossing over to it? What did God want him to do?

Besides stop wallowing in indecision. Stop pouting. That was a given.

He'd told Kaci he felt like striking out on his own and riding Pepper away from Sweet River.

Was that truly a temptation? When his life had been hard before, it hadn't been by choice. If he picked it now, he'd be leaving Mom and Weston behind. He'd not only be leaving financial security behind, but both his old and new families. Which was one family now.

A tractor made its way down a row in a vast market garden below, leaving a weed-free brown loam behind it.

God wanted to weed Jude's life, too.

Everywhere he looked, another metaphor seemed to leap at him. Distract him. If he eliminated running away, what were his choices?

Walk away from Kaci... or embrace Kirsten.

Of course, she might be the one to do the walking once she was free to return to Dallas. Jude could never fit into her Texas life. But what if she asked him to? Wanted him to?

The thought of rubbing shoulders with the Duncan Atkinsons of this world, pretending to be their peers, didn't sit well. Was it possible that Duncan had grown up since that trip to Mexico?

Jude had. He'd been 16 then. That whole trip had opened his eyes. Yes, he'd seen the entitlement of rich kids like Duncan and Joey, but he'd also seen true poverty that made his family's struggles on the Circle K pale by comparison.

He couldn't ask Kaci to give up everything and stay in Montana with him.

But what if it were her choice?

Trigger shifted under Jude's weight.

"Right-o, boy. Let's carry on." Jude clicked his tongue and nudged the gelding's flanks. The horse tossed his mane as he ambled out, and Jude grinned. That's how he felt, too. Impatient. Wanting to get in motion.

A glance at the wide blue sky revealed the contrails of several jets. The Jude of yesteryear would have longed to know where they were going and wished he were onboard. The Jude of today could do it, whenever, wherever, however he wanted.

He had the means to get away, but where?

"Where shall I go from your Spirit? Or where shall I flee from your presence? If I ascend to heaven, you are there! If I make my bed in Sheol, you are there! If I take the wings of the morning and dwell in the uttermost parts of the sea, even there your hand shall lead me, and your right hand shall hold me."

Psalm 139 again, just a few verses past what he'd quoted to Kaci the other day when she shared her struggles with identity.

He couldn't get away from God. Didn't want to. So, it became vital that he followed whatever God wanted him to do. God had brought Kaci into Jude's life. Had smiled upon their friendship. Was He smiling for more?

Why was Jude clinging to his outdated perceptions of what wealth did to people? Each person on the planet was only responsible for properly managing what was at his or her disposal. He could embrace his own situation and see what good he could do with it.

He could choose to love Kaci regardless.

In the grand scheme of things, it didn't matter where Jude went or lived. What mattered was God's hand holding him, God's Spirit present with him.

And Kaci.

THIS MORNING, it had been Jude pacing the Sullivan mansion. Now it was Kaci. Jude had been gone for hours. He'd left disgruntled as he'd been since their conversation in the truck on the evening before last.

He wouldn't have gone so far as to have abandoned her, would he?

Not Jude. He was upright, and he'd vowed to keep her safe.

She fingered her phone. She could call him.

Or she could trust that he'd return when he was ready. She could pray that God would settle his heart and guide him, which was the same prayer she asked for herself.

So many uncertainties!

Maribel was holed up in her office, and she'd taken Princess in with her. Dominica bustled around in the kitchen. When Kaci offered to help, the cook shooed her out.

That left pacing. Or, you know, praying. She could do both at once, but not aloud out here in the corridor.

Her guest room was large enough for a few circles, unlike staff housing at Sweet River. How were Trish and Kylie managing with all the cleaning? Had Tate replaced Kaci already? Maybe he'd hired the older woman who'd come for an interview the other day.

How many days ago was that now? It had been Monday and this was... she'd lost track. Thursday, maybe?

When had she last cracked her Bible open? Just as long, but Paisley hadn't thought to include Kaci's leather-bound NIV when she packed. No surprise, since Paisley used an app — when she remembered to keep her device charged, anyway.

Kaci headed into her room, settled into the easy chair by the window, and opened her burner phone. Only a few basic, pre-installed apps were present, but she could download YouVersion. A few minutes later, she tapped into Psalm 139. Jude had reminded her of these verses just the other day. Before he'd gone dark.

O Lord, you have searched me and known me! You know when I sit down and when I rise up; you discern my thoughts from afar. You search out my path and my lying down and are acquainted with all my ways. Even before a word is on my tongue, behold, O Lord, you know it altogether.

None of this was a surprise to God. He knew whether Dad was innocent or guilty. He knew Kaci's fears and trepidation. She didn't even need to know how to express her thoughts to Him. He knew.

You hem me in, behind and before, and lay your hand upon me. Such knowledge is too wonderful for me; it is high; I cannot attain it.

Where shall I go from your Spirit? Or where shall I flee from your presence? If I ascend to heaven, you are there! If I make my bed in Sheol, you are there! If I take the wings of the morning and dwell in the uttermost parts of the sea, even there your hand shall lead me, and your right hand shall hold me.

Not only did God know who she was, He was with her every step of the way. With Jude. Without Jude. In Montana. In Texas. Even in Kansas.

Kaci leaned back and closed her eyes. "I surrender, Lord. I don't want to fight with You anymore. You know I love Jude… but I love You more."

Did she?

Did she choose God's path even if it meant leaving Jude behind?

"Lord, I'm willing. Help my unwillingness." A bit of a paraphrase, but it was right where she was at the moment.

A truck rumbled up the quiet street and stopped in Maribel's drive. Jude was back.

But which Jude? The calm cowboy who was her dearest friend, or the confused man she'd thrown into a tailspin this week?

She loved him, whichever version he displayed. And it

was maybe time she told him so and laid everything on the line. She tucked the phone into her pocket and made her way to the garage entry.

The door opened. Jude stepped inside, lifting his cowboy hat with one hand and running his other through his hair. Then he caught sight of her. "Kaci?"

She took a few steps closer. "Hey. How was the ride?"

A shadow crossed his face. "Good. Not like home, but good."

"I have something to tell you."

He rocked back on his heels. "Oh?"

"A couple of things, actually. But one is more important than the other."

Jude nodded, his eyes still wary. "Okay?"

He wasn't making this any easier on her. She stood right in front of him, wanting to reach for him, but his hands clutched that hat like his life depended on it. "Jude Kline, I want you to know that I love you."

Surprise rippled over his face before his expression settled back into wariness.

Why the change? Oh! He thought there was a but.

"I talked to your grandfather, who has talked to mine. They think we should head to Dallas, that whatever is about to go down will be tomorrow. But that doesn't matter. What matters is you. I love you."

Jude gulped, his gaze riveted to hers. He stretched to hang his hat on a hook behind the door, but he missed, and the Stetson whooshed to the floor. He ignored it, like he'd forgotten it existed the instant it left his hands. Slowly, he reached for her.

Kaci wrapped her arms around his waist and squeezed

tightly. It still took a few seconds for him to reciprocate. But then he clutched her as though his life depended upon the connection.

Maybe it did. She felt like hers did.

After a long moment wrapped in each other's arms, Jude tucked his thumb under her chin and lifted her face to his. "I love you, Kaci. Or Kirsten. It doesn't matter to me, if it doesn't matter to you."

"I'll always be Kaci to you. I'm not sure who Kirsten is anymore. She's only a small part of what makes me, me."

"Okay." He bit his lip. "God and I had a bit of a chat while I was out riding."

"Oh?"

"I've had a chip on my shoulder for eons. I convinced myself I was the good guy, the normal guy because I'd grown up poor. I saw my wealthy relatives as the pretentious enemies. And I hated myself for having taken advantage of that privilege to get my pilot's license."

She searched his eyes, but the wariness seemed to have dissipated.

"And now?"

"There are good things that can be done with money. We don't have to be fakers. We can be genuinely nice people who care about others and help them."

"I think your grandfather is one of those good guys. As is mine."

"Maybe someday I'll get a chance to meet yours. If you want me to."

"I definitely want you to. He's going to be so happy to meet you."

"Oh, yeah? That sounds good." Jude's gaze flicked down before his thumb brushed across her lips.

Every nerve ending in Kaci's body flared with the contact. "Kiss me," she whispered, rising to tippy-toes. "Enough with the talking."

"Gladly." And he did.

Kaci had no idea how much time passed before the sound of a clearing throat intruded in her blissful bubble.

"If I may interrupt…"

Maribel. Jude's aunt.

Kaci kissed Jude again before loosening her grip on the front of his shirt and returning her heels to the floor.

They turned together, arms still holding tight as they looked at Maribel.

"What's up?" Jude asked.

"I think you two need to come and sit down for this."

Uh oh. Sounded ominous.

CHAPTER TWENTY-SIX

W hen Jude had first arrived in Chicago for flight school, Uncle James had taken him up in a stunt plane. Had it been to see what Jude's stomach was made of? To act as a warning to an interloper? Or merely to show off?

Jude had never figured out the reasons, but the gamut of physical and mental contortions had left him queasy for days.

That dissociative feeling had nothing on the past week. Updrafts, downdrafts, and air currents from every imaginable direction had buffeted his relationship with Kaci. And by the current expression on Aunt Maribel's face, the ride had taken another twist. Maybe a tailspin.

She led them into her office, and Jude closed the door before realizing there was a fourth person in the room, a woman in a crisp business suit, who stood as they entered.

"Good afternoon. I'm Special Agent Jane Jones from the FBI." She held out her badge.

Not that Jude had any idea if that sort of thing could be

faked. The sensation of plummeting in an out-of-control aircraft deepened, but he needed to anchor himself. He stretched to shake her hand. "Jude Kline. But you're likely here to talk to my girlfriend, Kaci Moore."

Kaci's shoulder bumped his arm as she reached to shake the agent's hand. "Formerly known as Kirsten Catriona Moorehouse-Atkinson."

Of course. In a formal — legal — situation like this, she'd be all Kirsten.

Jude's head swam. Her name didn't matter. She loved him. He loved her. They could get past the rest. Right?

"Please, have a seat." Ms. Jones gestured to the other two chairs as she sat.

Aunt Maribel sank into the cushy office chair behind her walnut desk and steepled her hands as she looked between them.

Jude seated Kaci then pulled the other chair close beside her so he could interlock her fingers with his. "I'm sure this isn't a social visit."

Ms. Jones smiled, softening her austere lines. She must be 40-something, her dark hair in a low ponytail reminiscent of Kaci's usual hairstyle.

"You're correct." The agent turned to Kaci. "The investigation of Douglas Atkinson and his law firm in Flower Mound, Texas, has been completed."

Kaci's fingers gripped Jude's tightly enough to cut off circulation. "Has my dad been arrested?" Her voice was tiny. Fearful.

"He has not. Douglas Atkinson and his son Duncan Atkinson have been exonerated."

"But…"

"The FBI wishes to thank you for your part in drawing attention to the unusual situation. However, a deep probe proved that Mr. Atkinson was undercover as part of a complex case to bring a corrupt law firm — a different one — and the clients it was protecting to justice. Multiple arrests have been made in the past two hours in a major drug cartel bust. You'll find the story on all major news outlets this evening."

"Masterson?" Kaci breathed.

Special Agent Jones blinked. "Yes."

"So... my dad has been cleared? My brother?" Her shoulders trembled.

"They have."

Jude slipped his arm around the back of Kaci's chair and rested his hand on her shoulder. "That's great news," he whispered.

"My dad..." Kaci's voice broke. "He probably hates me for not trusting him."

Special Agent Jones rose. "I don't believe that's the case, but you'll need to speak with him. I believe he's waiting to hear from you."

Jude smoothed Kaci's sleeve. "We can leave in ten minutes. Or we could fly commercial."

She turned to him. "You'd come with me?"

He hated that she questioned him. "I'll come with you anywhere, my love. To Texas. To anywhere on the planet or in the skies above it. I never want to be apart from you again."

"I've taken the liberty of checking flights from Wichita to Dallas." Aunt Maribel looked up from her screen. "By the time you drive to the airport, clear security..." She shook her head. "There isn't a flight for several hours, and you could already have arrived by vehicle before it lands. I can't believe I would ever be the one to recommend driving over flying."

"We should have flown down, after all." Jude squeezed Kaci's shoulder.

"We had good reasons not to. I'm up for the drive if you are."

"Absolutely, though I'm not sure if anyone wants to see us at nearly midnight."

"I'll call Grandad. And then—" Kaci let out a long breath "—my parents in the morning. I can't believe Dad doesn't hate me. Why didn't I trust him?"

"Mr. Atkinson understands your dilemma," Ms. Jones replied. "He had to stay in character. In fact, your disappearance heightened his cover and increased his legitimacy to the ones he was bringing to justice."

That seemed too simple. If Jude was having trouble buying the story, he'd bet Kaci was less convinced. He'd call Aunt Bridget to verify before escorting Kaci into a potentially hostile situation.

"It's been a pleasure to meet you." Special Agent Jones shook Kaci's hand.

Jude surged to his feet. "Let me show you out."

The agent pointed at the French doors leading to the private, gated patio. "I'm parked right through there. Thank you, but I can see myself out."

Jude watched her until she rounded the shrubbery before turning back to his aunt's office. "Well, that was quite a turn of events."

"Indeed." Aunt Maribel rose. "I'll have Dominica pack up food for your trip."

"Thank you. For everything."

"My pleasure. I'm glad this has had a happy ending." She looked between the two of them and smiled. "With more happy endings to come, it seems."

"I hope so."

Maribel slipped from the room as Kaci rose to grasp both Jude's hands. "This is surreal. I can't believe I misjudged my own father so badly."

"The agent said he had to play his part convincingly. I don't think you can take it personally that you believed what you saw and heard."

"Jude?"

"Hmm?" He rested his hands on her waist.

"I'm glad you're coming with me. I want my family to meet you. You're my safe place. Always will be, if you want to be."

"More than anything." He kissed her, somehow managing to keep it brief. "Pack up? We can be on the road in under half an hour."

"I'll call Grandad and let him know we'll be in late tonight."

Jude would be glad when this cross-country escapade would be over, and he could take his time kissing Kaci. Maybe forever.

THEY WERE an hour south of Gilead before Kaci was done talking to her legal counsel and Grandad. She turned off her phone with a sigh and tucked it in the cup holder before eyeing Jude across the cab.

He grinned at her then turned back to the road. "Everything okay?"

"More than okay."

"I'm not sure which direction is up."

She laughed. "I know what you mean. It's all been a little disorienting, but it's almost over."

"And you'll be Kirsten again."

"Right. Kirsten." She pursed her lips. "There are a few things I haven't told you about her."

"Oh?" His gaze turned wary again.

"Kirsten got her Bachelor of Science in Nursing from Baylor three years ago."

"She — you — *what?*" The truck swerved as he spoke.

"The road, Jude."

"I'm fine." He glowered at her. "You're a *nurse?*"

"Is that a horrible thing?" Her parents certainly hadn't been in favor.

"No! Of course not. It's good. It's just… I had no clue. What else don't I know?"

Kaci flinched. "A lot, but I think that's the only important thing I left out. I couldn't tell you about my entire life before we met at Sweet River Ranch. Just like you had dozens — thousands — of experiences I don't know about, I have a history, too. I don't want to keep anything from you anymore, but it will take a while to catch you up on pertinent bits. Just like it will take years, maybe a lifetime, for me to hear all your stories. I know almost nothing about your dad, for instance."

He sighed, staring straight ahead. "Sorry for over-reacting. Again."

"You're nervous about meeting my family. I am, too. A lot has happened, and not all of it good. But Jude? I love you. I'm committed to us."

Jude slapped the turn signal lever and swerved into a rest area. When the truck was parked, he turned to Kaci. "I'm committed to us, too. I'm sorry for how I've come across. I've been struggling. I told you."

Kaci nodded. There hadn't been much of a break in the tense, evolving situation for the past few days. "I get it."

"I guess I thought you were an ordinary person." His eyes searched hers. "I was thrown for a loop to realize you were actually in hiding and not just being private. Paisley didn't talk about her past much, either, and it turned out she didn't know who her father was, and her mother was a druggie. I guess… I guess I thought your story might be something like that."

"I'm sorry?" It wasn't like she could change her past.

"And that came out just as I was conflicted about the trappings of being Sullivan. Feeling guilty for taking advantage of my grandfather's money to get my PPL."

She couldn't think of a reply.

"But here's what I thought about while riding Trigger at Walker Ridge this morning. Was that really only today?"

"Yes?"

"All those disciples of Jesus back in the day… most of them were poor, uneducated fishermen and tax collectors and such. They weren't anyone special when Jesus called them. Right?"

"Right." And Kaci felt a tendril of hope.

"Romans eight says… here, let me look it up." Jude poked at his phone. "Okay, starting partway through verse 15: 'The Spirit you received brought about your adoption to sonship. And by him we cry, "Abba, Father." The Spirit himself testifies with our spirit that we are God's children. Now if we are children, then we are heirs — heirs of God and co-heirs of Christ, if indeed we share in his suffering in order that we may also share in his glory.'"

"Heirs of Christ," Kaci breathed.

"I know, right? It's crazy! We didn't do anything to earn that adoption, but He still showers us with all the riches of His kingdom. I didn't do anything to deserve the Sullivan name, either, but that hasn't stopped my grandfather from taking me in — me and my mom and my brother — and treating us like his family, pouring blessings on us. Because we *are* his family."

"That's beautiful, Jude." Tears pricked Kaci's eyes.

"I kept forgetting that I'm not worthy of any of it, but that's not what matters. What matters is love. God's love. Grandfather's love. It's love that *gives*. It's not about me."

Kaci reached for Jude's hands. "But you *are* lovable."

"And not worthy of that, either." He huffed a laugh.

"We can do a lot of good together. I want to nurse again… I will probably need to take a refresher course, since it's been so long. I need to look into what it would take to nurse in Montana."

"You'd come to Montana but leave the ranch?"

"Maybe?" That part was up to Jude, but she wasn't ready to point it out. "You know Maxwell's building a house for him and Eryn in Agate Bay. Bryce and Madison will probably live in town, too. It's not a long commute from there to the ranch… or to a hospital in Missoula."

"True."

"What matters most is that we talk to each other. Now there's nothing to hide, so we can just be open and honest and figure out each step as we face it."

"You're right." Jude leaned across the console to caress her lips with his own. "I'm the guy who likes to have all the i's dotted and the t's crossed. I like to have contingency plans on top of probability plans on top of emergency plans."

"That makes you a great pilot."

"It does? I guess you're right." He kissed her again. "I'd say, let's go for a walk here, but it will already be late when we get to your grandfather's place."

"It will. But we can talk while we drive." She slid her finger across his lips. "We can discuss all the layers you want in the next few hours."

"You know the saying, right? Man plans, and God laughs."

"I don't think He's laughing at us, my love. We'll get through this together… with His help."

CHAPTER TWENTY-SEVEN

When Mom had packed Jude's bags a few days ago, she hadn't dreamed he'd need his best suit, or any dressy clothes at all. At least he had clean, newish Levis and a button-down shirt that looked a little less redneck than his plaid, flannel snap-front ones.

Kaci, of course, looked classy no matter what she wore. Paisley had thrown in a variety of leggings and tunics as well as jeans and tees. After all, in Paisley's book, more was nearly always better.

Jude tugged on his cowboy boots. Frederick Moore-house's servant had polished those babies overnight as well as cleaned Jude's sweat-stained Stetson. He ought to be thankful Kaci's grandfather had thought to help, but he wasn't sure.

He shook his head. That was the old Jude speaking, the one who resented being judged for his financial lacks... and apparently his wardrobe lacks. And did he want to make the best possible impression on Douglas Atkinson? Absolutely.

You can't have it both ways, Jude.

But... couldn't he?

A tap sounded on his door. "Jude? You about ready?" Kaci.

"I'm ready." *As ready as I'm going to get.* He opened the door and let his gaze rove over her. "You look incredible."

Her fingers went to the hair brushing his collar. "You clean up pretty nicely yourself."

Jude gathered her close and kissed her. "Thank you. I'm pretty nervous here, just so you know."

"Me, too. It's going to be awkward, no doubt about it."

"Is that supposed to be a comfort?" He was only half joking.

"We're in it together."

"That *is* comforting." He kissed her lightly. "Let's go. Would you like to drive?" After all, she knew where they were going.

Kaci eyed the key fob dangling from his fingers for a minute before snatching it. "Sure."

They descended the wide staircase holding hands to find Kaci's stately grandfather waiting at the bottom.

"Ready to go, Grandad?"

Frederick nodded. "If I need to come home before you kids are ready, I'll call George to pick me up."

The old guy even had a chauffeur... but so did the Sullivans in Chicago. Jude had had a taste of elite ways. It wouldn't be so different here.

Keep telling yourself that.

He held the front passenger door for Frederick, who

protested that he could sit in the back just fine. "No, sir. You're our guest." Not that Jude was accustomed to the backseat anymore himself, but he did know how to honor his elders.

In less than twenty minutes, Kaci turned the truck into a paved lane between white board fences. Jude craned to see. Were there any horses? No, Kaci had said her parents sold them when she and her younger brother left home.

She drove into a circle drive and parked in front of a massive stucco-and-brick edifice. "This is it." She bit her lip as she glanced over her shoulder at Jude.

Jude gulped then swung out to open Frederick's door. By the time the elderly gentleman stood beside him, Kaci had rounded the truck and joined them.

The dark wood door swung open, and a middle-aged woman flew down the stone walkway. "Kirsten!"

Kaci rushed to meet her. "Mother!" The two embraced, rocking from side to side.

"That's better." Frederick Moorehouse nodded with a satisfied smile.

"Mother, I want you to meet my boyfriend, Jude Kline."

Boyfriend, huh? He liked that moniker. For now.

"Jude, this is my mother, Lillian."

He shook her hand. "I'm pleased to meet you, Mrs. Atkinson." The resemblance between her and Kaci was strong. Similar build, similar facial structure, right down to the high cheekbones.

"Jude?" Mrs. Atkinson — Lillian — gripped his hand with both of hers as she searched his eyes. "It seems we've missed much."

"I hope you can forgive me." Kaci stood with her arms tight around herself.

As soon as her mother released Jude, he moved beside Kaci and tugged her to his side. If he was going to be introduced as her boyfriend, he was going to keep his claim staked.

"You are forgiven, darling. But, please, all of you, do come inside. Welcome, Father." She air kissed Frederick's cheek.

He patted her shoulder. "Good to see you under such pleasant circumstances, Lillian."

"Indeed." She seemed to blink back tears as she gestured toward the house. When none of them moved, she led the way, with Kaci and Jude behind her and Frederick bringing up the rear.

Inside, the mansion seemed more homelike than Theodore and Bridget's residence, and Jude relaxed slightly. The worst would hopefully be over in the next few minutes.

A man in a business suit entered the foyer from the left. "Kirsten, honey."

"Dad!" Kaci let go of Jude's hand and flung herself into her father's arms.

The man held her for a moment before setting her at arm's reach and studying her face. "Montana has been good to you."

"I do love it there. But, Dad, I want you to meet my boyfriend, Jude Kline."

Jude shook the man's hand with a firm grip. He felt the man's measuring gaze even as he returned it. He could hardly blame Douglas Atkinson. Someday, Lord willing,

Jude would have a daughter, and he'd also do his best to intimidate any potential boyfriends.

"Jude Kline?" another male voice drawled.

Jude turned to see a man about his own age — one who looked a lot like the teen he'd known a dozen or so years back. "Duncan Atkinson."

Duncan shook his head and strolled closer. "It's really you? Imagine meeting you here."

Lillian frowned, looking between them. "You boys have met?"

Jude would let Kaci's brother answer that.

"Mexico. Remember the mission trip I went on with the church years ago?"

Lillian's gaze still ricocheted as though watching a tennis match. "Yes."

"Well, if I'm not mistaken, this here cowboy was on that trip, as well."

Jude held his shoulders squared. "That's right."

"I'm guessing I didn't make the best impression back then." Duncan raised his eyebrows.

"Also true."

Duncan laughed and clapped Jude on the shoulder. "I'd like to think I turned into a better man than anyone expected in my misspent youth." He turned to his sister. "Better than you've believed the past few years as well. Give me a hug?"

Kaci hugged her brother, who then shook Jude's hand.

"Now that we've cleared the air, maybe we can pretend Mexico never happened." Duncan laughed.

Douglas rocked back on his heels with his hands in the pockets of his slacks. "I'm sorry I gave you the impression I was on the wrong side of the law, Kirsten. When I realized your suspicions — just before you disappeared — I didn't know what to do. I felt we were so close to trapping the cartel at that time that I hoped everything would blow over quickly. I never dreamed it would take nearly three more years."

"I hated to believe it of you, Dad."

"Daughter, I'm truly thankful for one thing through this all."

Jude felt his eyebrows rise just like Kaci's did.

"I'm thankful for your sense of right and wrong, your sense of justice, and your faith in the Lord. I can only imagine how difficult this time has been for you, but I'm grateful you stood up for your convictions."

"Misguided as they were," Kaci mused.

"Your convictions weren't misguided. They were faithfully placed in the Lord. You had no way to know I was playing a double game."

Kaci's fingers clenched Jude's as she looked at her mother. "Did *you* know?"

"Not right away. I confronted your father after you disappeared, and he swore me to secrecy." She turned to Frederick. "I wanted to talk to you, but the fewer who knew the truth, the better. And the FBI seemed to think that the more of our close family who believed the worst, the more secure we were. It has been a difficult three years."

Kaci's chin jutted toward her brother. "And you?"

Duncan shrugged his shoulders. "It was my idea through a few things Joey let drop on several golf excursions. I went to Dad, and we decided to take it to the FBI. I had to keep making Joey think we were best buds. It was Joey who sent you the threatening text, by the way." He winced. "All I wanted to do was smear his face in—" He cut off his words as he glanced at his mother.

Lillian frowned at him.

"Well, you know," he finished lamely.

Huh. So, now Duncan Atkinson was a hero. Guess that proved he had grown up since the lazy brat in Mexico.

"Shall we adjourn to the lanai for refreshments?" Lillian suggested.

SURREAL. That was the only word for the sensation of standing in her parents' home — Kaci's no longer — after so long. Only Jude's grip on her hand kept her grounded.

"You okay?" he whispered as they trekked through the house toward the lanai.

"I think so," she whispered back. "How about you?"

"Surprisingly so."

She bumped his arm with her shoulder. "Good." Then, through the glass French doors beyond, she saw a woman and a toddler. "Deena?"

From the other side of her, Duncan turned. "Yeah. She wanted to wait out of the thick of things with Tyrell. You haven't met our little guy yet."

"I've been tracking his age and stage since he's within a couple of weeks of Jude's cousin's son, Simon."

"Toddlers are into everything. This kid is so much trouble."

Kaci laughed. "You deserve it."

"Gee, thanks, sis."

Kaci let go of Jude to dart ahead and hug her sister-in-law, though her nephew stared at her shyly from just out of reach. That was okay. He'd warm up to her after a while. Only... how long would she and Jude be in Texas? They hadn't discussed that part in all the turmoil of the past few days.

Behind her, she heard Duncan's voice. "So, what have you been doing with your life all this time, Kline?"

"Nothing much," Jude replied.

Kaci held back a laugh.

Jude continued. "Got my PPL — private pilot's license — last year. I'm currently flying sightseeing tours for tourists."

No mention of whom he worked for? Still with her back to him, she bit her lip. He'd probably not be impressed if she blurted that out.

"How did you land up in Montana, anyway, Kirsten?" Dad asked.

She turned to face the group again then met Jude's guileless gaze. "Grandad connected me with his old friend Walter Sullivan, who'd recently bought a guest ranch in Montana. It was a good place to disappear to."

"And that's where you work, Jude?" Dad went on. "I'm trying to figure out how you two met."

"Yes. Sweet River Ranch, not too far out of Missoula."

"I've been a lot of places, but never Montana. Is it as beautiful as they say?"

"It's better, sir. No hype could do justice to our big sky country. We have everything from the Rocky Mountains to the plains. We have lakes and rivers and wildlife and few people to spoil the natural beauty."

"Sounds amazing."

"You'll have to come visit sometime."

Dad looked at Kaci thoughtfully. "What are your plans now, Kirsten? Or have you had time to think about it?"

She couldn't stay apart from Jude one second longer, but crossed the space to take his strong, warm hand in hers. "Montana is my home now, so I second Jude's invitation. Come visit anytime."

His fingers squeezed hers.

"Just like that?" Duncan asked incredulously.

"I've been there over two years," she reminded him. "And another thing. I go by Kaci now. I'll answer to Kirsten, but I don't feel it's who I am anymore. The past few years have changed me. Have changed all of us, I think. But I'm Kaci Moore from Montana—"

"You dropped the rest of your name?" Mother sounded aghast.

"She was in hiding, sweetheart," Dad murmured. "Even so, Candy Masterson figured out where she was. Who she was."

"Kaci. Like your initials, only it sounds like a name." Duncan chuckled. "I like it."

"But you can't live in Montana, darling," Mother went on. "We're your family. We've missed you dreadfully, and we're here."

"I have a job there, and I've already put my boss in a bind by disappearing with little notice. I'm committed to working this season, at the very least."

Mother frowned. "Are you nursing?"

"No." Kaci inhaled. Exhaled. "I'm the head housekeeper at a ranch resort."

"You're *what?*" Mother fanned herself.

"I clean cottages after tourists leave, and I oversee a small group of chambermaids."

"But…"

"It's an honest living."

"And I thought nursing was bad."

"One more thing."

Everyone but the toddler was watching her now: Grandad, both parents, Duncan, and Deena. "I love Jude, and when the time is right, I hope you'll come to our wedding."

She heard Jude's sharp inhale. Right. It wasn't quite as though he'd proposed yet, though they'd circled around talks of their future, but she wanted to be sure her family understood. Yes, she was happy and beyond relieved to see them again, to know that her doubts had been unfounded, but her loyalty and her future lay with Jude.

Even though he hadn't come clean about his own family connections to hers. That would come. She was proud of him for not using that as a way to get her family to take him seriously. She wanted them to know and love the real Jude.

Like she did.

CHAPTER TWENTY-EIGHT

Weston nudged Jude's arm. "She's handling that well."

Jude's heart swelled at his brother's praise. "She is. She wanted to get ahead of rumors and let everyone know what had been going on."

They were seated in the back of the conference room, where Tate had called a staff meeting for those who needed to know Kaci's situation.

"You guys don't seem to be *just friends* anymore."

Jude chuckled. "You got that right, bro."

"When's the wedding?"

"I haven't proposed."

"Why the heck not?"

"We've been kind of busy."

Weston snorted. "You drove something like twenty-five hours to get home from Texas. Two people stuck in a truck for miles on end. Are you chicken? Still scared she'll say no? Because I gotta tell you, bro, she doesn't look at you like a woman who plans on sending you packing for the hills."

"I'm not worried about that." Jude couldn't help his smile. "But that's not a question you just drop on a woman without a plan." He had the ring, thanks to Frederick, but a proposal required a strategy.

"Paisley's good at plans."

Jude elbowed his brother. "Paisley is not doing my proposing for me."

"Turn her loose, and she'd be glad to."

"No doubt." Thankfully, at the moment, Paisley was at the front of the room to support Kaci. Better Jude's sister-in-law than him, or speculation would distract everyone from the real purpose of the meeting.

"Need help picking a ring?"

"Shh!" Did his brother have to whisper quite so loudly?

Weston's grin was unrepentant. "Valid question, bro. You could talk to Eryn — she has all kinds of artisan connections because of the gift shop. Or me and Paisley would be happy to accompany you to the jewelry store if you want something quicker, like today."

Jude's eyebrows shot up. "You'd willingly go in a jewelry store with me? I think I'll take you up on it, just to see this play out in real life." Even though the ring box had been in his pocket for days now.

"Deal. Don't let this girl get away.'"

"I'm not planning to."

The Q&A at the front of the room continued.

Weston's elbow found Jude's ribs again. "Hey, I got something to tell you."

Did his brother have no respect for the meeting in

progress? Apparently not. Jude glanced at Weston. "So, spill."

"Paisley's pregnant."

"*What?*" Jude shot to his feet. It took a few seconds to realize everyone had turned to look at him. His face reddened, and he glared at his smug brother before striding out of the room.

Weston followed him, chuckling. "Guess that was bad timing."

"Ya think?"

"Hey, just wanted you to know before everyone starts guessing. Those friends of hers are already eyeing her curiously. Paisley's no good at secrets."

Jude had known Paisley hoped to have half a dozen kids, so this shouldn't be a huge shock. It wasn't. Not really. It was the timing of the announcement. "Uh, congrats, bro. Really." He pulled Weston into a back-slapping man-hug. "Can't believe I'm gonna be an uncle. When?"

"February first, or thereabouts."

"You didn't waste any time."

Weston smirked. "No point to that, bro. Now you need to get married and get Kaci popping out babies so ours have cousins."

"Tell that to all the married guys first."

Weston jabbed Jude's chest. "You're the only sibling I've got. Jamie and Simon will be our kids' second cousins. Paisley explained to me how it all works. So, get going, bro."

"Where are we going?" Bryce's voice interrupted. The conference room door stood open, and others were filing out past them.

"Nowhere!" Jude blurted, Weston's voice echoing his.

"Sure." Bryce laughed. "Methinks thou dost protest too much."

"You're bringing Shakespeare into this?"

"Hey, whatever." Bryce slung an arm over each set of Kline shoulders and propelled them further from the busy path. "Haven't seen you since you got back from Texas, Jude. Good to see all that mess cleared up for Kaci. When are you proposing?"

Weston snorted. "That's what I asked."

Jude pulled away from Bryce. "You guys are all way too much in my business."

"Dude, it's been a long time coming."

"Think I don't know? I lived it." Jude looked between the guys. "Do you recommend eloping?"

Bryce grinned. "We didn't exactly elope. We just didn't want to invite all you yahoos to the wedding or wait for all the due process."

Yahoos? Once Bryce's word choice would have offended Jude. Now, it just made him laugh. "Montana has no waiting period for marriage licenses. Pennsylvania has, what, three days? There's less due process here."

They were staring at him.

"No waiting period?" Weston drawled. "How would you even know that if you haven't been researching?"

"Didn't say I hadn't been thinking ahead. Just didn't know when or if the moment would ever come."

"Anyway, eloping — or whatever you want to call it — has its benefits." Bryce clouted Jude's shoulder. "You should try it sometime. Ten out of ten recommended."

"I'll keep that under advisement."

"Course, Kaci's family would want to be in on a wedding, right? They only just got her back."

Jude narrowed his gaze at his cousin. "Like *your* family might have wanted to be present, not just Madison's?"

Bryce shrugged. "Big family. Too many opinions. Have you even met my mother?"

"Point taken. I spent a few days with her last week."

"Then you know… and also there's my father. But hey, weddings aren't all that bad. Maxie and Eryn's is coming in a few months. You should double up with them."

"Double?" Jude stared at his cousin.

"It's a thing. Two couples get married in one ceremony then share a reception. Saves on money, I hear." Bryce smirked. "And if the fam is all gathered already, they're happy not to make the trip twice."

Money wasn't even a blip on the radar of considerations, shocking as that thought still was. The Atkinsons would never go along with a wedding where their daughter wasn't the star of the show.

KACI HAD HEARD Jude's exclamation of surprise before he and Weston had bolted out of the room. What on earth had been going on in that back corner of the conference room? She'd have to find out later, but for now, she was one-on-one with Jane Mitchell, who'd been hired to cover for her absence.

Kaci shook the middle-aged woman's hand. "I'm so glad you're on board. It was such a relief to hear that cottages and guest rooms were still getting cleaned without Kylie and Trish being too overworked."

"I'm happy to be here, hon."

"Tate says you have a fair bit of experience?"

"Yes… but good opportunities are hard to find in rural areas like this, and I'm done with cities."

Done with cities. Huh. "Yeah, me, too. I love it out here."

Tate looked between them, clearing his throat. "I've been talking to my grandfather, and we have a proposition for you."

"Excuse me." Jane turned away.

Tate's hand caught her arm. "A moment, please. It affects both of you."

"What's up?" Kaci asked. She'd chatted with Mr. Sullivan a couple of times since her return, but he hadn't hinted at anything other than hoping she'd give Jude a chance to win her heart.

Too late for that. He already owned it.

"We'd love to offer you the position of camp nurse, Kaci. We're far enough out of town that it would be wise to have some medical expertise here to triage injuries or illnesses. Not that it's been a big problem thus far, but that's the thing with emergencies. You never know when they'll show up."

"Oh!" Kaci stared at him, her mouth agape until she realized she should shut it. "I'd be interested in hearing possibilities. Thinking about them. Praying about them." And discussing options with Jude. Or was it his idea? Had he put a bug in his grandfather's ear?

"If Kaci decides to move forward with that," Tate said to Jane, "we'd ask you to take on the head housekeeping duties. While it's true the other chambermaids have been here longer, they don't have the experience or connections you do, and neither is interested in more than a seasonal job at this time."

"Thank you for your trust in me." Jane nodded with a smile then turned to Kaci. "But you go ahead and make the best choice for you, hon. I'm good, either way."

"Thank you."

Jane turned away.

Kaci eyed Tate. "Camp nurse, huh? I didn't know you were thinking of hiring one."

"It hadn't come up, but Grandfather suggested it a few days ago, and I concurred. There have been just enough sprained ankles and allergic reactions and what have you to make me think an onsite nurse could be a good thing."

"I haven't worked in so long that I'll need to refresh my certification."

"Whatever that takes."

"I may need to work in a hospital setting for a bit."

"You're in charge, if you want to do this. Tell us how we can best accommodate you, and we'll make it happen. My grandfather wants to talk about it with you in more detail. In fact, he's invited you and Jude to have dinner with him and Eleanor this evening. Part of the purpose is this topic."

Kaci glanced around, but the room was empty save for her and Tate. Where had Jude gone? He wouldn't be far. "That sounds lovely. I'll check with Jude."

Tate's smile was warm. "You do that. We don't need an immediate decision, so make sure you look at his offer from all angles. We're just thankful you've decided to stay in Montana at all."

"Where else would I want to live?"

"Where, indeed?" Chuckling, Tate closed his laptop.

Kaci rested her hand on his arm. "One more thing."

"Yes?"

"Thanks for hiring Jane. I'm so sorry I left you in the lurch, both at the interviews and then again after Candy burst into the dining hall."

"No worries, Kaci. Are you sure you don't want to be called Kirsten now?"

"I like being Kaci. But back to the apology—"

"No need. There were extenuating circumstances. I'm only glad I thought to mention the names of those interviewing to you ahead of time."

"I panicked."

"I would have, too."

"You?" Kaci laughed. "You're unflappable. It's what makes you such a good CEO for Sweet River Ranch. I'm glad your grandfather saw that in you."

"Well, thanks." He shook his head, grinning. "I'm not sure Stephanie would agree that I can't be ruffled. She manages to do so on the regular."

Was there trouble at the helm? Kaci raised her eyebrows and discarded several replies.

"Oh, don't worry about us," Tate said. "We are getting loads of practice at apologizing to each other, forgiving each other, and leaning on God together. Even though we got married rather suddenly — and didn't know each other well at the time — we've grown together over the past two years. No regrets."

"I'm glad to hear that. Marriage seems like a pretty big challenge."

His eyes twinkled. "It is that, but the good kind. If and when my cousin pops the question, you be sure to say yes. Or here's an idea." He glanced around at the empty room and lowered his voice. "You could ask him."

Kaci took a step backward. "Is that a thing now?"

"Could be! We were engaged by accident after my mother jumped to conclusions in front of Stephanie's dad. You've met my mother."

Kaci managed an awkward smile.

"So you know she can be a bit manipulative to get her way. The thing was, it was what I wanted, anyway, but I'd planned to wait a little longer. We'd known each other such a short time."

"I remember."

"All that to say, Jude's a good guy, and he's crazy for you. I also happen to know that he's super careful. Which makes him a great pilot, but maybe not the swiftest at commitment. But when he's in, he's all in. So, if he thinks there's the remotest chance you'll say no, he'll hold off."

Kaci had to know. "Am I giving off negative vibes?"

Tate shrugged. "Ask Jude. Or just ask him the big question. He might be worried about your family's status. Money — or lack of it — has always been a sticking point for Jude."

"Hmm." Kaci thought they were over that. "You're not completely wrong. I'll think about it."

"Better yet, pray. At the end of the day, that's all any of us want, right? God's will. His blessing."

CHAPTER TWENTY-NINE

"So, you're going to be the camp nurse, huh?" Jude spoke into his headset and glanced across the helicopter at Kaci. Anything to make casual conversation and not give away his hand. She probably suspected, though.

"Is it a camp nurse if there isn't a camp?" She raised her eyebrows.

"Fair question." He laughed. "Ranch nurse? Resort nurse? They just don't have the same ring to..."

Ring. He should zip his mouth shut.

"To answer the question, I'm excited about the possibility. I hadn't even thought of using my training here instead of in a hospital. Maybe that's why I specialized in emergency procedures. I once thought about going for paramedic training, but my parents threw such a hissy fit that I backed off to nursing."

Huh. How had Jude not known that? But hopefully he had a lifetime to learn all the nuances of what made Kaci tick. She'd never be Kirsten to him. Thankfully, she seemed to prefer Kaci. "I'm sure they just wanted what was best for you, and the irregular hours of paramedics can be brutal, or so I hear."

"They were so controlling."

Jude glanced at her pensive face. "Maybe it was out of love?"

Kaci rolled her eyes. "Right."

"I'm serious. I saw how relieved and happy they were to see you last week. Their love and concern were palpable." He might have felt differently if she'd given in to their pressure to stay in Texas.

"I'm sure it's true. I just have so many adjustments to make in my mind about my dad's ethics. I thought he was a criminal for so many years that it tainted every memory, every thought I had of him. And my mom — how could she *not* know? Which meant she was in league with him. And Duncan."

"It looks like your brother turned into a decent human, despite what I thought of him in Mexico."

"Right? He seems to be a devoted husband and father. The big brother I once knew wouldn't have changed his baby's diaper."

"Heard from Owen?" Not the topic Jude wanted, but it kept his mind and mouth busy until they landed at the butte overlooking the lake. Just a few minutes away now.

"He was so wrapped up in his law classes he was totally oblivious. He's going to have to become a whole lot more observant if he's going to make it as an attorney."

Jude chuckled. He'd thought the same thing himself. Now he banked the helicopter toward the flat-topped rock. "Here we are."

Kaci bounced a little in her seat. "I was hoping we were coming here. Have we named it yet? I keep thinking of it as Butte Lake."

"I like that." He settled the bird and shut down all the systems before grabbing his backpack and ushering Kaci down the steep path. "We still haven't brought my grandparents here."

"Do you think they'll ever get married?" Kaci's muffled voice came from behind him.

Jude stopped to give her a hand down a tricky spot. "If they live long enough. Grandfather is nothing if not patient."

"Patience is good." Kaci's gaze flicked to his then away.

What did that mean? Maybe nothing. They descended the rest of the way, and Jude set his pack near the firepit. Within a few minutes, he had a fire crackling.

Kaci sat on a boulder nearby, staring out over the lake.

He clambered up behind her and settled her between his knees as he wrapped his arms around her. "Beautiful sight."

"It is."

"I meant you." He nuzzled her ear. "And the lake's not so bad."

She twisted a little. "Not so bad? You went to all this trouble to fly me to a not-so-bad place?"

"Busted." He cradled her close, inhaling the scent of her along with the gentle breeze. Soft waves toyed with the water's edge while the sun angled toward the western horizon. If the dictionary contained an illustration of peace, this would be a contender.

"Kaci—" he began, but she was already speaking.

"Jude, I have a question for you."

"Hmm? What's that?" He tucked his chin on her shoulder, reveling in the feel of her pressed against him.

"Actually, I have something I want to give you along with the question."

Hmm. This was curious. "Okay?" Wait. She had a box in her hand, longer than the one in his pocket. Was she...?

"Jude, you've been so patient with me. You've steadfastly shown love to me, even when I was hiding my identity from you. When I was afraid to love you in return. But I do love you." Kaci squirmed out of his arms and knelt to face him. "I know my family is intimidating, but I want you to know that I will choose you every single time. Will you marry me?" She held out the box.

Jude froze, staring into her eyes. She'd stolen his lines. He opened his mouth to reply then closed it again.

Confusion crossed her face as she looked down. "I'm sorry. I thought—"

"Kaci." He lifted her chin. "Kirsten Catriona. I love you more than I ever dreamed it was possible for a man to love a woman. I would be honored to marry you. But only if you marry me."

Hope filled her brown eyes as she studied him. "Yes?"

He tugged the little velvet box out of his shirt pocket and set both boxes side by side on the rock. "What do you say?"

A little grin played at Kaci's lips. "I say we open these at the same time."

"That seems fair." When they were both ready, they tipped the lids, but he watched Kaci's face.

"Oh! Jude, this is gorgeous! It's—" Her gaze flew to meet his.

"It was your grandmother's. Your grandad gave it to me for you."

Kaci threw herself at Jude, knocking him backward onto the rock. Thankfully, he wasn't close to the edge. He kissed her for a long moment before sitting Kaci back up against his chest. He tugged the ring from its nest and slid it on her finger. Man, it looked good there.

She held up her hand and let the sun catch the diamond surrounded with blue topazes, Texas's state gemstones. "It's beautiful, Jude. I had no idea you talked to my grandfather."

"I also talked to your parents while you were trying to win over your nephew. I know it's not required these days, but I wanted them to know I was devoted to you forever."

"So that's why they didn't argue when I said I was moving to Montana permanently!"

"It may have helped."

"You haven't opened your gift yet."

He had, but he'd been too busy watching her to look. What had she gotten for him? He looked down to see a leather bolo tie fixed with a blue topaz. If he hadn't spoken with Frederick about the Texas state gem, he wouldn't have understood the significance. Kaci was giving him a little bit of Texas along with a firm nod to his cowboy heritage.

"Kaci, I can't even tell you how gorgeous this is." Jude's voice choked over the words.

"I know how you feel about neckties and bowties."

"Just because I complained every time I had to wear one for a wedding."

"You can wear this one to ours." She kissed him. "Along with a tuxedo, a ruffled shirt, and a cummerbund."

He groaned around his laughter. It would be worth it.

"SURPRISE!"

Kaci giggled and looked at Jude as their friends erupted out of the conference room. Uh... he looked as shocked as she felt. Which was not at all. Instead, he smirked down at her before a questioning glint came into his eyes.

"You two are too cute!" Paisley hollered. "I take it you both said yes? Come on in!"

"You..." Jude laughed at the expression on Kaci's face. "You planned this?"

She gave a cautious nod.

"So did I!"

Kaci pivoted to stare at Jude's family and their friend group. "Did you all know we were both proposing?"

"We sure did!" Stephanie chortled. "And we thought it was hilarious that you both wanted us to plan an engagement party. It certainly made it easier."

No wonder they'd arrived back at the lodge at 8:00 sharp and somehow both accidentally steered the other toward the conference room. "You're sneaky." Kaci jabbed Jude with her elbow.

"So are you." He put his arm around her and tugged her to his side. "Party time?"

"We want to see the ring!" Cadence called.

Somehow Kaci was separated from Jude as the girls crowded around her. "This was my grandmother's ring.

Grandad offered it to Jude last week. I didn't even know he was talking to my family about marrying me!"

"It's stunning." Eryn smiled and gave Kaci a hug. "I'm so happy for you."

Madison was next. "I'm glad you guys worked things out."

"Me, too. And aren't you happy you braved up and confronted Bryce about being a father?"

"So glad." Madison beamed. "Not gonna lie, it was rough there for a while."

Kaci remembered the intervention she'd helped stage with the other women surrounding her. They made a formidable team, and they were her friends. Soon to be her family, too, since all of them were married to Jude's cousins or, in Paisley's case, to Jude's brother.

"How's married life?" A question Kaci hadn't wanted to hear the answer to before the crazy jaunt to Kansas and Texas.

"Amazing." Madison winked. "You should try it."

"You know, I think I will!"

Cadence huddled the group close. "Just want everyone to know that Graham and I are expecting a baby."

Paisley giggled, and everyone looked at her. "What?"

Cadence laughed. "You, too?"

"Yes! Early February. You guys?"

"About Christmastime."

The two hugged each other while Kaci eyed the others. "Stephanie? Anything to share?"

"Nope!" The woman held both hands up in self-defense. "Two boys under the age of four is enough right now. After Simon turns two, we'll start talking again."

"Talking is what you call that now?" Paisley teased.

"Hey, enough out of you," Madison scolded. "Have a heart for Eryn and Kaci here, still waiting for their weddings. When's the big day, Kaci?"

Kaci's gaze snagged on Eryn's. "We talked about a variety of possibilities, but we're not sure."

Paisley linked arms with Eryn. "Bryce told Jude they should have a double wedding with you and Maxwell."

Eryn pulled back, eyes wide.

Kaci tugged Eryn closer. "And we told him no way."

"Sorry, that just caught me by surprise. There would be a lot of reasons it would be a good idea. All the folks from the Sullivan family traveling, for instance."

Kaci rested both hands on Eryn's shoulders. "I want my own day, and I think you do, too."

Was that relief? Probably.

"But we were thinking maybe the day before or after for that reason. Or we can totally wait until Thanksgiving."

"The weather is pretty iffy for traveling at Thanksgiving," Paisley bulldozed in. "Remember we had that big storm two years ago?"

Kaci turned to Paisley. "You're not helping."

Paisley mimed zipping her mouth shut.

"You four should talk about that on your own time," Stephanie inserted. "Right now, we have an entire party planned, and the food is getting cold."

Paisley rubbed her hands together. "We'll play Pictionary!"

Stephanie turned on her. "We are *not* playing Pictionary."

"Charades?"

"Not that, either."

"Who let you plan this party if we're not going to play fun games?"

Stephanie stared at Paisley. "We are going to play *fun* games."

Kaci caught Jude's laughing gaze across the group.

He elbowed his way through the guys and then bumped Cadence aside. He captured Kaci's left hand and held it up to admire the ring. "Looks good, my love."

"So do you." She turned and straightened the bolo tie she'd placed around his neck up at the lake. "We're a matched pair."

"Always and forever."

Jude's lips on hers had the power to make the entire room drift away. Kaci could hardly believe they'd found each other in the midst of the entire mess that had been her life. She was hidden no longer, and whether Grandad rewrote his will — again — didn't matter.

Jude was her home.

Always and forever.

EPILOGUE

What was 83 supposed to feel like?

Walter Sullivan wouldn't feel a day over 60 if the young man standing beside the fireplace at Sweet River Ranch awaiting his bride wasn't Walter's youngest grandson, Maxwell... who insisted he was 28.

The love of his own life had passed away too young. She'd missed so many family events, including all of her grandsons' weddings and the births of three great-grandchildren, soon to be five... although the fifth wasn't one of Gladys's. It was hard to remember that his grandsons had different grandmothers.

Walter glanced at the woman seated on his right, who was looking down, perhaps at the hands clenched together in her lap, or perhaps praying. He reached over and covered her hands with his. "Eleanor?" he whispered.

She shot a tentative smile toward him, and he resisted the urge to wrap his arm across her shoulders and squeeze her to his side.

"What are you thinking?"

Eleanor shook her head with a tiny smile.

She was right. The answer to that was hopefully lengthy and might include him, and this wasn't the time or the place. Soon, though. She was softening toward him; he was sure of that. But when a man had just celebrated his 83rd birthday, he kind of figured time wasn't on his side anymore.

The pianist at the electronic keyboard by the windows segued into The Wedding March, taking Walter back to that wintry Chicago day over 60 years ago when he'd stood at attention, waiting for Gladys to come toward him. He'd loved her with his whole heart, forgetting for years on end of his indiscretions prior to meeting her.

He caressed Eleanor's hands, reveling in the grounding for today's wedding. He'd wronged her back then, never dreaming he'd planted a child in her womb, a child he wouldn't meet for many decades.

A row of stalwart young men stood shoulder-to-shoulder by the fireplace beside young Pastor Eli from down at Creekside Fellowship. Walter's six remaining grandsons. He allowed himself a moment to mourn his namesake, the eldest, who'd passed on to join Gladys almost three years ago now. So much — all this — had transpired in the wake of Wally's death.

Eleanor rose, tugging Walter to stand beside her, as she turned to face the bride coming down the staircase on the arm of her father. "Eryn is beautiful," Eleanor whispered.

"She is," Walter whispered back, "but not as beautiful as you."

"Oh, shush." She elbowed him lightly, but he could see his compliment pleased her.

Eleanor's step-granddaughter's entire face was lit with the love she had for Walter's grandson. It got complicated, the way their families had intertwined into one over the past three years.

What would Gladys have thought if Walter's indiscretions had come to light before she'd gone to heaven? She'd known he'd had a fling before their marriage — it had been the mid-sixties, after all. Expected. But he'd been faithful to Gladys all her remaining years.

Walter felt a twinge of guilt. He'd placed her second much of the time, with Sullivan Enterprises taking first place... and his Lord and Savior, Jesus Christ, in third, if even there. How his priorities had changed of late. He'd accumulated enough wealth to secure the futures of those six young men and their families, but at what cost?

"Who gives this woman to be married to this man?"

"I do." Keith Ralston kissed his daughter's cheek then took his place beside Nadine, who sat on the other side of Eleanor. Keith's wife. Walter and Eleanor's daughter. So complicated.

Maxwell took his bride's hands, and Walter's mind drifted back by only a day this time, to a similar moment when Jude had accepted Kaci from her parents. It had been so good to visit with his old friend Frederick Moorehouse last evening and to meet Frederick's daughter Lillian and her husband and sons. So many years had passed since Walter and Frederick had known each other in their youths, but it was good they'd stayed in touch, if only so that Kaci had had a safe place to land while the FBI investigated her father's law practice.

Yesterday Jude and Kaci had pledged their lives together right here in the lodge. They'd chosen to spend their wedding night in one of the upscale treehouses Maxwell's crew had built over the summer so they could attend Maxwell and Eryn's nuptials today. They'd be off on a Caribbean cruise out of Galveston tomorrow, then spend a few months in Texas where Jude would gain more flying experience and Kaci renewed her nursing certification.

Maxwell and Eryn would be off to Italy for their honeymoon.

Then it wouldn't be long before Graham and Cadence welcomed a little one into their home. From where Walter sat in the front row, he couldn't see Theodore and Bridget, but he'd caught them holding hands yesterday. The imminent arrival of their first grandchild seemed to have softened the pair of them. Praise the Lord for that.

Walter wasn't quite done praying for a reunion for James and Maribel, though it seemed farther off than ever. Their daughters-in-law, Stephanie and Madison, sat between them across the aisle from Walter and Eleanor. Maribel had Simon and Everly vying for space on her lap, while Jamie leaned against his grandfather's thigh as he peered to watch. That bony elbow had to hurt.

And then Weston and Paisley would welcome a little one later in winter, Eleanor's first great-grandchild.

Walter tried to focus on young Eli's wedding sermon and Maxwell and Eryn's vows, but all he could think of was the phrase "'til death do us part." He was under no illusions. The end could come at any time. No one had expected

Wally's and Ashley's deaths at such a young age, but the older a person got, the nearer the trumpet blast.

He wanted to spend what remained of his days with Eleanor. Not just an occasional visit or game of cribbage or family event, but every day. Every night.

Was it a sign of age that it seemed he blinked, and Eli was presenting Mr. and Mrs. Maxwell Sullivan? The beaming couple turned to face their families and friends, who cheered and applauded... and that shrill whistle had to come from Paisley.

In mere seconds, the grandson brigade had paused for their wives and children to join them, then Keith and Nadine followed, hand in hand, with James and Maribel stiffly behind them an arm's length apart. Eleanor tucked her hand behind Walter's elbow as they followed the processional to the foyer.

Behind Eleanor, Walter squeezed the bride's hand and clapped the groom on the back. "Congratulations."

"Thanks, Grandfather." Maxwell stepped in for a tight hug.

Walter blinked in surprise. They didn't do hugs... but maybe it was time to start. He took Eleanor's arm and steered her off to one side.

She smiled up at him. "What a beautiful wedding. I can't believe that's all of them."

"It doesn't have to be all."

She angled her head and looked up at him quizzically. "You have six grandsons, and Maxwell was the last of them to be wed."

As though he couldn't count. "Would you consider..." This was not how he'd intended to have this conversation.

"Consider what, Walter?"

He gulped for air. "Would you be open to marrying me?"

"If you asked me, I'd think about it."

"What would it take to get an affirmative?" If it meant getting her two sons on board, he'd work harder at the relationship, but both Reggie and Kenneth eyed Walter with suspicion. They seemed to think that their mother would leave them behind — forget them — if she went all in with Walter.

Maybe he should let them know that Maxwell and Eryn had taken his suggestion to add a suite over the triple garage at the new house they'd be building in town over the fall. Walter wouldn't be taking his new bride to live in the Windy City. Oh, they'd visit at times, but home would be right here in Jewel Lake.

Eleanor stretched and brushed her lips against his cheek. "A straightforward question might do the trick."

Oof. He hadn't been direct enough! But he'd save the real proposal for another day, when he had time to prepare and the privacy to do so. For now, he leaned down and touched his lips to Eleanor's forehead. "It's coming, my love. Be ready."

Soon.

DEAR READER...

Dear Reader:

I hope you loved Jude and Kaci! I bet you'd been getting curious about Kaci's secrets, and I hope I did justice to them in your mind. I'd sure appreciate a review on Amazon, Bookbub, and/or Goodreads.

I also hope you've enjoyed the entire Sweet River Ranch romance series and spending time with Walter's grandsons as they found love as well as a closer walk with Jesus. I'm so grateful for each and every one of my readers. May my stories consistently point you and me — all of us — to the Author and Finisher of our faith.

One more thing...

Would you like a sneak peek inside Eleanor's journal? *Dear Diary* is Eleanor's side of the story in her own words. It's a short ebook exclusive to my newsletter subscribers — if you're already a subscriber, you'll find a link in my next email! If you're not, you can subscribe right here:

https://valeriecomer.com/dear-diary

Oh, and one MORE thing...

Did you notice a few glimpses of Emma Cavanagh in the Sweet River Ranch series? Her six brothers' stories were told in the Cavanagh Cowboys series, but it's time for the sisters to shine! Come along for the ride as Emma, her twin Alexia, and their half-sister, Vivienne, each finds a love of her own. Check out Emma's story, *Take the Reins, Cowgirl*, today.

https://valeriecomer.com/reins

BOOKS BY VALERIE COMER

You'll find the complete list of titles by Valerie Comer on her website: fifty books (and counting) in ten series! Come on over to find farm-fresh romance, cowboy romance, and small-town romance, all with distinctly Christian themes.

https://valeriecomer.com/books

ABOUT VALERIE COMER

Valerie Comer is constantly amazed that living, talking, dreaming characters appear in her mind and flow from her fingertips and, from there, to her delighted readers. She only hopes her creations enjoy their happily-ever-afters as much as she does hers, sharing rural life in western Canada with her husband, adult children, and adorable grandkids.

Valerie is a two-time *USA Today* bestselling author and a two-time Word Award winner. She is known for writing engaging characters, strong communities, and deep faith into her green clean romances.

To find out more, visit her website at www.valeriecomer.com, where you can read her blog, explore her many links, and sign up for her email newsletter, where you will find news, giveaways, deals, book recommendations and more.

Welcome!